WHISPERED BONES

NC LEWIS

CHAPTER 1

Viv Gill came late to the Pow Beck bridge.

It was 9:00 p.m. Friday, when she tottered out of her one-room flat, red stilettos clicking on the bare wood steps, her strappy gold handbag across her shoulder. A sheen of thin mist covered the lane like a freshly spun spiderweb. Her hurried footsteps left tiny smeared dots behind. She didn't want to be late to meet the Dragon.

It was dark and frigid. In the distance, the sea crashed against the cliffs. The squat stone cottages in the village of St Bees huddled together as if for warmth. Viv hoped no one peered through their windows into the lane. She didn't want to be seen, couldn't risk that. The village was like a giant fish tank, with everyone peering and watching each other. What would they think? What would they say? She tightened the belt on her coat and pulled up the hood.

But at this time of night, the villagers would be settled in with a warm cup of cocoa and glued to the television. Or reading a book in front of the fire. That thought eased her, but she kept her hood up, just in case. She had to be careful. She slowed to pick her way around the rough patches. Should she even be doing this? This isn't what normal people do. Her feet kept walking, although her mind warned her to go back home.

A patchy fog blew in from the sea. Viv knew the path by heart. Still, she slowed to a crawl. As she picked her way through the dense darkness, she suddenly had the feeling she was being watched. She stopped, listened, and slowly turned around. A lamp post's orange hazy light was too weak to reach the path. Stone cottages lined this part of the lane, the glow from their windows like eager eyes. From some unseen house a dog barked. A front door opened and closed. Other than that, the lane was silent. Viv carried on, unable to shake the feeling of being observed.

At last, the fog gave way. She hurried on until her shoes clacked on the wood slats of a thin footbridge. It spanned the gurgling waters of a stream locals called Pow Beck.

The Dragon stood waiting.

It was too dark to see his face, but Viv knew he wasn't happy. The Dragon, that's what he liked to be called, looked more like a toad. A sour toad at that.

The Dragon blew cigar smoke. Tight curls like hissing steam.

"Sorry I'm late," Viv said.

The Dragon sucked on the cigar till its tip

glowed orange, then let the smoke out slowly but didn't speak. Viv knew this meant trouble. What did he expect? It was bloody freezing, and with all that fog and wet, how could he expect her to be early? He paid her less when she was late. She'd have to work harder now, get him in a good mood.

Viv said, "I'm in school uniform, as you requested, sir."

It had been a long time since she was in school. Thirty years would be a generous count. But blokes around here weren't that choosy, and in the fog and the dark... well, they could use their bloody imagination, couldn't they? Anyway, she'd worn her hair like Marilyn Monroe, with bright red lips and giant lashes. The Dragon liked the wide-eyed look. Paid well for it when he was in a good mood.

And she knew how to get him in a good mood. Viv Gill knew how men ticked.

Viv took a step closer, hand on the side rail to steady herself. *Come close, so Mama can take the candy from the baby*, she thought. Her lips curved into a seductive smile. She fluttered her lashes and unbuttoned her coat. A gust of wind flapped it wide like a cape. Another frigid blast tore through her braless blouse, and cold swirled around her nether regions. The miniskirt offered no resistance against the icy tentacles. "Bloody hell," she grumbled. *Why do the blokes with cash like to do it in weird places?*

But she needed to do this despite the icy chill.

She wanted the money and had to get closer to get a good look at his face. See if he was smiling. That would tell her how hard she'd have to work tonight. So she tottered forward, everything frigid and frozen, but somehow managing to swing her hips.

It was the sharp *clink* Viv heard first. Through the gloom, she caught a glimpse of something metallic. Pointed.

Edward bloody Scissorhands, she thought. *Well, he'll pay double for that.* She continued to totter forwards, hand on the rail and her coat flapping open like the cape of some ancient mystic about to give a blessing. She stopped; a sudden confusion filled her face.

"Who the hell are you?"

Time slowed to a crawl.

She took in the wild eyes and savage grin. And those hands. Each finger glistened with a blade designed to shred. Her feet became lead, her body ridged.

The figure lunged.

The quick movement threw Viv out of her frozen trance. She screamed and ran, kicking off her stilettos. Her bare feet pounded against the footbridge. She might have been long in the tooth for a schoolgirl, but she moved like a whippet.

And got away.

The figure hurried behind, blades *snip-snipping* like the claws of some hideous crab. Viv's flailing coat snagged on the side rail. For a moment, her legs turned to water. She struggled with her coat. The fight turned her insides to acid. She yanked and broke free. It only cost a second. Might as well have been an hour. The blades were upon her.

Frenzied.

Viv Gill's world went from red to brown to black.

CHAPTER 2

Fenella couldn't believe it. It was 8:30 a.m. on Saturday morning. She swept her shoulder-length, grey hair into a tight bun and stood amongst a chattering throng on the Port St Giles beach. Frigid gusts from the Solway Firth swept across the sands under a clear ice-blue sky. It wasn't the time or the cold that she couldn't believe. It was that she had persuaded Eduardo, her husband, to come with her. Park runs were not his thing. Like a well-fed scullery cat, he preferred to curl up in front of the fire, except with a steaming mug of coffee, on his weekend mornings.

He'd done that for years and gone from trim to plump to fat. It didn't help that he worked as a comic artist. The job involved staring at a computer screen, where he'd munch digestive biscuits to help his creative inspiration. Nan's fried breakfasts, grilled lunches, and stodgy dinners with desserts, which usually involved custard or ice cream, didn't help his waistline either. Not that Eduardo minded. But Fenella did, and she got her mother, Nan, on board. There'd be no more fried breakfasts or grilled lunches at their cottage on Cleaton Bluff. Not until he'd lost fourteen pounds or one stone in old money.

Eduardo liked Nan's fried breakfasts and grilled lunches and stodgy dinners with sweet desserts. But one stone was a lot of weight to shift, so he stood with Fenella and Nan amongst the throng. He claimed he'd not lost his high school physique, but his old school shorts were too tight, and his thin, polyester, breathable T-shirt no match for the frigid January blasts. At least his old running shoes fit, although he wore his orange office socks rather than the usual garb of flannelled white or black.

"I'm freezing," Eduardo said.

"Do some jumping jacks," Nan replied. She wore thick, black leggings under her shorts, a long-sleeved tracksuit top with a scarf wrapped tight around her neck, and a blue bobble hat to keep her head warm. "That will get your blood moving."

"That's just the thing," grumbled Eduardo. "My blood was quite happy where it was: at the kitchen table in front of the fire with a steaming mug of milky coffee while I read the news on my laptop."

Fenella smiled. She didn't mind the complaints. This was their time, family time—a few days with her loved ones where she didn't have to think about work. Didn't have to think about the unsolved crimes. Or the pile of paperwork that sat on her desk at the police station. She switched off on the weekends. And what better way to begin than a brisk jog with her fellow townsfolk along the beach?

"You don't have to run, luv," Fenella said. "You can walk."

That was too good for Nan to let pass without comment. "Him walk? The bugger's so fat, he'll have to roll, and I ain't pushing."

Eduardo laughed and stretched out his arms and spun in a slow circle like a giant cannonball-sized ballerina. That was one thing Fenella loved about her husband: his sense of humour.

"Silly sod," Fenella said, giving him a hug.

They stood in silence for several minutes, listening to the low mumble of the crowd and the distant crash of waves against the shore. Port St Giles Park runs brought out all ages, from families with young children to pensioners with their grandkids. Everyone was welcome. Fenella liked that.

"Fenella, that you?"

Fenella spun around.

"Gail. Gail Stubbs. What on earth are you doing in Port St Giles?"

"Moved here about a month ago from Whitehaven. I'm working at the cottage hospital in town and was going to look you up."

They'd met years back when Fenella was in

uniform and working a domestic violence case. She was the first officer to arrive on the scene, a derelict house in a run-down street in Whitehaven. She found a woman face down and lifeless at the bottom of the stairs. Her boyfriend sat at the top with his hands on his knees. It was his grin that sent a chill down Fenella's spine. She'd never forget the glint in his eyes and the satisfied look on his gnome-sized face.

Fenella took the woman to hospital, where she was nursed back to health by Gail. And the boyfriend? Fenella didn't know what happened to him. She wrote her report and passed it up the chain. Uniforms rarely got time to follow a case through the system. But she'd returned to the hospital, and a friendship formed with Gail, although they had lost touch over the years. *When was the last time they had chatted? Five years at least,* Fenella thought.

Fenella said, "Let's jog together. And if we don't push too hard, we can talk too."

The starter counted down and waved a flag. The crowd cheered and poured over the starting line as the five-kilometre event began. Some ran, others jogged or walked. There was even a group of teenage boys who hopped. But Fenella and Gail were both competitive and pushed hard as they ran over the starting line.

"I'll walk with you, Nan," Eduardo said. "We can take our time, so you don't get too tired."

"Catch me if you can." Nan power-walked off. "I'll not come in last."

Eduardo tried to keep up but dropped back after a few steps. He fell in with a group of pensioners who encouraged him to keep going.

CHAPTER 3

Ten minutes into the run, and breathing hard, Fenella and Gail approached the barnacled pilings of the pier. It was a glorious January morning, crisp with a fragrant breeze from the sea. Farther out, where the waves lapped the shore, a handful of beachcombers scoured the sands. Fenella watched as they picked through their finds. It was like a scene from a timeless oil painting, so quaint that it brought a smile to her lips.

"So what brought the move to our out-of-the-way town?" Fenella asked as they passed under the pier and out onto the broad flat sands.

"A change, you know how life is."

"And how is Leo?"

"We split last year." Gail breathed hard. "Fifteen years of marriage gone with the flick of a judge's pen."

"Is it what you wanted?"

"Aye. It is. Leo and I drifted apart years ago. With no children to keep us together, it is for the best. That's why I'm here, to make a fresh start. Leo is still in Whitehaven, shacked up with a younger woman."

They ran on in silence for several minutes. A pair of guillemots wandered along the shoreline, their webbed, crimson feet like winter boots. A teenage girl played with a young toddler in a red coat. Fenella remembered the game. It was the same she'd played with her own children when they were small. They would run backwards and forwards to avoid the surf, their voices filled with laughter. She watched the teen and the toddler, remembering.

It was hard going on the soft sand, and Fenella wondered whether she could keep up the pace. She glanced at Gail, whose face seemed set and determined. That was Gail for you, knew what she wanted and went after it until she got it. Then Fenella thought about Dexter, her detective sergeant, twice divorced and with no girlfriend these days either. Her matchmaking brain cells whirred.

"Help me!"

The young teen's desperate plea rose above the crash of surf against the shore. Fenella's head turned automatically to the sea. A moment later, she ran towards the surf.

A toddler struggled against a wave and fell face first into the water.

Fenella sprinted. She hit the frigid sea hard

and gasped in shock as she waded out to her knees. Another wave came. Bigger. The currents would make light work of sucking the child into the deep sea. In the frigid water and weighed down by winter clothes, there was no hope of survival. The churning waves of the Solway Firth prepared to take its next victim.

Fenella couldn't let that happen.

She squinted through the salt spray and scrambled to reach the child. Her hands caught hold. Fingers stiff with cold, closed too slow. The child slipped away from her grasp.

The roar of the waves sounded like a stampede of horses. Fenella saw nothing but the white surf and the glint of a red coat spinning away from her.

She clawed at the coat as salt water again sprayed into her eyes. It stung like drops of bleach. Her fingertips made contact again, and she yanked with all her strength. The child spun and drifted closer. Fenella scooped the pint-sized body into her arms and staggered back to shore.

She placed the child on the dry sand—a little girl, her face tinged with blue. Now she and Gail went straight to work. There was no time to talk. They communicated through their actions.

"Oh my God!" cried the teen. "One minute she was with me, the next she was in the water. We finished playing jump the waves and had started on hide-and-go-seek. But I only turned my back for an instant."

In the distance, Fenella heard the sirens and saw the blue and red flashing lights. Someone had called it in. Help was on the way.

CHAPTER 4

Fenella sat inside the closed doors of the ambulance and shivered despite the warmth, a thick blanket draped over her shoulders. Eduardo's arms held her close. They were alone for the moment. The quiet air was heavy with the scent of medicinal smells.

Eduardo squeezed Fenella and whispered, "You are a hero. You saved that young girl's life."

Fenella heard his voice but not the words. What would have happened if she slipped when she ran into the sea? Or grabbed at the child a mere split second later?

Eduardo said, "They've taken the girl and her sister to the cottage hospital. Gail went with them."

Fenella's heart thumped in her chest. It wouldn't slow down. She knew why, and said, "A moment later, and it would have been different."

"You saved her life."

"I was out for a fun run on the beach with a friend."

"You were there for the child when she needed

help."

"I should have been there for Eve."

"Don't, luv."

"My sister vanishes without a trace; her husband dies, and I can't do a damn thing to help."

Seven years earlier, Eve had a terrible car crash on a narrow lane in the village of St Bees. She was with her husband, Grant. They were on their way to Port St Giles for an evening out, a meal and dance and chat with friends. They hit a patch of black ice on a bridge that crossed a narrow stream. The car skidded, tumbled, ending upside down on a grass bank.

Grant died.

They rushed Eve to hospital, but she vanished from the ward before Fenella arrived. No one knew where she went. Not the nurses or the doctors, but CCTV cameras recorded Eve stumbling along a hall, seemingly confused. Then she walked through a door and was never seen again.

Fenella said, "If only I could turn back the clock."

Eduardo drew her close and kissed her gently.

"I've lost my sister," Fenella said. "I can take that, just. But what about Nan? She's lost her daughter. For a mother, to lose a child is..."

"Hush now, luv," he said. "We'll not let Eve or

Grant out of our memories. We'll not let them go."

A knock thudded on the door.

"Sorry to disturb you, ma'am," said a female officer in a crisp tone. "I've a message for you."

Fenella knew the woman, PC Beth Finn. A good cop. They both worked in the Port St Giles police station.

"The medics about the young girl?" Fenella asked.

"No, ma'am. But I hear the child is doing just fine. The superintendent would like a word in her office."

"But it's Saturday," Eduardo said. "And my wife is drenched from the sea and still in her jogging clothes."

PC Finn said, "I'm to drive you to the station, ma'am. It is urgent."

Eduardo's mouth opened. Before any words came out, Fenella placed a hand on his arm. His mouth closed without a word. She turned and gave him a quick hug of thanks. He never made a fuss about her job. She loved that about him. She stood. Her weekend with the family was over.

CHAPTER 5

Superintendent Veronica Jeffery didn't look happy.

She sat at her vast oak desk, her eyes narrowed. Folders were piled in an untidy stack. There was a faint trace of leather wax and polish in the still air. The winter sun glared through the tiny window of the oak-walled room but did little to lift the gloom.

"I'll not beat about the bush." Jeffery's voice buzzed like a wasp poised to sting. "This is one hot mess."

Fenella had no idea which mess Jeffery meant. Perhaps it was to do with the cottage fires? There'd been a string of blazes in the old stone cottages that dotted the villages and towns. They'd not found a link, and put it down to age. Now she half wondered if it might be arson. And there was the child-smuggling ring that snaked along the coast. The regional crime squad in Carlisle were rumoured to be close to nailing the kingpin, a big shot high up in officialdom. Did the boss have new information?

But it was Saturday and her boss was in full

uniform. It had to be something else. Full uniform meant big trouble. She let Jeffery blow off some steam and waited. She was good at the wait.

Jeffery leaned back in her leather chair. It was edged with gold and looked like a throne, although the boss didn’t look very regal at the moment. "I've some sensitive information which requires our full attention. Facts from a reliable source about Hamilton Perkins."

Hamilton Perkins had a love of two things: sharp knives—that's why the newspapers called him Mr Shred—and schoolgirls in uniform. It had been almost two months since he escaped from Low Marsh Prison.

Fenella tilted her neck from side to side, a trick she'd learned in yoga to ease tension. "What about him, ma'am?"

Jeffery closed her eyes, as if in prayer, but did not speak. The media went wild when Mr Shred was first caught, the trial of the century, they said, as huge as Jack the Ripper. News of Mr Shred's murders spread like wildfire around the globe. His trial was the biggest news ever to hit Port St Giles. He was born and raised a few miles away in the village of St Bees. That he lived and moved amongst the locals added to the sensational aspect of the story. How could one of their own do such evil things? It lingered like a shadow over the faded Cumbria seaside town.

Days before the trial began, American reporters arrived in droves. They booked out the hotels and boarding houses. They even rented huts in the East Side Caravan Park. Their shiny white teeth and perfect hair gave razzle to the show. Judge Grey wore a black gown and an old, white wig, so he'd look regal in front of the foreign cameras.

It had been a circus.

On the day the jury came back with their verdict, it was a rugby scrum at the court. Judge Grey, in a white wig and black gown trimmed with gold, gave Perkins life with no chance of parole. He'd not see a sunrise other than through the bars of his prison cell for the rest of his days. And that was just fine with Fenella.

Jeffery opened her eyes and said, "He's been quiet since he broke free. We thought he'd gone to ground, left the country."

Fenella felt sick. Ever since he'd escaped from prison, she had worried there'd be new deaths. Two months had passed, and he hadn't been caught. That upped the chances he'd strike again. He was clever. Always a step ahead of the police. The thought of the victims' faces made her want to throw up. Mr Shred by name. Mr Shred by nature.

Jeffery was speaking. "There was talk he'd found a hidey-hole in France, Grenoble in the Alps. Our French friends were alerted but found nothing." She licked her lips. "There were two murders in

Spain. Copycat killings. Not our man."

Again, Fenella tilted her neck from side to side and waited.

While in prison, Perkins had shown remorse, and with the help of prison psychologist Dr Joy Hall, agreed to show Jeffery where he'd buried his last victim. Her name was Colleen Rae, a fifteen-year-old schoolgirl with learning disabilities and the niece of Chief Constable Alfred Rae.

Superintendent Jeffery was ambitious. She'd kicked and clawed her way into the superintendent's chair, and her sights were set even higher. If she found the body of Colleen Rae, she'd glow like gold in the chief's eyes.

Fenella's patience snapped. If there was news about Perkins, she had to know. She had a personal interest too. After the trial she had visited the last place Colleen Rae was seen alive and promised to bring her home. Until her body showed up, she kept Colleen alive in her mind. Alive or dead, she'd keep her word. Never break a promise to a child. She'd bring Colleen Rae home. Not for the glory or for promotion. For peace of mind.

Fenella said, "Do you have news, ma'am?"

Jeffery looked at the tiny window and let out a morose sigh. "It's been a media circus; it won't be long before the big politicians fly in from London to pick over our bones. We have not come up smelling like roses. Rather the opposite I'm afraid." She reached for the stack of folders. Her hand hovered over a grey docket marked Private, then slid it across the desk.

Fenella didn't move. For an instant she thought of Nan and Eduardo. They'd be in the kitchen with logs on the fire, the room bathed in a warm glow. Her mind drifted to the child she'd saved on the beach. With the medics at her side, she'd pull through. She felt good about that. Now she looked at the folder and thought of Colleen Rae. She loved her family, and she loved her work. Yes, it was Saturday, and she was on the job. Deep down, she would have it no other way. If they had anything on Hamilton Perkins, she had to know. She wanted him back behind bars.

Jeffery said, "The file is from Dr Joy Hall. We went to college together. You have met her?"

Fenella liked Joy Hall. Competent. Professional. A role model for young women.

Jeffery said, "Dr Hall is a good friend, but I still had to pull a few strings to get this. Her psychological reports take time to write, have to be assessed and rubber stamped. But they are worth their weight in gold." Her taut cheeks raised into a wolfish grin. "This came to us in record time."

Fenella picked it up and read. When she finished, she dropped it onto the desk, and stared hard at her boss.

Jeffery leaned forward, fingers steepled.

"That's right. Dr Hall's best guess is that Hamilton Perkins isn't in France or Spain. He didn't leave the country, hasn't even left the county. Mr Shred is right here on the Cumbria Coast. It seems he is lying low, waiting for a chance to kill."

CHAPTER 6

PC Sid Hoon knew he deserved more.

He sat at the kitchen table in his two-bedroom stone cottage and thought about how much more. There was his job. Being a bobby in the village of St Bees wasn't a fast and furious life. He hankered after the big-city lights and had great ambitions of being a detective when he'd first joined the force. The exams were easy enough. Nowt but a piece of cake. Child's play. And he would study to take them, but there was so much to watch on the television. An education in life. That's what he saw every night on the flickering box. It helped him relax, as did his nightly four-pack of beer. Yes, he would be a detective one day, knew he was more than a uniform, although he had grown round and fat and comfortable in that skin.

"You still here, you lazy sod?"

And there was Maude. He watched as she marched into the kitchen, her hair in tight curlers. A cigarette dangled from the corner of her nicotine-stained lips.

He'd met Maude in a bar in Carlisle a dozen years back, on one of his fun nights out in that town.

She had given him a cute smile. They'd talked. She'd found out he owned a cottage in the country and came back with him that night. He wasn't sure he'd asked her; it was all a drunken blur. She made herself at home and cooked and cleaned and slept with him. It wasn't long before the wedding bell tolled. He wasn't sure how that happened either.

They hadn't any children. "Bad seed," Maude had said as though she'd been to medical school. She smirked. "You're firing nowt but blanks."

But he knew in those early times she took the pill and these days growled if he got close. Now she just hung around stinking the place out with her tobacco smoke, dropping ashes on the floor, and spending his money. It had never occurred to him that married life would be like this. He hadn't seen it coming.

"How can you expect to be taken seriously as a village bobby if you're sitting around supping tea when it is nearly ten a.m. in the morning?" Maude sucked on her cigarette and snorted a twin spiral of smoke through her nose. "If you had a bit more bite, you'd be a detective by now, and we could live in a big house. Not this poky place."

PC Hoon said nothing.

"Are you listening to me, you lazy sod?"

Surely, he thought, with a morose sigh, life owed him more than this.

"And bring me back two packets of fags and a bottle of Diet Coke."

PC Hoon didn't like to go to the village store, didn't like the way the shopkeeper looked at him. His name was Chad Tate, and he watched PC Hoon with a distrustful eye as if he knew what he had done. But how could he know? Nobody knew. So PC Hoon shopped there most days to stop Maude from nagging him. It was the only store in the village.

"Did you hear me, you deaf bat?" Maude yelled. "Fags and Coke, and don't forget."

PC Hoon couldn't stand to look at Maude. Her sly face filled him with anger. He felt his body tense, sinews pulled tight in his neck. He wanted his cottage back. He wanted Maude gone. Life owed him more than this. How come he'd married a viper when he was such a nice bloke? She wouldn't leave until she'd sucked him dry. He felt it deep in his bones.

"Right," he said and licked his lips. "I'll pop into the village store on the way back."

Maude snorted. "Why didn't you make me a cup of tea?" She didn't wait for an answer and shuffled to the kettle to turn it on. "Bleedin' lazy sod. Just as well you've got me to cook and clean for you, else this place would be a pigsty. I'll slap a joint of that fatty beef in the oven for your dinner. You like all that grease, don't you? Oh, and there are six cream doughnuts in the fridge. Eat them all, don't want them to go stale."

The clock on the kitchen counter chimed the top of the hour.

PC Hoon looked at his mug, and he looked at the clock, and he looked at his wife by the kettle. He rose to his feet, left her words in the kitchen and replaced them with the frigid air of his village beat.

CHAPTER 7

Chad Tate felt the rapid beat of his heart as he stared at the empty aisles.

He stood at the checkout in the village store, a middle-aged man with a growing gut, and a hairline receding at speed. In front of him an elderly woman in a long, brown coat and green headscarf, wheeled her cart, pausing here and there to take an item from the shelf, look at it with a scowl, and put it back. This was it. The Saturday morning rush.

He picked up his mug of coffee and gazed blankly out the shop window. St Bees Priory stood on the opposite side of the lane, its red-clay brick covered in moss and lichen. He'd only been inside once, for a funeral.

That was the day everything broke in his life.

He was in the hallowed halls of the church, thick with the sweet smell of incense, and in his black suit. The pews were crammed, jowl to jowl in a sea of sympathy, singing solemn hymns of forgivingness. All the officials were dressed in high uniform, PC Hoon one step behind the priest.

Chad's cheeks reddened at what he had done,

at what happened next. He swallowed hard to forget, heard a *click-click* in his throat and refocused his eyes on the St Bees Priory. Yes, he loved the view through the shop window. It was different from New York City, where he grew up. The Big Apple was always in motion. Always changing. He preferred it here, where time stood still. He tried to enjoy the view as yellow sunlight filtered through the window.

Nothing's changed in twenty years.

Except this morning as his eyes scanned the lane, he couldn't slow the rapid beat of his heart, and he didn't want to remember the last time that had happened.

"Do you have any tins of beans?" The elderly woman leaned on her cart, sharp eyes alert. She asked the same question every Saturday. It was best to play along with her game.

"What type of beans, Mrs Lenz?"

"Oh, any type will do. I'm not fussed."

"How about black beans? They are popular in Mexico."

"My Alf don't like to eat foreign muck."

"Black-eyed peas, they are great in rice."

"Baked beans, that's what my Alf likes. Do you have any Heinz baked beans?"

Chad had taken over the St Bees village store with high hopes and big dreams. It would be a slice of New York City right in the heart of the English countryside. He'd sell matzo-ball soup, arepas, calzones, and celery soda. He brought a big freezer to store the Big Apple's delights. But the locals wanted white bread, bacon, milk, and baked beans.

"Let me get you a can," Chad said with a mix of frustration and kindness. He loved his store. Loved the village. Loved serving the needs of his community and never wanted to leave. He just wished their tastes were more exotic.

"That won't be necessary, young man," said Mrs Lenz. "I'm not past it yet. Ask my Alf."

Chad joined in her laughter. If he didn't, she wouldn't buy the beans, or the bread, or the milk. Then she would tell all her friends, and they would stay away from the store. It had happened before. Not long after what occurred at the funeral. So Chad stretched his lips into a clown's grin and laughed.

Mrs Lenz said, "I've not had anyone call about that card I placed in your window."

"It's next to the poster of the fundraising fête at St Bees Priory," Chad replied. "A prime spot for eyeballs."

Chad had read the card:

A cheap room with all the mod cons and a meal thrown in on Sunday. Gas on metre. Lights out at nine. No overnight guests. No eating in room. No loud music. Coin-operated hot shower. Must be in full-time employment. Call for rate.

He would not want to live with Mrs Lenz, could see the yellowed net curtains and stained bedspread as he read between the lines. *No, thank you.*

Chad said, "It's a mystery why they are not fighting over it."

"If this were New York City, I'd have a dozen folk on my doorstep," Mrs Lenz replied. "Fifty pence for nothing!"

"It has a good spot in the window."

"You ought to give me a refund." She stared at Chad. "Am I right? I am."

Chad rubbed his chin. The store opened from 6:00 a.m. to 9:00 p.m. six days a week. It ran on a shoestring with only a handful of customers. He wished there were more. And so did his bank manager. "How about we give it another week, Mrs Lenz? No charge."

The doorbell tinkled. Chad turned in the hope that his smile would greet an eager customer.

It was the postman.

Each day this week he had walked into the store with his sackful of mail and a white envelope clutched in his hand. Each day Chad took the envelope as if he didn't have a care in the world. At first, the postman said, "Looks official, are you opening another store?" and then, "I suppose it's about your loan?" And finally, "For a bank manager, Mr Clarke is not as bad as they say. A bit of a ladies' man, but where is the harm in that?" This morning, he didn't say anything at all. He simply shook his head, avoided Chad's eyes, placed the white envelope on the counter, and left.

Mrs Lenz was at the counter before the door squeaked shut. "Postman brought you something nice, am I right? I am." Her sharp eyes scanned the envelope. "From Mr Moneybags Clarke, eh?"

Chad forced a smile, picked it up, and weighed it as though it might tell him something about the contents. He'd wait until she left the store to open it. "Oh, it is nothing. Are you done with your shopping?"

Mrs Lenz said, "Mind if I settle up with you at the end of the month? Not that I'm asking for credit. No. Just my Alf gets his pension at the end of the month."

"That is fine," Chad said.

"You are such a good man," Mrs Lenz replied. "Kind and considerate and big hearted. Respectable. I like a respectable man with an American accent. Bet the ladies are always after you. Am I right? I am. Not found the right one yet, I suppose?"

Mrs Lenz said that every week too.

Chad stretched his lips into a clown's grin once more and waved as she left the store. That's when he saw the young girl with her mother. She couldn't have been more than five years old and had a pink ribbon in her raven-black hair. He liked that. And the grey coat with white socks and the small black shoes, which shone in the bright January sunlight. His heart sped up.

The girl straggled two paces behind her mother, head down as though examining the cracks in the pavement. Chad couldn't take his eyes off her. He liked little girls. *So young,* he thought. *Innocent and sweet. But she didn't have a teddy bear. They looked cuter with a stuffed animal.*

When he was young, the kids ran about on their own. Even in New York City. These days they were always with their sharp-eyed parents. He let out a frustrated grunt and wished it was like the old days. It was easier then.

Still, he hoped they'd come into the store. He'd give the girl a lollipop and ask her name. Quickest way to win the heart of a child is with a piece of candy. Best not let the mother see, though. Maybe he should get a small dog? One with a wide mouth so it looked like it was grinning. Kids like them. Might lure little girls into his store by the dozen, and he could write the dog off as a business expense. He pressed his face against the cold glass of the door to watch the mother and child.

But they didn't come into the store.

Chad scowled as they continued along the

lane and disappeared around a sharp bend. If he were back in New York City, the store would be brimming with kids on Saturday. He'd have to fill his storeroom with boxes of lollipops and could take his pick of which little girl he'd give one to. He wouldn't need a grinning dog to attract them through the doors.

He reached under the counter for Bert, a three-legged, stuffed sheep with one eye. He wouldn't show it to the little girl. It would scare her. He kept it under the counter so that wouldn't happen. But when the store was empty, he'd bring Bert out and have a quiet chat with the sheep.

"Shall we take a look, see what's in the white envelope?"

Bert didn't answer. He never spoke.

Chad turned back to the white envelope, opened it, and read. Then he placed it on the counter and gazed blankly through the window. On the opposite side of the lane stood St Bees Priory. The green grass was mown, neat borders were edged at sharp angles, ready for the bright flowers in the spring. He thought about the little girl with the raven hair tied with a pink bow. Maybe it was time to visit that church, get on his knees and pray.

Really pray.

For forgiveness.

CHAPTER 8

An orange sun was up over the hills now, and the sea mist had cleared from the flat brown fields. PC Sid Hoon strolled along the lane and breathed in the chill air. Birds twittered in the barren trees, and a slight wind whistled through the branches murmuring like a contented crowd. *This is the life*, he thought as he watched a jay work an acorn. Its wings fluttered with flashes of blue, stark against the browns and greens of the countryside.

To the casual observer, he looked like a village bobby on his way to work. He carried an oversized sandwich box filled with cream doughnuts and the flask topped up with tea. And indeed he was on his way to open the police station. Not that it was much of a station, only a single room in St Bees train station. It had a telephone, computer, kettle, and space heater, which took ages to warm the room. On Saturday mornings he sat behind the desk and read the local newspaper or surfed the news on his work computer. There'd be no hordes waiting outside, no urgent matters requiring his attention, so he took his time. No rush. No hurry. The same pace he'd used for years.

Except today was different.

Today PC Hoon thought about Maude. He shouldn't have rummaged through her dresser last Tuesday. He didn't even know what he was looking for. But something told him to search. He waited until she was out of the house, then crept up the stairs. He should have been at work, but he came home to search. Under a pile of bras and knickers, at the very bottom, he found a pile of letters and a large, slim brown envelope, the type lawyers use. He tossed the letters aside and opened the envelope —a life insurance policy taken out on his name! His scrawled signature was on the paperwork, but he didn't remember signing. If he croaked, Maude got a wad of cash. He stared at the amount and gasped. Then he shoved it back under the letters, bras, and knickers. What to do about it?

If he confronted Maude, she'd know he'd been snooping. That wouldn't go down well. Maude knew his secrets. But how could he keep quiet?

Married life had been a living hell, but a divorce would wreck his meagre finances. He couldn't have that. He felt like a sparrow with a cuckoo chick in its nest. He couldn't go on like this. His nerves were shot through.

"Till death do us part," he said to the whispering trees.

A soft gurgle of water broke into his thoughts. He stopped to listen to the gentle slosh of the Pow

Beck stream. It began near the country house of Mirehouse and flowed through the village and out into the Irish Sea. Locals said it washed the flesh from the bones of King Arthur and spewed them into the surf. "Nothing good happens over them waters," they'd say. "Nothing but bad luck from Mirehouse to the salt sea."

On impulse he left the lane and made his way across a field towards the stream. He strolled along the bank following the flow of the Pow Beck and stopped under the brick stilts of the footbridge. Last year at this time, he'd spotted a rose-coloured starling and a spoonbill, which local legend said brought good luck. He stopped and watched for a few minutes, heard nothing but the call of a crow. So he poured a cup of tea from his flask, ate all his cream doughnuts from his oversized lunch box, and brooded over the question of Maude.

Twenty minutes later, with a lazy gait and contented belly, PC Hoon climbed the wood steps of the Pow bridge. He felt the strain in his legs. Warmth rushed to his face. *Eh, Sid, you need to work out at the gym,* he told himself. *Won't take but a few weeks to get into shape. A piece of cake.* He gasped for breath as he heaved himself onto the level slats.

He took three steps, then stopped. For a long moment, he stared. He staggered backwards and felt the breath being sucked from his lungs. It was the shoes he saw first. A pair of red stilettos scattered on each side of the bridge. He lifted his eyes to see a coat caught in the railing, and two paces beyond, a girl face down on the slats in a cream blouse with a thin, strappy, gold handbag across her shoulder and a short dark miniskirt hitched up to expose bare skin.

Now PC Hoon's training kicked in. He walked quickly along the slats of the bridge, heart thumping in his chest, eyes fixed on the girl.

The skin on her legs was grey with patches that were almost purple. It wasn't a schoolgirl; he could tell that now. An instant later, he knew it was Viv Gill without seeing her face. Blood pooled around her matted hair. He didn't have to get any closer to know she was dead.

An urge to see her face seized him. He told himself it was to confirm her identity but knew otherwise. He edged a step closer.

They tell uniforms never to enter a crime scene. The risk of contamination is far too great. Leave it to the crime scene techs and the suits. PC Hoon recalled this as he took two more steps and squatted next to the body. He mustn't touch Viv Gill. Still, he leaned forward and tried to look at her face. It pressed against the slats. The part he could make out was bloodied and bruised. Red, raw. Shredded.

Acid churned in his gut. PC Hoon felt light headed, felt the blood drain away from his body, saw black spots before his eyes. For a long while he remained frozen, how long he could not tell.

A sudden noise came from behind. A flutter

and scrape. Startled, PC Hoon glanced over his shoulder. A jay sat on the wood rail watching. It was only a bird, but he didn't like the glint in its sharp eyes. It reminded him of the way the shopkeeper, Chad Tate, looked at him. What had happened years back was water under the bridge. Case closed. Forgotten. He stared at the jay, wanted to shoo it away. Throw a stone, knock it dead. He barked an angry shout. He growled and swore. Wings fluttered, flashes of blue. The jay flew.

Now he was alone, but the gurgle of the Pow Beck made him uneasy. He kept hearing footsteps on the slatted steps where he'd just walked. His imagination, he knew. Still, it put the hair up on the back of his neck.

Somewhere, a crow squawked. The wind whistled through the barren trees as though in a warning shout. Once again, he thought he heard footsteps. He looked up and down the slatted bridge. There was no one about. No unwelcome eyes watching. He put on a pair of latex gloves, undid the clasp of Viv Gil's handbag, and rifled around inside.

Bingo!

With a satisfied grunt, he pulled out Viv Gill's purse and slipped it into his jacket pocket. He searched the gold handbag again, found her mobile phone, and took it. Then with a greedy grunt, he shoved the handbag into his lunch box, pushing hard to force the lid shut. Next, he peeled the gloves off his hands and reached for his own phone to make the call.

CHAPTER 9

The call came through when Fenella was at the police station.

She'd just left Jeffery's office when the duty sergeant called her over.

"A suspicious death in St Bees," he said. "I know it's not your shift, but we are short staffed today. We need to send a detective. Could you drive over and take a look?"

When she arrived, there was a small crowd of locals at one end of Pow bridge. Under a clear, blue January sky with the sun the size of a melon, they stood in silence and watched. There was an air of quiet expectation about the townsfolk. A low hum, like the mumble before a carnival horror-house ride begins.

A thin line of police tape stretched across the narrow footbridge. In front, a tall constable stood with his thick arms folded.

"Good morning, ma'am," he said as Fenella crossed the tape.

"Not for the poor sod in the crime scene tent," she replied.

The crime scene techs had already put up a tent of sorts so Fenella couldn't see the victim. She paused for a long moment to take in the scene. Figures in white suits flitted about as if ghosts. They changed colour as they moved—splashed in the red, blue, and white of flashing lights.

Fenella wondered who was in charge of the techs, hoped it was Lisa Levon. Fenella liked Lisa, thought she'd look good on the television, knew the head crime scene tech was as tough as nails. Thorough and professional. She scanned the scene but couldn't make her out in the sea of white suits.

Now she glanced about, her eyes taking everything in. The footbridge was very narrow, barely enough room for two people to pass. And the rails were lined with a mesh wire to prevent things falling through. On one side were bushes and trees. On the other side, about ten feet away, was the arched stone of the road bridge where the police vehicles were parked. Below the slats, the water of Pow Beck gurgled. So what had happened here, then?

"Guv, over here."

There was Dexter, her detective sergeant. He knelt by the handrail and peered down at the gentle waters below. Fenella knew Dexter struggled with drink, and half wondered whether he'd been at the bottle already. She stepped closer: he smelled of sour rum, but when she saw his face, it was stone-cold sober.

"Thoughts?" Fenella asked the question, although she had not yet seen the body.

He stood and shook his head. For a long while he didn’t speak. When he did, his voice was an octave higher than normal. "Nasty one, Guv. Not what you would expect in an English seaside village. Can't say you'd expect to see it in a big city either. Right nasty."

She knew, then, he had been inside the crime scene tent, already saw what she had yet to see. They'd worked together for years. Had each other's back. But she couldn't recall his voice that high-pitched. Ever. Her stomach roiled.

"Not an accident, then?" Fenella knew the answer but asked anyway.

Dexter opened his mouth, closed it, then said, "Best go see for yourself; make up your own mind. I'll have a word with the crowd, never know who saw what." He pulled out his notebook and strode with big steps towards the crime scene tape, dipped under, and disappeared into the gathered crowd.

Fenella glanced towards the crime scene tent. Three figures in white suits walked by, followed by a police constable who lingered. There was already a lot of activity, but it seemed to be increasing. The growl of a generator tore through the air as it whirred into life with a mechanical cough.

"Do we have a name?" Fenella said to herself out loud. She liked to know their name. It made it more personal.

"Viv Gill, ma'am." The answer came from a police constable, more round than stout. The one who lingered after the three white suits walked past. "She moved here six months ago, rented a room just off Station Road."

"And you are?"

"PC Hoon, ma'am. I'm the local police constable. I found the body."

Fenella's sharp eyes took him in. She'd met him before. Or rather him and his wife. What was her name? Marge... no, Maude. Maude Hoon. And she'd met the couple at a police do in Whitehaven, must have been three years ago. They'd shared a table and small talk. An odd couple, she had thought then. She remembered wondering how they'd got together. But opposites attract, don't they? Now, she racked her brain for his first name and got it in a heartbeat.

"Sid Hoon, eh? I'd forgotten this was your beat."

He took a step back.

"Have we met?"

"Aye, a couple years ago, at a police event in Whitehaven. Christmas party." Fenella liked to keep on good terms with the uniforms. She had walked the beat herself years back. So she treated police constables with respect and always made time for small talk. Then she remembered what happened at the Whitehaven Christmas party. The officer had got into a drunken argument with his wife. They'd called each other names, too tanked up to think about shame. Eduardo got between the couple and split it up before it got out of hand. "You were with Maude; we shared a table. How is your wife?"

PC Hoon smiled, but it didn't extend to his eyes. "Loving life in the country. We two are like milk and honey, belong together. My Maude is a credit to me."

"Aye," Fenella said, eyeing him with uncertainty. "Happen you're right about that. We'll have a chat later. I'll need your help to confirm the details."

"At your service, ma'am," PC Hoon replied. "Us uniform blokes are always willing to lend a helping hand." He gave a slow smile. "I'd best get back to the job. It'll be a long day." He walked quickly away from the crime scene tape, glancing twice over his shoulder.

CHAPTER 10

Fenella turned her attention to the crime scene tent. A figure in a shapeless, white suit walked from the entrance. They moved as though their legs were made of rubber. Not quite a stagger, but very close, as if they were about to collapse.

Fenella hurried forward, took the person by the arm. "It's okay, pet. Is this your first time?"

"I'm fine," a woman's voice whispered.

Fenella stared in shock. It was Lisa Levon, the head crime scene tech. Gorgeous, sexy Lisa Levon. Except today her auburn hair hung limp, dark eyes dulled, and her almost forty-something face, usually glowing with the vitality of a teenager, crinkled into the scowl of a woman twice her age. There was no doubt she was less than fine.

"You don't look fine, pet." Fenella couldn't hide the concern in her voice.

"I thought I'd seen it all," Lisa said in a dry voice. "But her face..."

"Come on, luv, this way." Fenella led her to the rail. Lisa leaned against it for support. "That bad in there, eh?"

"Worse."

Fenella glanced at the crime scene tent, then looked at Lisa with deep-felt sorrow. Whatever happened here, she would get to the bottom of it, put the perp away. Her detective mind kicked in.

"Handbag?"

"No sign of one," Lisa replied.

As Fenella thought about that, she could hear the low murmur of voices above the bubble and splash of the Pow Beck. When she glanced towards the crime scene tape, she saw PC Hoon, watching.

She turned back to Lisa and said, "Do you think it was a mugging gone wrong?"

Lisa managed a shrug. She looked sick, with sunken rings of puffy, dark flesh around her eyes. "You are the detective; we just look for clues amongst the blood, guts, and bile."

Solving crime was like reading Chinese to Lisa Levon. All strokes and squiggles. Incomprehensible. She never speculated about why a crime was committed or who did it. As the head crime scene tech, she organised her team to sift the scene for forensic clues. That was her job, and she was damn good at it. It was Fenella's job to solve the crime.

Fenella said, "Time of death?"

"Last night late or early this morning." Lisa's voice became hoarse, and she suddenly turned another shade of pale. "Viv Gill died no later than two a.m., and mercifully, it would have been quick."

Fenella knew it could not have been a mugging gone wrong. Who would wait on a bridge in the middle of a small village in hopes of mugging someone? She had checked the weather report for the previous night. A fog had blown in from the Irish Sea. Not an opportunistic thief. Not a mugging gone wrong. Someone had lain in wait, knew Viv Gill was coming.

Lisa said, "Dr MacKay is on his way to examine the body. We'll have a better estimate of time of death once he's gone over her in the pathologist lab."

Dr MacKay liked to visit the scene of a crime, get a feel for the place, see where the grisly deed was done. It was as though he got a thrill from being on-site. Fenella wondered what he'd make of it but didn't get far with that thought.

Lisa grunted, leaned over the rail and threw up into the Pow Beck stream. After the third heave, she turned to Fenella and pointed at the crime scene tent.

"You'd better go inside and see for yourself. It looks like the work of Hamilton Perkins. Mr Shred."

CHAPTER 11

Chad Tate stood at the back of the crowd watching so he wouldn't be seen.

He had closed the store after ringing up the bill on Mrs Lenz's baked beans, white bread, and small box of black English breakfast tea. Her Alf loved strong tea with his beans on toast. But she came back to the store because she forgot the milk, so Chad went to the fridge and brought back a carton, full fat.

Mrs Lenz was the rush hour, and when she left, he knew it was over. He'd planned to reread the letter in the white envelope and think about what to do next, but he heard the wailing siren of a police car, then an ambulance and another police car. Curiosity got the better of him, so he shut up shop and followed the flashing lights to the footbridge over the Pow Beck.

There were police cars all over the place. An ambulance. Even a fire truck. Chad felt an excited thrill as he watched them hurrying about like worker bees. He'd already heard that Viv Gill was dead, her body discovered by PC Hoon on the footbridge over the Pow Beck. He'd also heard the victim was a backpacker who travelled up from London, from the old widow who lived on Brown Hen Lane. The crowd were awash with the chatter of rumours. But there was only one question in Chad Tate's mind—would the police find any clues?

"Those waters are cursed."

Chad spun around.

Mrs Lenz tightened her headscarf. "My Alf always said those waters were blighted ever since they washed King Arthur's bones into the Irish sea, and with Viv Gill dead, I've half a mind to believe him."

"Now, Mrs Lenz," Chad said in a measured tone, "that is just a myth. What happened here can't have anything to do with King Arthur."

Mrs Lenz said, "Poor lass was out and about last night in all that fog. Don't suppose you saw anything?"

"I just got here," Chad replied, voice suddenly hoarse.

"That's odd." She stared at him with her sharp eyes. "You like to walk about the village in the wee hours. I'm surprised you didn't find the body. Did you walk across the bridge this morning?"

Chad turned away. He didn't like the way her sharp eyes looked at him. "Let's not jump to conclusions. It might not be Viv Gill."

"Mr Tate, there is a dead girl on the footbridge

over the Pow Beck with police swarming like ants. And the vicar says he couldn't get an answer when he knocked on Viv Gill's door. Am I right? I am."

"But we don't know the facts," Chad replied. "It might have been an accident. Are you sure it is Viv Gill?"

"Whoever the poor lass was, she died an unnatural death." Mrs Lenz's eyes seemed to cloud for a moment. "Pity you don't sell fresh fish in your store; my Alf likes his fish pie."

"We have fish fingers," Chad replied automatically. He always tried to provide what the villagers wanted so the shop would be profitable. Not that he was bothered about the money, he just wanted to stay in St Bees. Forever.

An excited murmur rose from the gathered crowd. Two figures clad in white suits hurried from the crime scene tent.

"They've found something!" Mrs Lenz placed a veined hand on his shoulder and squeezed softly. "I hope they catch the bugger who killed her, don't you, Mr Tate?" She tugged at her headscarf, gave him a sad smile, and hurried to the police tape to get a better view.

Chad watched as she nattered with the crowd, then gazed at the crime scene tent. He wished he could see inside. See what they were doing. Watch like a fly high on the wall. He felt his heart thud against his chest. The police wouldn't find anything, would they?

His heart pounded so hard, he forced his mind to think of something else. It settled on his village store and the white envelopes under the counter. He sighed. If he were a real businessman, he'd be back in the shop. With so many people about they'd want a bite to eat, and his was the only store for miles. He'd make a killing if he opened up now.

But Chad Tate didn't want to open the store.

He wanted to stay here all day and watch from the back of the crowd where the police wouldn't see him.

CHAPTER 12

The following day, Fenella paced restlessly at the front of Incident Room A, waiting for the team to settle down and the real work to begin. She had seen to a tea urn and brought breakfast sandwiches made by Nan. A coffee pot bubbled in the corner; its aromatic brew drifted through the air. At 7:00 a.m. on a cold Sunday, where darkness and fog still clung to Port St Giles, hot drinks and warm food would be welcomed by her team.

She loved this part of the job, leading her team, calling the shots. Today they'd focus on Viv Gill, build a picture of her life. What secrets would they find?

The superintendent was late; hence, the wait. Jeffery had called the meet at a time when the police station would be quiet. Less ears to hear their hushed talk. Less mouths to flap their plan to the press. What happened next was to be top secret. Fenella was keen to hear all the details, keen to get started, hoped Jeffery wouldn't be much longer.

The tea urn let out a gurgle. Steam twisted in gusty spirals vanishing like a ghost in the bright room. Fenella paused her anxious pacing and wondered what was holding up her boss. Probably speaking to the top brass in Carlisle or smoothing things over with the town hall. She pecked at a sandwich and took a quick swig of tea. If she'd known what lay ahead, she'd have done more than nibble. She'd have gobbled the whole bloody thing down in one bite and grabbed another.

But Fenella was in a bright mood, and her team were at full strength once more. She felt good about that. Dexter sat in the front row poised like a coil about to spring. He drank his coffee black and munched on a bacon-and-egg roll. His dark eyes shone bright. No sign of booze on his breath. No sign of a drunken slur. He was ready. So was she. The death of Viv Gill came as a shock to many. Not Fenella. She left surprise at the door the day she joined the force. Replaced it with a tenacious curiosity for the truth, no matter what stones had to be upturned.

Detective Constable Zack Jones stood by the coffee pot with a small cup in his hand. He joined her team from the national detective school. At thirty-five, he was no newbie and had worked in business for years, then made a mid-career switch. What he lacked in uniform streetwise, he made up for in brains. He came top of his class in finance forensics and a history of art degree from Cambridge. He had a masters in photography from the Royal Academy and was easy on the eyes too. A smooth talker, he'd charmed Fenella on their first meet. Charm had worked for Eduardo too. All he had when Fenella met him was a sketch pad, pen, and a head full of dreams.

Muffled laughter drifted from PC Beth Finn. She hovered around the coffee pot, her eyes on DC Jones. She was the new member of the team. PC Beth Finn had been asked, and agreed, to help. She'd work in plain clothes. A short-term job, which Fenella thought she'd relish. Out of uniform, PC Finn looked even younger than her twenty-seven years.

The tea urn let out another hiss. The lights in the room flickered, and there was a moment of darkness. Someone shuffled into the room. The lights came back on. PC Hoon stood in the entrance, his gaze uncertain.

"Grab a bite to drink and eat," Fenella said, waving him into the room. She had a soft spot for uniforms. Village bobbies were a kind of police royalty in her eyes. They knew what went on in their patch. Knew the secrets and the lies. She hoped he'd help with the locals, sort out the wheat from the chaff. "Plenty to go around. We'll start when the superintendent is here. Won't be long now, though."

"Right you are, ma'am," PC Hoon said, lips twitching up at the corners. He shook himself out of his coat and filled his plate with three bacon-and-egg rolls and chose the large-sized paper cup for his tea. "Guess it will be a long day, with even longer to come."

The door opened. Jeffery marched into the room. She stopped to pour a coffee and grabbed a bacon-and-egg roll, then gave Fenella a quick nod and went to the whiteboard. For a long while, she stared at the crime scene photographs, the only sound, her muffled grunts. Then she turned and gave one of her smiles that always reminded Fenella of a wolf. It made her stomach churn because the superintendent's lips only curved that way when there was bad news.

Jeffery said, "Inspector Moss, from the regional crime squad, will lead the Viv Gill murder investigation. He is due here any moment, driving from Carlisle."

CHAPTER 13

Fenella sat on the front row next to Dexter and Jones and PC Beth Finn. She sipped a cup of warm tea, nibbled the edge of her bacon-and-egg roll and stared at Inspector Tom Moss. Outside, the fog had cleared, with the darkness of dawn having turned into bright light. A crisp January morning in Port St Giles. No clouds, just an orange-globe sun in an ice-blue sky. A perfect day. A day to cherish. But it was tough to enjoy the weather when acid slowly bubbled in your gut.

Fenella and Moss had a history.

A bad history.

Yes, he was from the regional crime squad and had been on the force for as long as she could recall. That gave him street cred and a sharp nose that got things done. He caught the perps and put them away as efficiently as a machine. But the man was a dinosaur who had survived the wind of change that swept aside the bigots.

Maybe he had changed?

Moss surveyed the room with his cool grey eyes.

He said, "The top brass have asked that I lead the team." He glared at Fenella. "They thought it wise to bring in a man with experience."

There he goes again, Fenella thought, *trying to needle me*. She sipped from her cup, kept her eyes on his face, but didn't say a word.

Jeffery said, "We picked Inspector Moss because we want to keep the investigation local for the moment. If it goes to the regional crime squad, the press and media will be all over it. Let's stay one step ahead of the pack and clear this up quickly. We don't want any fuss."

The door opened. Everyone turned. Tess Allen, the press officer, hurried into the room with a large folder under her arm. Tess wore a sharp business executive jacket, matching skirt, cream blouse, and dark shoes. Fenella thought Tess brought a touch of class to the station. And Tess had one of those plum-filled accents, all posh, like she'd grown up in Windsor and hobnobbed with the royal family. A perfect voice for the media, perfect for calming the public mood too. She went to sit on the back row, but Jeffery waved her to the front.

Tess said, "All questions from the press are to come to me. Until the media have worked up a head of steam, we maintain radio silence. Remember, if Rodney Rawlings comes calling, the answer is no."

Rodney Rawlings worked for the *Westmorland News* and was a tenacious news hound, who liked his stories big. He drank hard, chased leads like a fox, and foxed around with women, like a dog in heat. No one crossed Rodney Rawlings. He knew where the skeletons lay and was not shy about digging them up and putting them on public display.

Jones glanced at his phone and said, "I've not seen anything on the social media sites yet. Nothing from the *Westmorland News* either."

"We might be a day or two ahead of the media," Tess replied. "No one has come sniffing at the press office either, but it is Sunday. Even Mr Rodney Rawlings likes a lie-in."

Everyone laughed. It was the first time Fenella had seen Moss chuckle. His shoulders jiggled as he wiped a tear from his face. It was hard to dislike a man with a good sense of humour. She warmed to him, a little.

Jeffery held up a hand. "We are going with the theory that Viv Gill was killed by Hamilton Perkins. He escaped from prison two months ago, is believed to be lying low in the region, and her mutilated body has all the hallmarks. We have hired Dr Joy Hall to assist. She doesn't know about the death of Viv Gill yet. I will brief her on Monday."

Jeffery nodded at Moss, touched Tess Allen's arm, and the two women left the room.

"Right, then," Moss said. He spoke as though he were spitting out a distasteful flavour from his mouth. "Let's see who I'm working with. Sallow and

Dexter, eh? Gawd, a man can dream of an elite team, can't he?"

Dexter shifted in his seat. Fenella touched his arm; she didn't want him to swing for Moss. They'd exchanged physical blows before. She had to pull every string to get that swept under the carpet. It would have cost both Dexter and Moss their jobs.

Fenella said, "We are happy to have a regional detective work at our level. Our own Constable Zack Jones studied at Cambridge." She pointed at Jones. "If you don't understand anything, please let him know, and he will simplify it for you."

Moss chuckled, but his eyes were sharp as a hawk. He turned to PC Beth Finn.

"Name and rank?"

She responded and smiled. Moss seemed to like that, for his lips curved into a grin, and his eyes lingered on her breasts.

He hadn't changed.

Moss licked his lips. "Welcome aboard the express train, PC Finn. It is going to be a wild ride. You'll get a peek at how the big boys work and..." He paused as if there was more to come. They waited. He shook his head, pointed at PC Hoon who had got up to grab another bacon-and-egg roll. "And who the hell are you?"

"Police Constable Sid Hoon, from St Bees at your service, sir."

"Out!"

"Pardon?"

"Get out! I'll not have any bleedin' village bobby bugger up my investigation. Get lost."

That riled Fenella. She stood. "We need all the help we can get here, sir."

Moss pulled a face. "I'm not buying, Sallow. Uniforms are only good at two things, screwing things up and getting things wrong."

It wasn't her call, Moss could do as he pleased, but she couldn't back down now; he'd got under her skin. She kept her voice level. "PC Hoon's knowledge of the locals could be the key that turns the lock to Hamilton Perkins."

"No. I've told him to bugger off." Moss glared at PC Hoon. "Clear off."

If Fenella were a cat, she'd have exposed her claws. It should have been her case. Now, five minutes on the job, and Tom Moss was throwing his weight about. She wouldn't put up with that. She'd seen Viv Gill's mutilated face. They needed help to solve the case from wherever it came and that included the village bobby. There was no way she would back down. Dexter sensed this and touched her arm, but it was too late.

"We can't leave PC Hoon out of this," she said in almost a shout. "There'll be an appeal for someone in the village to come forward, tell us what they saw.

It will be easier with the local bobby. We need him. You have to try everything in a case like this. Local police are the blood that runs through the veins of our communities." She stood and sensed Dexter standing at her side. "PC Hoon stays, or we walk!"

There was a long silence. The coffee pot gurgled. Everyone watched Moss as if he were a volcano about to explode. The tea urn hissed.

Moss licked his lips. Again, he chuckled. It didn't extend to his eyes.

"Fair enough, Sallow. If Hoon screws things up, I will hold you personally responsible."

CHAPTER 14

Fenella turned off the main road onto the gravel lane that snaked its way along the coast to her cottage on Cleaton Bluff. The sun had slipped below the pine trees so that shadows drew thin fingers across the windscreen. It was only three but would be as dark as midnight by four.

At the station, Inspector Moss had gone over the Viv Gill case with his sour wit and sexist digs. Dexter had almost swung at him when he made a jibe—something to do with Miss Gill's face being an improvement after the knife.

Fenella eased the Morris Minor around a sharp bend and let out a long breath. Now it was time to let go, to flip the switch and spend the rest of Sunday with Eduardo and Nan. As soon as she climbed into her car and pointed it towards home, the crimes faded away. As did the forms to fill and sign and file. She had long ago mastered the switch between work and family life. She reached for her radio and turned it on. Hits from the 1980s boomed through the car speakers. She sang at the top of her voice when Prince's "When Doves Cry" came on.

It was in London, the Ealing Dome, when she

saw him perform the song live. Eve, her sister, was there too. She had gotten the tickets for free from a friend of a friend. They danced and laughed and cried and giggled. Two girls out for a bit of fun.

At two in the morning, they'd walked from the Dome through Ealing Broadway on their way to a friend's house on Madeley Road. Eve suddenly stopped, turned, and went into a darkened doorway. She came back moments later with a small dog in her arms, a scruffy ball of fur with frightened eyes. She called the dog TJ and planned to take it to the Ealing dog shelter the next day.

At the house on Madeley Road, the small group stayed up all night drinking and smoking and making plans for their life. TJ ate, then slept. Eve never did take him to the shelter. He became part of her life.

Fenella slowed her car as she relived the memories long past: the rumble of the train at the bottom of the garden as it rattled along the track, a golden sun rising through the haze to light a new London morning—and she remembered Grant. That friend's home on Madeley Road was where Eve met him, and Fenella knew they would one day be man and wife.

A tractor huffed and coughed into view. Fenella pulled to the verge to let it through. The man gave a wave of thanks. She recognised him: Mr Bray. He ran a small organic farm which sold old-style apple trees. His broad smile lifted her mood even higher than Prince's music could. She'd pop in for a visit and take him one of Nan's steak-and-mushroom pies. Eve used to gobble those treats as if they were the last drop of water in an oasis. Fenella laughed out loud at that. An instant later, the pain of what had happened to Eve hovered over her like a ghost. Where had she gone?

All they had were the CCTV cameras of Eve stumbling along the hospital hall. The clip lasted less than thirty seconds. Eve shuffled with her hand on the rail, clearly the worse for wear. She'd been in a car wreck with her legs and arms bruised, and she knew that Grant didn't make it. At the end of the hall, she fumbled with a door latch and pushed. No suitcase. No coat. No car keys. Eve simply stepped through the hospital doors at 7:03 p.m. and was never seen again.

Fenella pulled out every stop to find out where her sister went. She drew a blank at every turn. No witness in the hospital. No one saw her in the nearby streets. No nameless body in the morgue. No lost-memory cases in the hostels. Nothing.

Eve's disappearance and Grant's death were double blows to Nan. Two loved ones lost in a split second. One to death and the other...? No one had the answer. Not the vicar who came to express deep sorrow nor the reporter Rodney Rawlings, who wrote a story. Fenella had no answers either. No one knew what had happened to Eve. No one could help.

After a week of dead ends, Fenella got onto a friend in the regional crime squad. The friend agreed to look into the case, got transferred before the file arrived, and passed it to Inspector Tom Moss. Another week passed. Fenella went to the offices in Carlisle. Moss hadn't looked at the file. It lay in a pile on the floor. Dexter was with her that day. How she regretted asking him to come along for support. It had turned into a bloody fiasco.

Dexter called Moss a lazy sod. The two men got into a tense standoff. Quiet curses at first until they were howling like wolves. What happened next seemed to go in slow motion. Dexter swung first. A solid left hook to the jaw. Moss stumbled back, then sprung forward like a wild beast. Fists flew. The two men slugged it out like old-time heavyweight boxers. Somehow, Fenella got in the middle and called out for help. It took five officers to break up the scrap.

Fenella yanked every string, used every trick to keep Dexter out of hot water. In the end, she had to save Moss as well even though she would have liked to have thrown him to the dogs.

When she saw Moss today, she'd thought of Eve and the missed chances to track her down those first few weeks after she vanished. Her feelings towards Moss were personal. Should she step down from the case, have a word with Jeffery?

No. She'd not do that. They had no idea what

happened to Eve, but she could help find out what happened to Viv Gill.

The Morris Minor eased around another bend. The tree shadows merged with the coming night. It was a straight shot into her driveway. As she pulled into a parking spot, she saw Eduardo, relaxing in a chair on the porch, his nose in a book. He looked up at the sound of the engine, stood, and smiled.

Nan always told her, "There's no place like home." Now she knew exactly what that meant.

CHAPTER 15

Late Sunday night, Dr Joy Hall sat at her desk in her spacious office. A faint trace of fresh paint hung in the air. The painters had left two days earlier; now she had the place to herself. The cottage had been remodelled to her satisfaction, a remote house on the edge of St Bees only a short walk from the salt marsh and sea. It beat the cramped flat she had owned in Carlisle. Here she could spread out and do some real research. Maybe she should get a dog?

The old house creaked and groaned and made strange noises that she'd never heard when she lived in the flat. Sometimes she thought they sounded like voices, muffled so the words were not clear. "It's the ghost of old Mrs Rye," one of the painters had said when she asked him about the strange creaks.

The widow had died in the house a decade ago, during one cold, hard winter when the snow fell deep and didn't break until May. They found her sat up in bed with a book on her lap. The maggots were huge, the smell damn awful. The house stayed empty, derelict, until Dr Joy Hall snapped it up at a low price. As good a deal as it was, the mortgage was much more than she could afford on her pay from

Low Marsh Prison, and she had a lot of big dreams to go with the house, the kind that don't come true on a prison psychologist's salary.

Joy was working on a secret project, funded with a big advance from a London publisher. She couldn’t believe the money. Her eyes were on stalks when they deposited it into her bank account. She used it for a down payment on the house.

The publisher said it was a sure winner. They said they'd sell a million books, that Dr Joy Hall would become a household name, and it would rocket her career to new heights. The royalties would more than pay the mortgage. But they wanted the book soon. The public were fickle and would move on to new things.

Joy leaned back in her chair and let her eyelids droop. When the book came out, there'd be chauffeured trips to London and free flights to New York. Even the Chinese were said to be keen. This was her shot, her one chance to break through to the big league. But she couldn't quell the sense of unease which nibbled at her mind like some unseen disease. Could she do this, set herself up as an expert? She felt like an impostor. And she had to keep it top secret. If they found out at work what she was up to, she'd lose her job. Maybe even end up serving time in prison for breach of her professional duty.

Now she had two weeks off from work ahead and only the last chapter to go. It would tie her years of research into a neat bow and required careful preparation, so she took her time. It was slow going, and she couldn't quite pull it all together. What she really needed was inside information, to be a fly on the wall, to see how things unfolded. Yet she couldn't quell the excited pulse of her heart as she sensed the end was in sight. If things went well and the book flew off the shelves, she'd be rich. And she would do everything in her power to make sure things went well.

It felt good to take time off her job in Low Marsh Prison to write. She felt like an undiscovered genius. An Einstein of criminal psychology. Didn't he work as a public servant before he was discovered too? *Don't be silly; you are no genius*. Still, the thought lingered like smoke from a fire.

So intense was Joy's focus that she forgot to eat. She glanced up — almost eleven o'clock. Her last meal was breakfast: half a slice of toast and a mug of black coffee. Hunger nibbled at her stomach as she stood and stretched. Suddenly she had the feeling that she was being watched. There were no curtains in the windows. She turned from the desk and peered through the glass.

A face stared back.

Her own.

Beyond her reflection there was nothing but shadows and darkness. *There'd be no one out at this time a night,* she told herself. It was freezing outside with an icy wind, which blew in sharp gusts from the Irish Sea. And anyway, she had only moved into the old house a few days ago. Hardly anyone knew she was here. Who would be watching?

But she was a woman, striking, in her fifties, who lived alone in the middle of nowhere. She should take precautions. She would look into that on the next trip to Carlisle. She turned away from the window. Grab a bite to eat or go on with the work?

She chose to keep at it for an hour, then break for a small, fat-free cup of cocoa. As she eased into her leather chair, picked up her notes and read, again came the disquieting sense of being watched. She glanced at the dark window and wondered if there was someone there.

"Don't be a damn fool," she said, but her voice in the still room made her jumpy. "You're working too hard."

It was almost midnight when Joy Hall next looked up. She thought she heard a key in the front door. She put her research to one side and listened. For a long while she stayed very still, like a small mouse on the watch for a cat. Why would anyone be at her door?

For an instant she was a child, face to face with Uncle Fred. The midnight chimes had just rung from the hall clock, and he was peering through the gloom of her bedroom door, ale can in hand and grinning. She sat up, and his face faded into the shadows. But she knew he was there. Knew he was waiting. Smelled the sour stench of cheap cigarettes and strong beer. Joy shook her head. It had been years since she saw Uncle Fred. Twenty, at least. How would he know she had moved to St Bees? It couldn’t be him at the door, could it?

There it was again. A jingling sound as if the wrong key had been selected. She crept into the hall and switched on the light but could see nothing through the glass panel of the door but her own reflection. She felt nervous and foolish. Who would have a key to her front door?

"Hello, is anyone there?"

No answer.

There was a low table with a lamp and an old-style rotary telephone near the front door. She had not bothered with the telephone landline; her mobile phone was good enough. But that was before she found out that the mobile phone signal was weak in St Bees. She got no bars in most of the house and one in the study, if she was lucky. Now she wished she'd had the landline connected. She turned on the lamp, her eyes fixed on the glass panel of the door and waited.

Three slow minutes passed.

Nothing.

After three more minutes, she padded to the door and peered out. Wind hissed through leafless trees. Clouds clustered low under a moonless sky with the garden bathed in shades of night blue. In the distance an owl hooted, and farther out, the low rumble of the sea. There was no one there. No one about. *The ghost of old Mrs Rye*, she told herself, nothing but the creak and groan of the house.

She made a cup of cocoa and took it to the study with two chunks of cheddar cheese. The lamp on the telephone table she left on, as well as the lights in the hall. Yes, she would definitely see to the landline and get a dog. Though she knew even a big dog wouldn't ease her nervousness. That wouldn't go away until her secret book came out.

It was about Hamilton Perkins.

Mr Shred.

The sooner he was caught and put away, the sooner Dr Joy Hall could put her last chapter to bed.

CHAPTER 16

Early Monday morning, PC Sid Hoon slipped out of bed, tiptoed across the bedroom and hoped Maude wouldn't hear. He wanted to get away from the house without having to explain.

He stepped on a floorboard.

It creaked.

He cursed.

"What the hell are you playing at?"

Maude flipped on the bedside lamp and sat up.

PC Hoon blinked into the bright light and stared at his wife. With those damn pink curlers and sagging skin on her chin, she reminded him of a giant lizard. Only a lizard's eyes had more warmth to them.

Best not tell, he thought. *Got to keep this to myself.* He said, "It's Monday morning, luv. I'm getting ready for work."

"For crying out loud, Sid, it's five thirty." She flashed a shrewd look. "What's going on?"

His mind seized. He watched the second hand move around the bedside clock for a full thirty seconds. If he told her where he was going, she'd get excited, make plans to sell the house, spend even more of his hard-earned cash. He couldn't have that.

He said, "I want to get in early today."

"Why?"

Again, he didn't have an easy answer. When did he last go to the police station early? Must have been years ago, he couldn't recall. Maude would know. The suspicious glare in her eyes gave him the answer: Never.

PC Hoon let out a morose sigh and realised he hadn't thought it through. Even if he had sneaked from the bedroom without waking her up, there'd be questions for sure when he came back late.

Better tell the truth. Sort of.

He said, "I've been asked to work with the detectives on the Viv Gill case."

Maude reached for a cigarette, struck a match, and sucked until her sunken cheeks gave her the look of a Halloween mask.

"You don't say."

"Just a minor role, really. The village plod on the beat who knows the locals."

A plume of smoke spidered from Maude's nose. "So you are driving to Port St Giles today?"

"Want to be there by seven thirty, briefing starts at eight."

"Well, pop into the village store and grab me a six-pack of Diet Coke. I'm running low."

"Okay, honey." But it was too early in the morning to face the accusatory stare of the shopkeeper. He didn't want to be reminded of the past. He'd give the St Bees village store a pass and grab the drinks in Port St Giles.

Maude said, "How long will you be working with the detectives?"

"For as long as they need me."

"I see."

He could tell she was already planning to spend more of his money and said, "It's only a temporary assignment, and then I'll be back to a plod on a village beat."

Maude looked at him through narrowed eyes, sucked on her cigarette, and blew out another plume of acrid smoke.

"Someone has been rummaging through my dresser. Was it you?"

He stared back, but his denial didn't come; her words left him completely paralysed. An eerie silence hung in the room so that the second hand of the clock tick-tocked like a cannon boom. He didn't want her to know he knew about the life insurance policy. *What to say?*

At last, he said, "Are you sure?"

"I can tell whether someone's been in my sodding dresser, you idiot."

"Oh, your dresser! That must have been me. One of my tie pins fell down the back, and I had to move it, must have disturbed the contents too. Is anything missing?"

Maude stared at him and took another drag on her cigarette, then dusted the ash into the saucer on the nightstand.

CHAPTER 17

PC Hoon took a quick shower, then sat at the kitchen table listening to the radio and thinking. He needed to find a way to fix Maude good and proper. Get her out of his life for good without her sticky fingers grabbing any of his cash. He had to find a path to freedom, no matter how ugly it got.

He walked to the stove, poured hot water into a cup, and dipped in a teabag. Maude knew where his secrets lay. If he threatened divorce, she would dig them up and put them on display for the world to see. He'd lose his job. He could not let that happen. He had to be careful. He stirred the tea with a slow spoon. Sugar came next, a splash of milk, and back to the table to think and sip.

When he drained the last dregs from his mug, he listened for Maude and thought he heard a snore. With quiet steps, he walked to the slatted door that led to the basement. *Careful*, he told himself. He didn't want the steps to creak.

In a box of rusted work tools he found Viv Gill's gold handbag, purse, and mobile phone, exactly where he placed them Saturday morning. This was his first real look. He put on a pair of latex gloves and lifted the items from the box. With one hand on the rail and quiet steps, he climbed back into the kitchen. At the table, with a gloved hand, he pressed the on button. The phone flickered into life. *Piece of cake,* he told himself as he tried a swipe to unlock the screen.

It didn't work.

He tried again.

Still nothing.

He placed the phone on the table and stared at it for a long while. Once more he picked it up and swiped again and again and again until it gave four ear-splitting beeps which locked out any more tries.

He swore, realised too late to keep his voice down. He didn't want to wake his wife, didn't want her to hear or see. She didn’t know about this secret. So he shut his mouth, although he felt a vein throb in his neck. It eased a little as he continued the tirade in his mind.

Next, he turned to Viv Gill's purse and rifled around inside. A credit card, two debit cards, and twenty pounds in five-pound notes, enough for a nosh-up lunch.

Now he looked at the mobile phone, decided it was best to destroy it. He'd chuck it into the Pow Beck stream on his way to Port St Giles. The purse he'd add to his private hoard. The credit cards, he'd pass on to a fence in Carlisle, but not just yet, better to wait a while.

"Twelve," he said in a whisper, the number of women's handbags in his secret stash. This was the secret he'd kept from Maude. That made him smile. He knew he would outsmart Maude, outsmart the detectives, get away with it. *Piece of cake,* he told himself again as he ran a hand over the soft gold leather of the handbag.

He didn't hear the creak of the kitchen door or see Maude watching.

CHAPTER 18

Chad Tate liked to watch. But today he had to talk to someone.

He stood by the checkout and looked at his empty store. It was 10:00 a.m., seven customers since he opened: three loaves of white bread, four cartons of full-fat milk, seven newspapers, and two packets of Benson & Hedges cigarettes. He let out a morose sigh and turned to stare through the window. The sun was above the rooftops in an ice-blue, cloudless sky. It dappled St Bees Priory in shards of glitter and coloured the neat lawns in soft shades of green. Freezing outside, but pretty enough to watch. It was his life, watching.

It's what old folk do when there's nothing else left, he told himself. *Watch.* He ran a hand over his receding hairline and patted his gut. The store was supposed to be the heart of the village, and it drove him crazy that none of his customers had stayed to gossip about the death of Viv Gill. That's what he wanted to talk about.

The local bobby hadn't been in yet either. Where was PC Hoon? He always came in on Monday and blathered on like a broken steam pipe that released white mist in the winter streets of New York City. Chad wanted to hear the details of Viv Gill's last moments. Again and again and again, until it seared an image deep in his mind. One that would stay with him forever.

He trudged to the fridge to check the dates on the cartons of milk. Then he rearranged the loaves of bread and tins of baked beans. If this were a deli in New York, he'd sell sliced hams and salami. But the villagers only wanted bacon and sausages and quick-frozen peas. *No point thinking about New York,* he told himself. *You're not going back. Ever.*

He thought for a moment about going into the storeroom to check the contents of the freezer. The thought of opening the lid made his heart pound. Now he felt edgy. Better to not look inside; let sleeping dogs lie.

Chad went back to the cash register and pulled out Bert, the one-eyed, three-legged sheep. *At least Bert will listen,* he told himself, *and he won't repeat what I tell him.* He gazed through the window to collect his thoughts. That's when he saw Vicar Briar hunched in the entrance of St Bees Priory, puffing on a cigar. He wore a black cassock and stood in a way that made him appear to be part of the shadow.

Chad watched.

The cleric leaned his head back and breathed out a long, slow plume. It curled in tight circles like a dragon's breath, to vanish in the gloom.

"It's time," Chad said to Bert, "for a quiet word with the man of God."

He flipped the store sign to CLOSED, locked the door, and hurried across the lane.

As Chad's footsteps echoed across the cobblestones, Vicar Briar moved from the shade into the light. He was a wiry man in his mid-forties with puffy, red cheeks, a purply bulbous nose, and deep-set, small, dark eyes.

"What is it, my son?" The vicar couldn't hide the alarm in his voice. He outed the cigar against the stone wall.

"It's this business with Viv Gill," Chad said. "Can we talk?"

"Not here," Vicar Briar replied.

"Inside, then?" Chad nodded at the church door. He'd only been inside the hallowed hall once, didn't want to go back in there again. Not after what happened last time.

"No, best if we don't go in there," the vicar replied. "Follow me."

Vicar Briar moved fast. The cassock covered his feet, so it appeared he was floating. A black shadow hurrying across the land as though time itself were running out. Chad followed. They made their way across the neat green lawn, around ancient tombstones and freshly dug turf, to an old stone shack with a corrugated iron roof and small, round, grime-stained windows, like portholes on a boat.

The vicar glanced over his shoulder and hurried inside. It smelled of soil and mould, and the only light came from the small, circular windows.

"Now," the vicar began, "what is all this about?"

"I like to watch," Chad said. He blinked as his eyes adjusted to the dark.

"I know, my son. I know." The vicar's eyes narrowed. In the gloom they looked like two bottomless pools of still water. "Thinking about the little girls?"

"I am. Don't you?"

"Of course, ever since the—"

"Please don't say it."

"Don't let it become an obsession."

"I can't help myself."

"This goes right to the top." Vicar Briar closed his eyes for a moment as if in prayer. "I've a meeting with the bishop at the end of next week. He is all in. Keep that to yourself. Our little secret, okay?"

"I don't want to leave St Bees."

"You might have to, if things heat up."

"But—"

"You have to think like a businessman. We all

do. Focus on the money."

"It's just that the death of Viv Gill makes things more—"

The vicar raised a hand, palm out, his voice tense. "You saw something?"

"It was dark, the night filled with fog. How could anyone see?"

Vicar Briar placed a hand in his cassock and pulled out a lighter and lit a cigar. "Dominus Deus tuus ignis consumens est."

Chad didn't understand. "What was that?"

Vicar Briar said, "The Lord, your God, is a consuming fire." He sucked hard on the cigar, and puffed out a great grey plume. Then he took a step and placed an arm around Chad's shoulder. "It is God's will that you saw nothing, my son. If the police ask you questions, you'll have nothing to say."

CHAPTER 19

"Three birds with one stone."

Fenella spoke out loud as she pulled into the car park of the St Bees Cottage Hospital. There'd been a long briefing about Viv Gill at first light. The full team were there bright and early. PC Hoon sat on the front row and wrote pages of notes. Inspector Tom Moss strutted about like a peacock. He barked questions at the team and cursed if he didn't like the answer. Where was the pathologist report? What about the crime scene techs' analysis? Has anyone been on to the labs yet?

Fenella had spent the rest of the morning on desk work. It was noon now. She'd planned to visit the morgue to have a quick chat with the pathologist, Dr MacKay, and then a catch-up lunch with her friend, Gail Stubbs. But there was one thing she had to do first.

It was bright inside the children's ward with cartoons drawn on the walls in more colours than a rainbow.

The desk nurse said, "Are you Inspector Sallow?"

"Aye, for my sins."

The nurse looked at her with something akin to admiration and said, "Her name is Ann Lloyd. She is asking for you."

Ann Lloyd sat up in bed, her face pale as dawn. She held a crayon in her small hand, and a large colouring book rested in her lap. An IV tube dripped into her arm. But her huge brown eyes were bright, and she chatted to herself as she drew. Her mother sat on a chair beside the bed with her face turned towards her daughter's picture.

They both looked up at the same time. *Spitting image*, Fenella thought. Just like she and her sister, Eve. She tilted her head from side to side to ease the sudden knots that staked a claim to her neck.

The mother stood. "Inspector Sallow?"

"The same."

The little girl grinned, but she didn't speak. She looked very small and very shy in a gown two sizes too large.

Fenella held out her hand to the mother, but the woman lightly batted it away and gave her a hug.

"Thank you," she said in a whisper. Then broke away. "Please, take a seat."

Fenella had five grown children of her own, and then there were the grandkids. She pointed at the colouring book and said, "So what are you drawing?"

"The beach," Ann said. "It's still my favourite place."

"Aye, happen you love it as much as me."

Ann looked at her for a long while, then said, "Are you a defective?"

"It's detective, darling," said her mother.

Ann grinned at Fenella. "Are you one of those?"

"That's right," Fenella replied. "I'm a detective, and my job is to help people."

"I want to be a detective when I grow up.... or a nurse... or live on the moon and fly a spaceship."

Fenella grinned. "Why not do all three?"

"Oh," Ann said, considering. She nodded and turned back to her drawing.

The mother said, "She remembered playing on the beach, the ambulance ride, a nurse telling her not to worry, that her mum was on her way. But nothing about being swept into the sea."

"Aye, maybe that's for the best," Fenella said.

They watched in silence for a while as Ann drew. Then Fenella eased to her feet, gave the mother a wave, and tiptoed from the room. She'd just wanted to check on how the girl was doing. Reports were one thing, but seeing for yourself was another.

Now she'd see for herself what Dr MacKay had

to say about Viv Gill. A sharp knot of tension gripped her neck.

CHAPTER 20

Fenella stared in shock.

She sat in Dr MacKay's office. It wasn't the glass jars filled with human body parts, which sagged on overstuffed shelves in the dim room, that caused her surprise, or the thick, sweet stench of death, which no amount of air freshener or potpourri could scrub from the cool, still air—it was the person who sat across the desk.

Dr Oz said, "Dr MacKay has taken some time off. We are short staffed, so I've stepped in to cover his role for the next few days."

Dr Paul Oz, an angular-faced man with keen eyes and an air of importance and impatience, was the medical director at the Port St Giles Cottage Hospital. He had risen through the ranks and secured the top spot at a relatively young age for a medic. He was in his early forties and had worked many roles: from heart surgeon to mental health specialist, and even served a stint as a family doctor. Now, it seemed, he'd turned his talented hand to the cut-and-slice of the post-mortem room.

Fenella said, "A week or two in the sun, eh?"

She'd never known Dr MacKay to take time off. He lived in the labs. He'd hovered in the halls of the post-mortem rooms for almost forty years. She'd heard he slept there too. That could not be true. But there were so many rumours about the long-time medic. They swirled around the hospital like leaves trapped by a city wall. His wife, it was said, was as thin as a wisp and wore African kanga dresses with pink sandals: on her head, a loose tartan headscarf, and she drove an ancient Volkswagen minibus with black windows, to keep folks from seeing what went on inside. None of that could be true either.

Dr Oz said, "He's gone with his wife to Kenya. I hear she likes the exotic shops and fills her bags with dashiki robes. Wouldn't be a shock if the good doctor filled his own bags with bones. They come home next Monday, late."

Fenella made a note, looked up, and said, "Shame, I just popped in to have a quiet chat about... things."

Dr Oz said, "I'm no sleuth, not bright enough, but are you here to discuss Viv Gill?"

Fenella took her time to respond. Inspector Moss had told the team to keep their inquiries low profile, not reveal any details. Not even to the medics. A local murder, that's all. Keep it under wraps until they had no choice. They didn't want to start a panic or alert the press, who'd start a stampede. Moss would blow his top if the news got out. And anyway, they'd not yet confirmed that Viv Gill died at the hand of Hamilton Perkins, although they were working under the theory that she did. But until they had official confirmation, there would be no need to alert the politicians or public. And they didn’t want to do that. Not yet. Not until they'd had a chance to work a few leads, shake the trees to see what fell out.

She said, "What can you tell me?"

"Too early for any detailed results."

"I know, but you have a sharp mind; what does it tell you?"

He shrugged. "My role is not to theorise, just report the known facts, which are not clear at this stage."

Not like Dr MacKay, then, Fenella thought. *He'd speculate until the cows came home and then bet a bottle of Glenmorangie whisky on his far-out ideas.* She'd learned not to take his bets. The strange ideas too often came through.

She said, "We want to build a picture, then we'll generate leads. It is early but your thoughts on the death would be a big help."

Dr Oz placed a hand into his pocket and pulled out a pair of blue latex gloves. "I've taken a quick look. Care to join me? We've got her on the slab."

Fenella thought about her lunch with Gail Stubbs. If Dr Oz's exam of the body were as thorough as Dr MacKay's, she'd not want to eat after it was over, only down a shot or two of a stiff drink.

"Oh, there's no need for that," Fenella said, watching him slip a glove on to his right hand. "Why don't we discuss what you have found here?"

"Like I say, it's only my first impression. The post-mortem is Tuesday." He rubbed a hand over his chin, slow as if in deep thought. "I think 'odd' is the word I would use to describe my first thoughts. Strange. Troubling."

Fenella's heart began to pound. She could read his body language and knew what came next wouldn't be good. She leaned forward.

"Go on," she said, "I'm listening."

"This is off the record?"

"Of course."

Dr Oz took off the glove from his right hand and placed it back into his pocket. There was a moment of silence, then he let out a slow breath.

"Have you heard of a Mr Hamilton Perkins, likes to go by the name of Mr Shred?"

CHAPTER 21

The glass-walled atrium of the hospital cafeteria was crowded with everyone talking and laughing at once. Fenella found a table and waved Gail over. They'd both gone for the chicken salad with a bowl of minestrone soup.

Gail said, "I've asked a friend to cover for me, so there is no rush to get back to my shift. Give us enough time to chat."

Fenella admired Gail's go-getter attitude and her professionalism. She wore her blue nurse uniform like a television model with her blonde hair, streaked with grey, tied back into a neat bun.

Fenella said, "How are you getting on now you've moved to Port St Giles?" She thought that was a safe place to start, although she wanted to hear all the details as to why Gail and Leo had split.

"I love it here. The people are so nice, and I found a little flat on Clearview Row." Gail forked salad into her mouth and munched. "The rent is low, and there is a discount for nurses."

"Sweet," Fenella said. "And it's near to the beach, so you'll get your daily jog in."

"That closed the deal. I try to run before work; at night I'm too tired."

Fenella thought she should do the same—go for a jog every morning. She dipped her spoon in the soup and stirred, realising it was only her competitive streak kicking in. She enjoyed her daily strolls along the beach with Eduardo and occasional jogs on her own. She didn't run every day because she didn't want to. It was not her thing. Still, if she did take to the sands every day before work, she might shed those stubborn few pounds around her waist.

Gail took a final forkful of salad and pushed the plate aside. She looked at Fenella, squinting. "I'm not dating, if that's what you are thinking about."

"Me?"

Gail wagged her finger. "Oh, come on. Your matchmaking mind never turns off."

Fenella stuffed salad into her mouth and tried to look innocent. She'd been thinking again about Dexter. Since Priscilla left, he'd been at a loose end in the romantic department. Gail would be good for him. And he'd be good for her. A perfect match. She held both hands up, fingers crossed, and said, "I've retired from interfering in other people's lives. 'Live and let live': that's my motto."

They both burst out laughing at that. A fit of giggles and snorts.

"Leo and I started dating at university," Gail said. "We were so young, and it was so long ago, it feels like a dream. You remember our wedding, don't you?"

"A month after you graduated," Fenella replied. She'd been a bridesmaid with her sister, Eve. That thought made her heart squeeze. "Thought you two would be married for life."

Gail gave a sad smile. "Like you and Eduardo?"

"Aye, luv. Like me and Mr Dumpling."

"I never wanted kids, nor did Leo. You have five, helps to keep the marriage alive, I suppose." Gail picked up a spoon and went to work on the soup. After several mouthfuls, she looked up. "The night we broke up, Leo and I went out for a date night to a fancy Thai restaurant in Carlisle. We shared a bowl of tofu pad Thai like we did when we were students. We laughed and argued over the last strand of noodle, like the old days. When the bill came, he told me he was having an affair with a younger woman and was leaving. Our marriage was over, just like that."

Fenella reached out to touch her friend's arm. "No chance Leo will see the error of his ways and be back?"

Gail shook her head. "It was over a long time ago. If it wasn't him, it would have been me."

Leo and Gail had seemed like a perfect match.

But when something was broken, it was best left alone. They looked at each other in silence for a moment.

Gail said, "I was angry when he left, but I don't feel bitter towards Lyn."

"That her name, then?"

"She is a nurse in Whitehaven. Very young. About six months after he left, she rang me. We met over coffee where she said she regretted what had happened, thought about it every night with a sense of shame. But she loved him, and I could see that she did in a way that I no longer could. It's strange, but I felt happy for her as much as I felt sad for myself. Now I'm in Port St Giles, a fresh start."

"Aye," Fenella replied, thinking. After a moment, she said, "So you'll come to our social, next Sunday?"

Gail squinted. "You are not going to matchmake me with anyone, are you?"

"Nan's making a big spread. And she'll make blackberry pie. Is that still your favourite?"

"You didn't answer my question."

"There'll be family, of course, and a male friend or two."

"Fenella!"

CHAPTER 22

"Veronica, you have to be kidding, right?"

Dr Joy Hall's elbows rested on the executive desk, her eyes fixed on Veronica Jeffery. They were in the superintendent's office and had just begun a working lunch which passed, in part, as a social. It had been years since they were in college together, but they'd kept in touch. Team Superwomen, they called themselves. Lunches were a regular event on their calendar. Tuna-and-mayo rolls with a tossed green salad. The meets followed a regular pattern. They ate first with small chit-chat, then talked about their professional lives. Networking and friendship rolled into one.

Jeffery's face flushed. "This is confidential... nothing has been officially confirmed."

"But you said there was a murder in St Bees?"

"Late Friday night or early Saturday morning."

Joy felt her throat tighten. "Was it a schoolgirl?"

"No. Well, not exactly."

"What the hell does that mean?"

Jeffery pushed her tuna roll away, studied her friend for a long breath and jabbed at the salad with a fork. "Viv Gill wasn't of school age. She left school over thirty years ago."

"An adult doesn't fit the profile." Joy let herself visibly relax. "So what makes you think her death is tied to Hamilton Perkins?"

Jeffery said, "I read your report and feel it to be of such merit, I've asked the team to take a look."

"Veronica!"

Joy felt a flush of frustration. Why wouldn't Jeffery give her it straight? What was going on?

Jeffery dropped the fork into the salad and pushed it next to the tuna sandwich. Her lips twisted into a wolfish smile. "We've taken the details in your write-up seriously. Your best guess is that Mr Perkins is lying low in the county?"

"I'm not some damn politician, and this is not a game," Joy said. She knew the smile, knew her friend, knew what came next was key. "Answer my question. What on earth has the death of Viv Gill got to do with Perkins?"

Jeffery drew in a sharp breath. "Viv Gill's face was... well, we all know Mr Shred's trademark."

Joy considered that for a moment. She felt her heart pound in her chest. "Could have been a copycat. The case has been all over the news. Didn't they lock up a bloke in Spain?"

Jeffery stood, walked to the window to peer at the courtyard below. She kept her back to Dr Joy Hall as she spoke. "It was dark when he struck, lots of fog. Viv Gill wore the clothes of a schoolgirl."

Joy was on her feet, shouting. "For God's sake, Veronica, I'm his prison psychologist. I should have been told."

Jeffery turned. "You know the rules."

"Don't give me that crap. Bloody hell, Veronica, if he has turned his hand to adults, there'll be no end to the bloodshed. I've got a target on my back. I want a police guard."

"Joy, let's not get this out of perspective. The victim was dressed as a schoolgirl and—"

Joy was at the window, face to face with Jeffery. "You don't get it, do you? I've bought a house in St Bees. Moved in last week."

Jeffery gave a start. "What?"

A tense silence settled over the room. They'd been having these lunches for years, a habit they'd started in college to push their careers to new heights. A fun treat to their crammed workday. This was the first time the air had turned sour.

Jeffery chewed on her lip, looked through the window for a moment, then turned to meet her friend's eyes. "Joy, let's sit back down, talk this through. We are both intelligent women, career blazers, at the top of our game. We can rise above this."

"Okay," Joy said. "Okay."

They sat at the desk, and Jeffery cleared away the lunch plates. The lettuce leaves had begun to wilt and turn brown at the edges. A faint trace of tuna hung in the warm air. As the plates clinked, the radiator by the window gurgled in a low hiss.

Jeffery gave her a wolfish smile. She said, "How long have we been friends?"

"Too long." Joy watched Jeffery's thin lips and knew there was a plan brewing behind those sharp eyes. She wasn't sure whether she would like it, but she'd hear it out.

"What a ride, eh?" Jeffery's lips curved into a full-blown smile. "One thing we have in our favour is our ability to get things done. We aren't passive little women. I want you to work on the Viv Gill case with our detectives—as a consultant. Help track down Hamilton Perkins, and put him back behind bars."

"What?" Joy hadn't expected that and needed time to think it through. But she felt her heart beat even faster. Fear or thrill?

Jeffery leaned forward on the desk. "You built trust with him in prison. He agreed to tell you where he'd buried Colleen Rae. You know his mind better than anyone."

"I don't know."

"Joy, I need your help. The top brass are all

over me on this one." Jeffery shot her a pleading look. "We have a briefing at four o'clock. I've told the team you will speak."

Joy said, "I feel like you are backing me into a corner. Do I have a choice here?"

"Listen, I'll get a uniform on your front door before our coffee arrives, and I'll make sure you are paid top dollar for your services, but you have to work with me. Agreed?"

Joy considered for a long while. Suddenly her lips twisted into a slow smile.

"You've got a deal."

Now she'd be a fly on the wall, see how things unfolded and get paid for the privilege as a consultant. It would make the perfect last chapter to her secret book.

CHAPTER 23

At 3:59 p.m., Dr Joy Hall waited with Superintendent Jeffery in the corridor outside the briefing room. She had always admired her friend's punctuality, although today with the news about Hamilton Perkins and the death of Viv Gill in her new home village of St Bees, she wished the meeting was over.

"Thirty seconds to go," Jeffery whispered. "Keeps the troops on their toes if their head is on time. I'll give the team a morale boost, then over to you. When you speak, be quick and clear. They appreciate that."

Joy's mouth felt dry, and she wondered whether she would be able to speak at all. This wasn't like a presentation in front of the prison board. What could she tell a team of seasoned police officers? Her psychological reports were only one strand of the investigation. *A thin strand,* she thought. Had Jeffery put too much weight on her suggestions? After all, that's just what they were. Suggestions. She felt like a fraud. Nerves tumbled in her gut. What was she doing here?

"I can't do this," she said.

But Jeffery's hand had already reached for the door handle. It flew open, and the superintendent walked in. Joy hurried behind as though the two were connected by an unseen cord.

The whole team was crammed into the small room. A tiny space, quarter the size of Incident Room A. More of a side room, really, where they would not attract attention. Jeffery didn't want word to leak to the press just yet. And police stations leak information like flour in a baker's sieve.

Joy looked at the faces and knew them by sight. Jeffery had shown her their photos over lunch with a short verbal bio as well. PC Hoon sat on the front row, pen in hand. Dexter, Jones, and Fenella sat at his side. PC Beth Finn stood by the small coffee machine at the door and downed the bitter brew as if it were a magic elixir. Someone had set up a whiteboard with photos of Viv Gill, and there were also images of St Bees and the Pow Beck footbridge.

Jeffery's marched to the front, with Dr Joy Hall behind. Inspector Moss greeted them with a smile.

"Okay let's get started," he said and handed the reins to Jeffery.

Jeffery planted her legs wide, arms by her side. Joy watched, liked what she saw, and decided to do the same when her turn came.

Jeffery said, "I want Hamilton Perkins tracked down. I want him brought to the station and put behind our bars. You want that too. Our work here is top secret. If anyone speaks to the press, I'll have their hide."

The words seem to fall flat. When her turn came, Joy thought she'd take a different tack. They didn't need motivation. They needed information so they could track down Hamilton Perkins, make an arrest, and put him away. What could she tell them?

Inspector Moss clapped his hands. He was the only one.

"Come on, folks. That's what we need, an energy boost from the boss. I hope you got the message." He turned to Jeffery. "They're all jazzed up, ma'am, raring to go."

Jeffery stood very still and watched their faces. After several moments, she took two paces back. "That will be all. Over to you, Inspector Moss."

She turned and marched from the room, her arms swinging at her side.

Moss said, "Dr Joy Hall will speak to us in a short while. First, I'd like to get a quick sense of our progress. PC Hoon, what've you got?"

"I've made a list of folks in St Bees who are known for their keen eye. If they didn't see what happened, sir, no one did."

"Okay, keep up with that. Once you're done, start knocking on doors." Moss placed his hands behind his back. "Anyone else?"

Jones said, "Still working Viv Gill's

background. She was not a local, moved here less than a year ago from Whitehaven. Her rent was paid until the end of March, no bills, no debts as far as I've been able to tell. I've sent a request to her bank to get more on her financials. It might take a day or two before they come back."

Moss turned to Fenella. "And what did Dr MacKay have to say?"

Joy watched the woman with the shoulder-length, grey hair hesitate as though she were performing some difficult calculation. This was Detective Inspector Fenella Sallow.

Fenella said, "He is out the country. In Africa. But I spoke with Dr Oz, who heads the cottage hospital. He's made an initial exam of Viv Gill's corpse, but it is too soon for him to come to a firm conclusion."

"Come on, Sallow," Moss barked. "He must have told you something. Spit it out."

"Nothing to report, sir."

"Don't give me that crap. Solving crime is a team effort, Sallow. Dr Oz is one sharp brain; the man has ideas. What's he thinking?"

Fenella said, "He thought Gill's face was... well, he mentioned Hamilton Perkins."

"Oh God!" Moss yelled. "I hope to hell that is not official yet. Bloody hell, it will be all over the press before we know it. Get on to Tess Allen; let our press officer know."

Joy watched as Fenella Sallow made careful notes in her book. Jeffery had said Detective Sallow was one of her best. She weighed that in her mind as she thought about her opening lines.

Moss was talking. "Anyone else? What you got?"

PC Beth Finn raised a hand. "Been checking out abandoned buildings, sir. Places where Perkins may camp without being seen. Noticed some activity at the Seafields Bed & Breakfast. It closed a month ago, and the place is up for sale. Someone has been living there, camping out, not local. I've asked uniforms to keep an eye out."

Moss leered at PC Finn as though his eyes were stripping away her clothes. "Follow up and keep me up to date. And while you're at it, check out empty properties in St Bees. PC Hoon will be your guide."

Joy caught PC Beth Finn's roll of the eyes. She doubted Moss noticed, and everyone else looked towards the front. But she saw it, all right, and knew in that instant PC Finn had more ambition than Jeffery had suggested. The woman wanted to be more than a uniform in plain clothes. The same couldn't be said for PC Hoon who'd never been up for promotion or sat for any exam. "A good, solid plod," Jeffery had said, "The backbone of our small communities."

She was still thinking about that when Moss

pointed to her and said, "It's all yours, Dr Hall."

"Okay," she said, trying to control the panic. "Okay."

She turned to the gathered faces and wondered what the hell to say.

CHAPTER 24

Dr Joy Hall stood at the front of the cramped briefing room, next to the whiteboard, throat bone-dry, her mind racing like a steam train on the track.

"Ladies and gentlemen, I'm here to talk about Hamilton Perkins, full name Harry Hamilton Perkins," she began, then told herself off for sounding so formal. She cleared her throat and started again. "Let me begin by telling you what I'm not. I'm not a police officer, not skilled in criminal investigations, no training in the law. I'll not step on your toes or get in the way of your inquiries."

"That's what we like to hear," said Moss, who had taken a seat on the front row. "I like a lass who knows her limits."

Sweet mother of God, Joy thought as she felt her neck tighten. She knew there was something about the man she didn't like, knew it wouldn't be long until she saw through him. It lay there just beneath his skin—sexist. She'd met his type in prison, on both sides of the bars. If she was going to work with this team, she'd need each person to perform a psychological assessment, so she could figure out how they would best work together. *Yes,* she told herself, that would be her first task.

"I'd like to begin with us," she said. "We are a team, and teams need to work well together. I'd like to suggest each person complete a psychological profile."

"Bleedin' hell, we ain't contestants for *Mastermind*," Moss growled.

"It will help build team spirit, enhance trust, and deepen respect," Joy replied.

"No."

"It is important we work well—"

"I said no." Moss took a step towards Joy, fists tight. "I've assessed my team, know all I need to know about them. Move on."

"Okay," Joy said. She'd drop the assessment for now but wouldn't be cowed. She had long ago found that doing what she was good at put the bigots back in their box. "There is one thing I know better than anyone else in this room—the mind of Hamilton Perkins. He was on my slate when you lot put him behind bars. I studied him like a scientist observes a specimen under a microscope. That's what I do, what I love, to grasp the motives of criminals and build psychological profiles to understand and help you lot capture them."

Moss gave a slow clap. "Come on, luv, we haven't got all day. We get you have fancy bits of paper hanging on your office wall, but we've got a murder to solve. What have you actually got for us?"

Joy wasn't sure whether he was a woman hater or just dumb. Either way, she'd watch him, report her observations back to Jeffery. She knew her friend loved breaking balls.

Dexter got to his feet. "Give her a bleedin' chance. We need all the help we can get with this one, sir."

Moss glared. Dexter glowered back. The two men stared hard at each other.

Joy was nervous, sensed it would break out into a full-blown fight, and said, "Like I said, I know the mind of Perkins, have insight into how he thinks."

"So where is the bugger, then?" Moss folded his arms, face twisted into a sneer.

There was something about this team, the atmosphere in the room, that reminded Joy of the lull before the storm. There was no way they would work well together. It seemed to her they were a bunch of dogs at each other's throats. There'd be no tears if Moss stumbled, no soft wails if he fell. She thought police crime squads were supposed to be like a solid brick wall with one goal, to trap the perp and put them away. Now she knew different and made a mental note to include it in her book. They weren't like her and Veronica—friends as strong as a chain. The team in the room were more like strands of dried grass that could be swept away by a gust of wind. How the hell would they catch Hamilton Perkins? That thought made her mad.

"Listen," she said and stomped over to the whiteboard to point out Viv Gill's photo. It hung next to a map of St Bees. "An adult. Hamilton Perkins killed a full-grown woman, not a schoolgirl."

"It was the dead of night, and there was a bleedin' fog," Moss said. "How'd he know Viv Gill was nowt but a bit of tough mutton?"

Fury boiled in Joy's gut. How did Moss rise through the police ranks to inspector? The way his eyes roved over her slender body, like the hands of a masked groper, the way he dismissed her words, and the smug sneer on his face, no longer filled Joy with fear, it made her mad. She'd show the bugger. Hadn't she lived and breathed Hamilton Perkins for years, penned a secret book on the man? She knew how Perkins's mind worked and said, "Where was Viv Gill killed?"

"Pow bridge," PC Hoon said. He didn't realise the question was only rhetorical.

Everyone laughed despite the tense atmosphere. Or perhaps because of it.

Joy's mind raced as it put the pieces of the puzzle in place. When the laughter died, she said, "Viv Gill was killed over the Pow Beck stream, and that is the key. Anyone else see what I'm seeing?"

She folded her arms and glared at Moss.

Everyone in the room knew her game and watched with intense anticipation. She'd thrown down a challenge. Could Moss figure it out?

Moss shifted in his seat. The sneer disappeared as he stared at Joy Hall with intense concentration. After two slow minutes, he shrugged.

"You're the damn psychologist. Why don't you tell us what it means?"

Joy took her time now. She was in charge and had the room's full attention. She'd spent years working with Hamilton Perkins, building his trust. It was only after she broke through his layer of ice and got deep into his mind that the idea for the book came. The advance was enough to put down a deposit on her cottage in St Bees. The book sales would be more than enough to pay the mortgage. She'd quit her job at Low Marsh Prison, work freelance as a consultant, and travel the world to give advice. Now, in her mind, she was acting out the last pages of her book.

With purposeful steps, she paced the front of the room, then back to the whiteboard and pointed at the picture of the Pow Beck stream. "We all know the rumour of King Arthur's bones, washed into the Pow Beck and tossed into the Irish Sea, symbolic of cleansing." Now she stared at Moss, smiling. "Perkins is telling us something."

"Go on," Moss said, leaning forward,

interested. "What's he telling us?"

Joy wasn't sure, but her thoughts moved fast. What was Hamilton Perkins saying?

Now she paused and looked at each face in the room as if encouraging them to speak up, share their ideas. A trick she'd learned in the prison consulting room. Smile and nod and wait it out; someone would throw out a thought. All she needed was a thread, then they'd brainstorm it to a solution.

But no one spoke. Worse, they looked baffled.

Panic.

What the hell was she going to say next?

Joy began to think fast. She had to put the pieces of the puzzle in place on her own. Her mouth was dry, her hands slick with sweat, and her heart pounded like a heavy metal drum. *A fool*, she told herself, *that's what I've been*. Yes, Jeffery was a friend, but she should have said no. All she wanted was to flee from the room. But right now she was between a rock and a hard place.

Joy took a deep breath, closed her eyes, and slowly let the air out. She wasn't an impostor, she told herself. She was a professional woman with years of experience. She'd studied Hamilton Perkins, knew his mind.

Her eyes snapped open. How had she missed it? She turned to face the whiteboard and spoke once again in a strident voice. "It's obvious, isn't it? He kills Viv Gill on the Pow footbridge over the Pow Beck stream. Legend tells us the water cleansed the bones of King Arthur. Perkins is telling us that..."

Everything suddenly clicked into place. Dear God, was it even possible?

"He has made the transition, cleansed his past. The bridge is symbolic of a gateway to a new self." Joy spun around to face the room, eyes wide. "Perkins is telling us that he has grown up. His next victim won't be a schoolgirl. It will be an adult. A woman, mature."

"That's a bit far-fetched, ain't it, luv?" Moss sounded sceptical. "Perkins made a mistake cos it was foggy and dark, thought he was getting a nubile schoolgirl, ended up with an old broiling hen. He's done the deed, satisfied his need. I don't reckon he's in the county, might even have left the country, taken the boat to France. It don't take a fancy bit of paper on the wall to figure that out."

But Dr Joy Hall didn't hear. She was staring at the map of St Bees and sticking pins into it.

CHAPTER 25

The next day, at 7:45 a.m., Fenella pulled her Morris Minor onto the drive of Seafields Bed & Breakfast. She wanted to look around the place. PC Finn had seen signs of camping on the site, but there was another reason for her visit. Not too long ago, she'd worked a case that involved the old brick house. She was nosy, curious to see how much the place had changed.

At the end of the gravel drive, on a patch of bare ground with tufts of brown grass, stood the Victorian red-brick house. There were no curtains in the windows, no light on in the house, and the front door was nailed shut with thick wood slats. A faded sign proclaimed, Seafields Bed & Breakfast. Luxury Accommodation at Great Rates.

Fenella cut the engine and climbed out.

The sun was rising quickly into the dawn sky, and the sea far out beyond the rusted iron rails of the fence shimmered like stars in the night. But the building looked like a haunted house from one of those old horror movies where you yell at the girl not to go inside. Somewhere a herring gull screamed a warning cry; somewhere the wind rattled dustbins. Fenella looked at the boarded front door and wondered if there was an easy way in.

But she'd wait for Dexter.

They had agreed to meet at eight fifteen. So she went back to the Morris Minor, settled down and began to read Dr Joy Hall's report. That's why she didn't hear the quiet footsteps approach or the soft tap on the car door. But she sensed the presence and glanced up to see a face staring through the car window.

He had a mop of bleached-white hair and sharp eyes.

"Oh, it's you, Fenella; thought I recognised the car," he said.

Fenella climbed out and shook his hand. "Malcolm Buckham! Long time, no see. Run here every day, don't you?"

"Wouldn't call it a run, more of a hobble and hop, but there's not a lot to do when a man retires," he replied. "Keeps me fit and passes the time."

Fenella smiled, took in the lime-green jacket and tight green shorts. He always wore those shorts, but she thought they could do with a wash. "How are things in the harbour?"

Malcolm Buckham, far from retired, ran the Port St Giles Harbour with his nephew, Councillor Ron Malton. Malcolm was friendly and cute with a deep voice that resonated like a soul singer, the opposite of his nephew, who was gnarled and hard and prone to kick the police just to see them jump.

He said, "Ah, forgot you know all my secrets, being a detective. But you forgot one."

He spoke in a smooth tone, like the voice on the telly advertising rich dark chocolate. Fenella made a note to buy a bar later in the day, and said, "Eh, what you on about?"

"Only my grandad called me Malcolm, and he died ten years ago. It's Malc to everyone else."

That made Fenella laugh. She knew that, had always called him Malc, but he'd crept up, taken her by surprise. She glanced at his jacket; it could do with a wash too, then recalled he was single and thought he'd make a good catch for Nan. Her mother remarried for the fourth time at seventy. The last husband croaked during an intimate moment on New Year's Eve. And Fenella wondered whether Malc might make a nice fifth husband for her mum. She wasn't one to beat about the bush when it came to matchmaking. It was like geese heading south in the winter to her. Instinct.

She said, "We are having a do at Cleaton Bluff this Sunday. Any time after two will do; consider yourself invited."

"Oh, I don't know… I mean..."

"Got something better to do?"

"I've my jog on the beach… no, not really."

"My mum is doing the cooking, and I'd like to introduce you two. Bring a bottle."

"Formal or casual?"

They both laughed.

Out beyond the broad flat sands, a wave crashed against the shore, spilling foam and froth onto the dry land. Malc ran a hand through his mop of hair. His lips were broad and wide and grinning.

He said, "You didn't drive all this way to invite me to a lunch date with your mum. Why are you here?"

Fenella didn't answer directly, better to keep the investigation under wraps.

She said, "Have they sold this old place yet?"

"Not much demand for these Victorian houses, too much work to bring them up to scratch."

"But you are the executor of the estate?"

"Aye, and I'll do my best to squeeze every penny out of the buyer. But in this market, it could be a year before this place sells."

Fenella considered for a moment. "I suppose you put up CCTV cameras or hired a security firm to keep an eye out?"

He shook his head. "Got to keep costs down; that's why I jog by every day, to keep an eye out."

Fenella said, "Seen anything unusual?"

"No," he said and shook his head and turned to look at the old house. "About two weeks ago, I saw a thin plume of smoke rising from the back garden. I went to take a look; that's when I saw him."

"Him?"

"The man. Shifty face, all scrunched up as if he'd chewed on a sour grape. There was a woman with him. I didn't see her, just heard her laughing. I asked him what he was playing at. The man said he'd only stay a few nights, then move on. I didn't think it was worth going to the police, and now he's gone, so I guess I was right."

Fenella thought about that for a moment. There wasn't much to go on, and she almost let it drop, but said, "Don't suppose you got a name?"

Malc half closed his eyes, remembering. "Harry... he said his name was Harry Perkins."

CHAPTER 26

Fenella opened her mouth to ask a question when Dexter's battered old Volvo rumbled along the track. He pulled up next to her Morris Minor, climbed out, glanced around, then moved with tiger-like strides to where she and Malc stood.

"How do," he said as his sharp eyes took in the situation. He exchanged a glance with Fenella. "What's going on?"

Fenella reached into her handbag, pulled out her phone, and scrolled until she found the right image. She showed it to Malc.

"Is this the man you saw?"

Malc stared at the phone for less than a heartbeat.

"Aye, that's him. That's Harry Perkins."

"Okay," Fenella said, trying to hide the excitement in her voice. "Okay."

But Malc was a canny old sod, saw right through it and said, "Thought his face looked familiar. Is he wanted by you lot?"

There was no point denying it, but she'd not

give him the full details.

"Aye, we would like to have a quiet word with Harry."

"P-e-r-k-i-n-s," Malc said, sounding out each letter as if trying to remember. "I know the face, and the name rings a bell. Where have I heard it before?"

The public knew him as Mr Shred, but Harry Hamilton Perkins was his full birth name. That was a mouthful for a news headline, while “Mr Shred” sold news copy. A cockerel crowed in the distance, its shriek an alarm call for the vanishing dawn.

Dexter said, "We'd better call it in, Guv."

"Let's have a look around, first." Fenella glanced at Malc. "Why don't you show us where you saw the smoke."

They followed Malc along the side of the house to a wire fence, six feet tall with barbed spikes on top.

"Put it up to keep the local kids out," Malc said.

They walked along the length and stopped at what Fenella thought was a random place. Malc stooped and tugged at the edge of the wire loops. A gap opened.

"After you," he said in his deep, rich voice.

It was a tired garden with a lawn of brown patches and a wilted pear tree next to a path that stretched out from the side of the house in an arc.

At the far end, half hidden by an overgrown hedge, stood a run-down shack with a rusted roof, cracked windows, and a makeshift door with a large gap at the top.

"They were burning a fire by the pear tree when I saw them," Malc said in a whisper as though they might be overheard. He pointed at a black patch of earth. "Damn stupid place to light a fire, if you ask me. That old tree is nowt but tinder, hasn't born fruit in years."

"They?" Dexter hadn't heard the earlier conversation.

"There was a woman with him," Malc said. "But like I said to Fenella, I didn't see her, just heard the laugh."

Fenella said, "Okay, Malc, wait here while we take a look."

They circled the ground around the fire, scanning for anything that caught their eye. A cigarette stub, ring pull from a can of beer, fast-food bag. Anything that might help give them more information. But there was nothing but a few burnt twigs, piles of dust and ash.

"They did a good job of cleaning up," Dexter said.

"Aye, very careful. Not your average day camper." Fenella placed her hands on her hips and glanced around the garden. "Don't suppose we'll find much in the shed, but let's take a look anyway."

Fenella stood by the door, flipped on the torch on her phone and swept the room in a long, slow arc. It was like a small cave inside, dark and dank with the stink of rot. The beam of light shone on a lawnmower, slats of wood, and a broken stool next to a low bench.

"Look!" she said, pointing.

A green canvas bag lay on the bench. Even as they peered through the gloom, they could tell there was something inside.

"I'll take a peek," Dexter said. He shuffled into the dark space, put on latex gloves, and reached for the bag.

"Looks like a cardboard box," he said. "Damp at the edges."

"Bloody hell, I got it!"

Fenella turned and saw Malc hurrying towards them.

"Harry Perkins! Why, that's the pervert Mr Shred, ain't it?" He'd passed the pear tree. "And the bugger's got the cheek to camp in this garden. Bloody hell!"

"Please go back. We will be with you in a minute," Fenella said. She raised a hand like a traffic cop. Malc halted, took two paces back, and watched.

Dexter lifted the box out of the bag, opened

the lid, and peered inside.

"Only an envelope, nothing else; can't make out the writing, too dark."

He walked to the door and handed it to Fenella. She stepped from the gloom of the shed into the bright light of the morning sun and blinked at the untidy scrawl that had been written for the address on the envelope.

"To Harold Perkins, Low Marsh Prison." She flipped the envelope over. "From Mrs Pearl Smith, Thirty-Eight Oak Grove Lane, St Bees."

CHAPTER 27

Before the first uniforms arrived at Seafields Bed & Breakfast, Moss was on the scene. He walked with quick steps to the edge of the gravel, stood listening, working the tip of his shoe into the ground as if trying to decide his next move.

He said, "And you found that envelope in the shed in the back garden?"

"Aye," Fenella replied. "We thought we'd take a quick look around after PC Finn said she'd seen signs of camping."

"I'd have ordered a search myself, of course, must have slipped my mind. There are so many things to juggle when you are the senior officer."

"Not many can do it," Dexter said.

Moss ignored the snide remark. "And you said a Mr Malcolm Buckham noticed smoke about two weeks ago?"

Fenella pointed to her Morris Minor where Malcolm sat inside. "Would you like to speak with him?"

"I leave the interviews to the plods on the

ground. Just answer my question, will you."

Fenella's gut twisted; it never took long for Moss to get under her skin. And now as she watched his smug face, she thought of Eve and felt a surge of rage. The search for her sister had fallen flat. Rightly or wrongly, she blamed Moss for that. If he'd been quicker off the mark... if he'd searched harder... She tilted her head from side to side. She needed a stiff drink, no matter that it was early and the cock had just crowed.

She said, "It's surprising what you find out when you meet people face to face. You should try it, sir."

Moss breathed hard. Short snorts of white mist shot through his nostrils. There was going to be a big ugly row. A quarrel right here at the crime scene. She'd tell him what she thought. He'd get the whole mother lode. Irrational, she knew, but she was ready.

Moss said, "All right. No need to be like that. I want Perkins behind bars as much as you do. We're a team, aren't we?"

Fenella felt suddenly foolish. She'd let him get the better of her, get under her skin. That would not help Viv Gill get justice or put Perkins back behind bars.

She sucked in a long breath and let it out slow. "Mr Buckham noticed a plume of smoke coming from the garden. He jogs by this place every day and is the executor of the late Miss Maureen Brian's estate. She owned this building."

"I see." Moss glanced about. "Garden that way, is it?"

"Aye," Fenella replied.

"To carry out a search, you begin with what you can see and then bring in the crime scene techs for what you can't," Moss said as though he were a schoolteacher speaking to a four-year-old child. "Think I'll have a brief peep for myself." He strode towards the side of the house.

When Moss was out of sight, Dexter said, "Wouldn't want to be in his shoes, Guv. He is in the Last Chance Saloon, one cock-up and he is out. I hear the top brass will have his hide if he doesn't solve this one quick."

Dexter kept his ears close to the ground. So close, it was as if he tapped the top brasses' phone line. There was barely a time when he got it wrong. If Moss was under pressure from the top, he'd make their lives hell. In the distance came the whine of police cars.

"How the hell did you get into the garden?" The angry shout boomed from the side of the house an instant before Moss reappeared, his face purple, white snorts shooting from his nostrils. "It's like a bleedin' prison fence."

"This isn't gonna be an easy one, Guv," Dexter

said under his breath." If we don't catch the killer soon, I'll be up for murder."

"Aye, you and me both," Fenella replied. She knew Viv Gill's case could go on for months. How on earth would she put up with Moss without snapping? And she worried about Dexter. Another mark on his record and he'd be out of the force.

By the time Fenella had shown Moss the gap in the fence, the black soil by the pear tree, the tumbledown shack, and the envelope, more uniformed officers had begun to arrive. They hurried about as Moss barked orders.

"A fingertip search over the whole place, and you lazy sods better not miss a thing, else you'll have me to answer to."

As police cars continued to arrive, Moss returned to stand by Fenella and Dexter. The three detectives watched the scene unfold in silence. When a forensics van arrived, and officers in white bodysuits with spades climbed out, Moss said, "I better call Jeffery," and stepped away.

Not far enough, though.

"Yes, it's Inspector Moss; good news," he said. "I found the camp of Hamilton Perkins, got crime scene techs on-site and officers on the search… yes, a hunch, that's how I found it… knew he'd be local just like Dr Hall said… might have him in the bag by nightfall… thank you, ma'am. I do my best."

He ambled back to Fenella and Dexter, an arrogant smirk on his face.

"The boss is on her way with Dr Joy Hall. I think you two had best make tracks. Go on, get lost, sharpish."

"Pardon?" Fenella stared as if she didn’t quite believe his words.

"Nothing personal, but you know where three detectives gather, the press are not far behind. If this leaks out, there'll be hell to pay."

Dexter said, "So what do you want us to do?"

"I don't care, so long as you don't speak with the press. Just clear off, will you?" Moss sighed. "Listen, I'm ahead of the game right now. If Perkins is anywhere near this place, I'll have him. Why don't you drive over to St Bees, track down Mrs Pearl Smith, and see what the old goat's got to say for herself."

CHAPTER 28

The terraced houses on Oak Grove Lane stood on either side of a crooked, narrow street that came to a dead end by the cliffs. They were built of grey slate stone with latticed windows and steps that led up to faded front doors: an old part of St Bees where those who worked manual jobs lived.

Fenella and Dexter arrived just after 10:00 a.m. in the blue Morris Minor, which they parked with its passenger-side wheels on the curb. It had turned into another bright day, although the chill from the sea hung in the salt air. In the distance there was a crash of waves at the base of the cliffs and a black-headed gull screamed from the rooftops. There was no one about in the street, no noise from the grey slate houses. The workers were out on their nine-to-fives; it wouldn't get busy till dark.

"Might be a wasted trip," Dexter said as he climbed out of the car and looked around.

They hadn't called ahead, best to take Mrs Pearl Smith by surprise. That way she'd not have time to think about her answers or call a lawyer, who would slow things down. It was only a friendly chat to gather facts, but experience taught them to be cautious.

"Do you feel lucky?" Fenella said, staring at the silent houses.

They rang the bell on number thirty-eight; the door opened a crack before the chimes faded.

"If it's cash you're after," came a woman's voice from the crack, "the gas bill was paid—"

"We are not here to collect the gas bill, luv. We are from the police." Fenella held up her warrant card to the tiny crack. "Are you Mrs Pearl Smith?"

The door opened and a short forty-something woman with a plump face and round belly emerged with her hands on her hips. She was very pale. Lardy, as though she only came out at night. She wore a tight bathrobe, had bare feet, and her tousled, black hair was streaked with grey.

"What do you lot want, then?"

"Can we come inside, luv?" Fenella said.

"I don't know... I'm on my own. Can you come back later?"

Fenella smiled. "Won't take long. A few questions. Best if we come in, so the neighbours don't hear."

Pearl glanced over her shoulder at the stairs. After a long moment, she turned and led them down the hall into a small kitchen with a large pine table. By the window there was a two-seat sofa with a green rug thrown over it and a burnt-orange handbag perched on the edge. Next to the sofa stood a sideboard with a photograph of Pearl and an elderly man. The curtains were drawn and it was dark, but Pearl didn't turn on the lights. Instead, she went to the kettle and flipped the switch.

"I could murder a cuppa, any takers?"

"That'd be lovely," Fenella replied.

"Two sugars for me," Dexter added.

In some minutes, they sat around the table with steaming mugs of tea.

Pearl said, "What do you want with me?"

"A chat, that's all," Fenella replied. She nodded at Dexter, who took out his notebook and watched Pearl closely as she asked her first question. "Do you know a Mr Harold Hamilton Perkins?"

Pearl made a face and rolled her eyes. "Course I do, else you wouldn't be here, would you?" She took a sip from her mug, watchful. "What do you want to know?"

"He escaped from prison—"

"Low Marsh, supposed to be high security." Pearl gave a sharp snort. "Harry's like a snake in a sack, won't stop wriggling until he gets free."

Fenella said, "Have you seen him since he got out?"

"Not likely." Pearl picked up her mug, placed it

to her lips, then put it back down. "Neither sight nor sound."

"Are you sure?"

"On my dead grandad's grave, I ain't seen him."

Fenella nodded towards the sideboard. "Nice photo of you and..."

"That's me grandad, Charles; took it last month."

"So he's not dead, then, luv?"

Pearl took a gulp from her mug. "It were only a figure of speech. We all die in the end. But I ain't seen Harry, if that's what you came here to find out."

Fenella wondered, *What was this woman hiding?*

"Ever visit Port St Giles?"

"Who doesn't?"

"Often?"

"Not very."

"Been there in the past few weeks?"

Peal looked at Fenella with wary eyes. "No."

"Ever visit Seafields Bed & Breakfast?"

Pearl ran a hand over her face as if trying to wake up her mind. "No. Never heard of the place."

"Okay," Fenella said, watching her like a hawk.

"Let's go over it again so Detective Sergeant Dexter can get it all down, and in case you'd like to change your mind, let me ask you again: Have you seen Harry Hamilton Perkins since he escaped from prison?"

Pearl breathed hard. "Of course not. Why would he contact me?"

"You wrote to him in prison."

Pearl stood, walked to the gas cooker, opened the door, and pulled out a frying pan. She fiddled with it for a long moment and seemed flustered. At last, she said, "I ain't denying that, guess you've seen the letters. Yes, I wrote to him, but I stopped with that over a year back."

"Come and sit down, luv," Fenella said. "Tell us all about it. I'm listening."

Pearl hesitated. She walked back to the table, sat, and half closed her eyes.

"It began at the trial; I wrote to Harry to ask if he was guilty. To my shock, he replied… a long letter about when he was a child and all the bad things that went wrong. I wept as I read." Pearl stared at Fenella with a saddest eyes she'd ever seen. "Well, I wrote back to him, said what happened to him as a child was wrong, but I understood. Our letters went back and forth for years. It was romantic, you see, writing to a man behind bars."

Fenella said, "Why did you stop?"

"He got angry with me."

"Why?"

Pearl looked away. "I don't know."

"Yes you do." Fenella reached out, touched her arm. "Come on, pet. You'll feel better if you talk."

Pearl stared back through narrowed eyes. "I... I told him I was moving on. That our friendship was over. Finished."

There was a silence, and Fenella said, "Don't suppose you've kept any of the letters he wrote you?"

"Oh yes! Harry told me I was the first woman he'd met who understood him."

Fenella folded her arms. "Where do you keep the letters, pet?"

"In a box in my bedroom."

Dexter was on his feet. "Mind if I take a look, ma'am?"

"No." Pearl was at the kitchen door. "I'll go get them. Wait here."

She stood, glanced at the two detectives, and left the kitchen. They heard her feet shuffle up the stairs.

Fenella said, "What do you make of that?"

"Got something to hide," Dexter replied. "I'd bet a jar of fine ale on that."

He got to his feet, went to the sofa, and put on

a pair of latex gloves. He glanced at the door, then grabbed the burnt-orange handbag and searched. They heard banging in the room above them, too loud for someone opening and closing dresser draws. What was she doing up there?

After a few seconds, they heard footfalls, heavy, and her feet shuffling back down the stairs. Dexter dropped the bag on the sofa, and they met Pearl in the hall with a cardboard box in her hand.

"Hey, I told you to wait in the kitchen!" Pearl yelled. "Why are you creeping about in my hall?"

"With all that banging, we thought something was wrong," Fenella replied. "Is everything all right upstairs?"

Pearl muttered something under her breath and handed over the box. "You can borrow them, but they belong to me. I want them back; do you hear?"

"Okay," Fenella said. "Dexter, can you give her a receipt?"

A tense silence fell over the hall. Dexter wrote out the details. Pearl opened the door to let them out. Upstairs, there was movement. A shuffling of feet. Dexter shoved by Pearl and bounded up the stairs.

"Hey," she yelled. "Come back!"

But Fenella darted after Dexter.

In the bedroom, a ratty-faced man struggled to pull on his trousers. Fenella stared in disbelief.

She knew him well. Rodney Rawlings, reporter for the *Westmorland News*. The local paper sold in towns across Cumbria.

"Oi, Fenella, ain't no crime in having a bit on the side," Rodney Rawlings said. He zipped up his fly, narrowed his eyes, and added, "What you working on, then?"

CHAPTER 29

Chad Tate was in the storeroom when the doorbell tinkled. He wondered if it was the police again. They'd stop by to ask questions—the local bobby PC Hoon and a woman officer called PC Finn. He'd told them he hadn't seen anything and sent them on their way. Now, nerves jangled, he wondered, *Why were they back?*

He crept back into the store. What had they found? What would he say? But it wasn't the police standing by the checkout. It was Mrs Pearl Smith from Oak Grove Lane. She carried a canvas shopping bag with a burnt-orange handbag slung across her shoulder.

Chad froze.

He peered from between the shelves at the back of the store, uncertain what he would say.

"How do, Chad," Pearl said, her voice warm but tense. "Come out of the shadows so I can see you."

"What can I get for you, Mrs Smith?" He carefully kept his face a blank.

"Please, call me Pearl. There is no need to be stiff and formal, now, is there?"

Chad hesitated, felt a vein pulse in his neck.

"What do you want, Pearl?"

"Thought you'd like to know the police have been snooping around, asking questions about Harry."

"Why would that be of interest to me?"

"Because..." Pearl walked to where he stood and placed a hand on his chest.

"Don't," Chad said. "Your policeman friend won't like it."

"PC Hoon?" Pearl moved closer and put her arms around him. "He is yesterday's news. There is still something special between us, Chad. I only want to help."

Chad sniffed her floral scent, remembering. It was a sunny day and they were on the cliff trail. He'd carried a picnic basket while Pearl giggled like a teen. Their first date. The only one out in the daylight. She had worn a long, floral skirt with sandals, and they'd drunk wine and made love while the waves crashed against the rocks below. He was petrol to her hungry blaze.

In the following months they met like clockwork at Pearl's house when Chad locked up the store over lunch. Their relationship flickered like a flame in the breeze. Briefly. It ended six months ago, when they'd got drunk and shared secrets.

Pearl eased him away and opened her canvas

bag. "I'm here for my weekly shop. Do you have any of those Alston pork sausages?"

"Cash only," he said.

"Come off it, Chad. Put it on the slate. I need a little credit cos it ain't been easy."

"I have bills to pay," Chad said. He watched her face. He'd never been able to tell what she was thinking. That made him uneasy.

Pearl turned and headed back to the checkout, swaying her hips as she walked. She placed the canvas bag on the counter.

"Fill it up, honey. My usual, and don't forget those Alston pork sausages."

Chad felt heat rise in his face. It wasn't right she still came in asking for free stuff. It wasn't right that he still gave it to her.

"I'll be back in an hour," Pearl said.

The door tinkled. He hurried to the window and watched. Pearl strolled across the lane to St Bees Priory. Chad couldn't take his gaze off her swinging hips, couldn't stop remembering.

A plume of grey smoke drifted out of the shadows. Vicar Briar stepped from the entrance, cigar hanging loosely between his lips. Pearl looped her hand around his arm. They chatted. Chad thought he heard Pearl's laughter ringing high and throaty like the peal of the church bell.

CHAPTER 30

Don's Café was PC Sid Hoon's favourite place in St Bees to sit and waste away the work hours. His favourite place used to be his living room, where he'd lie on the sofa and watch the afternoon television shows.

That was before Maude moved in.

This morning, he sat with PC Beth Finn in his usual spot at the back of the café where he couldn't be seen from the lane. It was dark and dingy but away from prying eyes. Especially the watchful stare of the village shopkeeper who ate here too. PC Hoon made a point of avoiding the place at those times. He didn't want to be reminded of the past. It was easy. Chad Tate was as regular as clockwork. He came to the café on Thursdays at two in the afternoon.

But today the café was empty. That's how PC Hoon liked it.

PC Beth Finn glanced at her watch. "About time we got on with the door to door, and let's look around some empty properties while we're at it."

"Righto, sounds like a plan," PC Hoon replied. "A bacon roll to go for me, Don, and while you're at it, you might as well top up our coffee."

"Coming up, my friend," Don replied. He was a short, middle-aged man with a greasy tangle of curly brown hair, who waved his arms about as he spoke as though he were Italian. "How about a side of chips to go with it, seeing as it's nearly lunchtime?"

"Aye, that'd be lovely, mate," PC Hoon replied. "Throw in some baked beans to round it off."

PC Finn closed her notebook and sighed. "Come on Sid, it's nearly eleven a.m. We'll have to make fast progress now, else Moss will tear us apart."

"Relax. It don't take long to get around; it's only a small village." He winked. "We can stay here till lunch if you like; just don't let on to Moss."

"Come on, we've been here half the morning already. Let's go. We've got a job to do."

PC Hoon didn't think there was any point asking the locals questions. No one had seen anything. He thanked God for that. Viv Gill was dead, and there was nothing anyone could do about it. Best leave well enough alone. But as a police officer, he knew it didn't work that way. With Moss on the scent, there'd be no end to it. The man was like a rat at a bone, wouldn't stop until he'd gnawed it through. And then there was Maude; she'd been acting funny over the past few days. That made his stomach uneasy.

"There you go," Don said, wiping his hands on his once white apron. He glanced at PC Finn and smiled. "It's a priceless thing of beauty, my bacon butty. Are you sure I can't tempt you with one?" he asked Finn.

"No, thank you."

"What about my famous King Kong fry-up? That would bring a smile to your lips."

"Coffee is fine, thank you," PC Finn replied. "Can you put it in a paper cup so I can take it with me?"

"For you, darling, anything." Don whistled as he strolled back to the counter.

"I'll wait in the car," PC Finn hissed. "Eat your food here. Don't want that grease to stink out the vehicle. And don't be long."

CHAPTER 31

PC Hoon lazily wiped up the last of the beans with a slice of bread when the café door opened. Mrs Pearl Smith walked in, burnt-orange handbag slung over her shoulder. She sat at a table by the window and called out for Don.

"King Kong fry-up for one over here, honey."

"Righto," Don replied from somewhere in the back of the kitchen.

Without being completely conscious of his actions, PC Hoon stared across the tables. His eyes settled on Mrs Pearl Smith's handbag. It reminded him of something he'd seen in one of Maude's high-fashion magazines. He wanted a closer look.

For several minutes he watched as Pearl stared idly out into the street. *Piece of cake,* he told himself, then popped the last bit of bread into his mouth, munched, wiped his hands on the tablecloth, and ambled across the café.

"Nice morning for it," he said as he stood at Pearl's table.

Pearl looked up and smiled, her pale-dough face, like an undercooked doughnut. "How do, PC

Hoon. Why don't you join me? Go on, luv. Grab a chair. It has been a hard morning, and I could do with a nice chat with an old friend."

He sat opposite Pearl with his back to the window, so he wouldn't be seen from the street and, in turn, could get a good look at her new handbag. It was a fancy design with a little brass plate above the latch: French or Italian. Expensive. Had she had a sudden cash windfall?

He said, "What's been going on in your world, Pearl?"

She wrinkled her nose. "Two of your lot came over this morning. Detectives Dexter and Sallow, do you know them?"

PC Hoon sat up straight. What were those two doing in St Bees? This was his village. The thought they were poking about, asking questions, sent alarm bells ringing in his head. His heart raced, and sweat oozed from his palms. Were they onto him?

"What was that about, then?" He tried to sound casual but felt the blood rushing to his head.

She peered at him with big, innocent eyes. "I've no idea what they wanted with me, but I answered their questions as best I could."

PC Hoon wanted to find out more, but Don appeared at the table with a large, greasy plate of his King Kong fry-up.

"There you go, luv," he said. "That'll put hairs

on your chest. Are you having a nice chat with PC Hoon?"

"Aye," she said, patting her handbag. "And bring me a coffee in one of those paper cups, large. PC Hoon's a gentleman: he's paying, aren't you, honey?"

PC Hoon felt his chest compress. Another damn woman's hand taking money from his purse, but before he could protest, Don said, "Right you are," then wandered to the counter where the coffee pot gurgled.

Pearl flashed a puppy-dog face. "Ain't been easy these past few months. Cash is so tight. Seeing as you are paying, I'll save the coffee for later and order another King Kong to go. Why don't you get one for your supper tonight? They heat up real nice in the microwave."

PC Hoon looked at Mrs Smith, and he looked at her burnt-orange handbag. Now that he'd relish what he planned to do, he'd enjoy it to the max. Like a dog that tastes human blood, there was no going back.

CHAPTER 32

It was a little before 3:30 p.m. when Inspector Moss and Dr Joy Hall met in the superintendent's office. A quiet talk to go over what they had found at the Seafields Bed & Breakfast and plan the next steps.

Dr Joy Hall felt a pang of sadness as she looked at her close friend. Veronica Jeffery seemed tired and tense. The death in St Bees weighed heavy, and there was pressure from the top brass to get a quick result. It showed on Inspector Moss too. His eyes were puffy with the stare of a man who'd already run out of ideas. She almost felt sorry for him. Almost.

"Thought I'd better put you in the picture," Jeffery said. "Carlisle are asking for an update, twice a day. The good news is we have kept the media at bay, but I don't think that will last more than another day or two. Still, tell the troops if there is a leak, I will have their head." She turned to Inspector Moss. "Any news?"

"I'm sorry to say we have made no progress at the bed and breakfast. Our officers have swept the grounds and worked through the house, but they have found nothing."

Moss spoke in a flat voice that made Joy wonder if he had already given up hope of a breakthrough. It felt as if they were one step behind and losing ground fast. Would they catch Hamilton Perkins?

Moss was speaking. "The team have worked hard, but I'm not hopeful they'll find anything new. The man is long gone."

Joy said, "What about the envelope? I heard it was addressed to Low Marsh Prison. Was there a letter inside?"

Moss shook his head. "Just a return address on the back. A Mrs Pearl Smith, who lives in St Bees."

Joy stood, walked to the window, and began to pace.

"What is it?" Jeffery asked.

"A Mrs Pearl Smith wrote to Perkins when he was in prison. He talked about her all the time, and told me her first letter showed up at the start of his trial." Joy paused, remembering. "Over time, the letters became quite intimate but stopped a year or so ago. Perkins never said why."

Moss said, "That's also been confirmed by Sallow and Dexter, ma'am. I sent them to St Bees to have a word with her."

Jeffery thought about that for a moment and said, "Any chance she is hiding Perkins in the house?"

Moss shook his head. "Not a chance. It appears she is in a relationship with another gentleman, local reporter by the name of Rodney Rawlings, and hasn't spoken with Mr Perkins in quite some time."

"Do we only have her word on that?" Jeffery asked, a sharp edge to her voice.

Again, Moss shook his head. "Dexter and Sallow caught her new fella with his pants down, as it were. It is quite clear that Mrs Pearl Smith has moved on."

They fell into an uneasy silence. Joy thought about her job in the prison service, the regular hours, the certainty of it all. This was very different; the police never knew what would come at them next. It made her mind dizzy. There were so many possibilities, with only one thin path to the truth. How could she help?

Moss said, "Here's an idea, ma'am, that you might want to float to Carlisle, give us a little bit of time, ease the pressure."

"Go on," Jeffery said. "Please go on."

Inspector Moss steepled his hands, and his eyes darted to Jeffery and Dr Joy Hall. "Okay, let's try this for size. We know Mr Perkins is in the area, know he killed Viv Gill, and according to Dr Hall, we know he will strike again."

"An adult, this time," Joy said. "I'm absolutely convinced of that fact."

Moss rubbed his hands and spoke in a low whisper. "So we wait."

"For what?" The question came from Joy.

"For him to attack some poor bugger. Adults ain't as easy as children. He'll slip up, and we'll nab him. All we have to do now is wait."

Joy was on her feet, shouting. "That is totally irresponsible, Inspector Moss. We can't leave it like that. Hamilton Perkins must be caught and put back behind bars before he kills again." She couldn't help herself, had to tell them what was on her mind. "It's time to go to the news media; tell them what we know; get them on board; make an appeal to the public. Someone saw something. Someone can help."

CHAPTER 33

Jeffery said, "Please sit down, Joy, and let's walk through this, see what is possible."

Joy felt embarrassed by her outburst, thought she saw Moss sneering, slumped back into her chair, her head spinning. She'd made a fool of herself by letting her emotions show through. But they were the police, and their job was to track down and capture and put bad people away. She'd never have imagined that the police would just wait and do nothing, not in a million years. If she ran Moss through a psychological assessment, she was sure he would fail. How could he suggest doing nothing? Nothing wouldn't look good as the last chapter of her book. Her stomach churned.

Jeffery drummed her fingers on the desk. "Carlisle wants a quick result. They know they'll be under immense pressure when this leaks out. To sit on our hands for Perkins to make the next move won't cut it. I'm sorry, Moss, but to wait is out of the question."

Joy said, "So we go to the press?"

Jeffery didn't answer for two heartbeats, then

said, "Anyone got a better idea?"

Moss spoke first. "We know Perkins is still in the county, right?"

"That's correct," Joy replied.

"And he'll strike again?"

"I believe so."

"An adult?"

"Absolutely."

"A woman?"

Joy understood his game now. He was tying her down, pushing her into a corner. He'd had years at this, but this was her first go round. And that look in his eyes was like a cat playing with a mouse, certain of the kill. How could she fight back?

Joy said, "Perkins thought Viv Gill was a schoolgirl, but she was an older woman." There'd be no emotional outburst this time. She'd put the bigot back in his box by being good at her job. The best. She'd worked with Hamilton Perkins for years, sensed what he would do. Her best suggestions, that's what she'd give them. Fate would take care of the rest. "Now that he has crossed the threshold into the adult world, he'll do what most wealthy men do."

Jeffery nodded. She understood.

Moss said, "And what's that, then?"

"Go for a younger woman," Joy said, like a teacher talking to a slow child. "Teen to early twenties with a schoolgirlish look."

Jeffery said, "The question is, where?"

Joy didn't miss a heartbeat; she was in her stride now. "These things can never be certain because we are dealing with the human mind. But there is a high chance he will go back to St Bees to finish the job he started."

"But how can you be so certain?" The question came from Moss.

"Perkins knows he made a mistake with Viv Gill and will want to correct that. It's a compulsion in him. He must have a perfect record."

"Okay," Moss said. "Only one more question—"

"I don't know," Joy said, before he had a chance to finish. "But he'll kill again soon."

They fell into silence. The radiator under the window grumbled. A cloud passed the window and cast the room into gloominess.

Moss said, "I've got a plan, ma'am."

"Go on," Jeffery replied.

"First, we put a tail on Mrs Pearl Smith. Two officers around the clock. One to watch the house, the other to follow her around the village. If she knows Perkins's whereabouts, it won't be long until we do too."

Jeffery leaned back in her chair, considering. Again the radiator gurgled. A wolfish twitch at the corner of her lips gave away the answer before the words tumbled out. "Not good enough, Moss," she said. "We have no evidence Mrs Pearl Smith knows his whereabouts, and she is in a relationship with another man, who happens to be a hound dog of a reporter by the name of Rodney Rawlings. If he gets a sniff, it will be all over the wires." She slammed her fist on the desk. "You are on the hook here, Moss. Another death, and there'll be hell to pay, not just from Carlisle but the press and the politicians too. What else do you have?"

It was suddenly quiet. Joy looked at her friend with admiration and understood why they called her Teflon Jeffery. Nothing stuck. She'd pointed the finger at Moss, made it his problem. If the crap hit the fan, the stink would land on him.

Moss licked his lips, beads of sweat shining on his forehead. Deep down, a sudden urge to cuddle and protect him surged in Joy. Was she warming to the man? It was the same feeling that drove her into psychology. A need to understand and help those who were not understood.

Moss smiled at Joy. "Dr Hall, at our first briefing, you put pins in the map of St Bees. What were you doing?"

Joy didn't want to say, but Moss knew the answer, else he wouldn't have asked. She said, "It was silly of me really. Just a stupid idea."

Moss said, "Why did you stick pins in the

map?"

He'd put her on the spot again, backed her into another corner. The man terrified her; he was capable of anything. "I only used three pins."

"Why?"

"To work out where Perkins might strike..." Joy spoke in a quiet, flat tone. "If there was a second attack."

"What did you find?" Moss said. "Where will he kill again?"

"I can't be sure," Joy said. "I don't know."

"Tell us where you stuck the pins!" Moss was on his feet, shouting.

Joy yelled back, "You are putting me in an impossible position."

Jeffery eased the tension, her voice as soft as mist. "Tell him where you put the pins. You don't need to worry, just let us know, so we can decide what to do about it."

It was of no use; Joy had to tell them. If it didn't play out the way she hoped, it wasn't her fault. "I placed the first pin on the Pow Beck bridge."

"Come off it, Dr Hall," Moss yelled. "He won't return to the footbridge with all that police activity."

Joy exhaled a slow breath. "The first pin was for reference, to help me get my bearings. Mr Perkins will not return to the place of his kill; he never does."

"And the second pin?" Jeffery asked.

"At the train station. It's a quicker escape than driving along the narrow lanes. He'll have checked the timetable so he can slip away with speed. But again, it's only there as a reference, a possible route of escape."

Moss snorted, "And the third pin?"

"It marks the place where I believe he will kill." Joy let her words hang in the air, waiting for the inevitable question.

"And where might that be?" Jeffery got in ahead of Moss.

Joy said, "Almost all of Hamilton Perkins's victims were attacked on woodland paths. If he strikes again, it will be at night and under the cover of trees and bushes. The third pin I stuck in Hemlock Woods, eighty acres of woodland that backs on to Old Hen Lane."

CHAPTER 34

It was 7:30 p.m. Moss stood at the front of the briefing room with his eyes fastened on PC Beth Finn. Fenella sat on the front row, tore open a bar of Cadbury's dark chocolate and tried to ignore the churn in her gut about the way Moss ran his show. The team wanted to go home, kick off their shoes, relax. It had been a long day. She wondered what was happening at home. Nan would make a hot cup of milk in an hour or so and sit by the stove with a book. She'd like to join her, knew it would not happen, and took a sharp bite from the chocolate bar.

Moss brought the team up to speed. The search of Seafields Bed & Breakfast turned up nothing new. The envelope from Mrs Pearl Smith was a dead end, or so he said, and the door-to-door inquiries in St Bees drew a big fat blank. No signs of a camp in the empty buildings either. He pointed a finger at PC Hoon. "In a village with so many windows and doors, how come no one saw a thing?"

PC Hoon said, "Some said it was too dark to go out the night Viv Gill was killed, sir." He paused. From the corner of her eye, Fenella thought she saw him smile, not broad and wide, just a slight twitch at the edge of the lips. "Others said the fog dampened all sound. A few old-timers, who like to talk, said they were sure it was King Arthur and the curse of Pow Beck that did in Viv Gill. I haven't followed up on those leads, though."

PC Finn jerked to her feet and walked to the back of the room. She sloshed tea into a cup. Moss tracked her like an owl peering down at a rodent. Dexter joined her, filled a cup, and the two spoke in an inaudible whisper.

"There'll be no whispering in my briefing," barked Moss.

Dexter turned and glared. Slowly he walked to the front of the room. He sat next to Fenella, all the while his eyes never leaving Moss. The room crackled like the dry air before a wildfire ignites.

Fenella let out a low sigh. Moss looked like a character from the *Wizard of Oz,* but she couldn't make up her mind which one. What did he want from PC Finn? She knew he wanted something and silently saw him as the Tin Man—heartless.

That's when the briefing-room phone rang. A call to Moss from Jeffery.

Moss picked up, dropping his voice to a whisper. His body posture changed from the ridged form of the Tin Man to the soft curves of the Cowardly Lion. It seemed the press were on the prowl in the form of Rodney Rawlings. It was clear from the one-way chat, the boss blamed him for the leak.

But when Moss hung up, the Tin Man persona returned. "Which one of you buggers has been speaking to the press?" He jabbed a finger at Dexter. "You!"

Fenella grabbed Dexter's arm before he got to his feet. He would make a swing for him if she didn't watch out. The mood in the room turned down a handful of notches.

"Point at me again and see what happens," Dexter growled.

Moss took a step forward. "No leaks to the press! I hope I've made that clear?"

Fenella squeezed Dexter's arm. He continued to glare but kept his lips sealed. If she was in charge, she'd have called it a day and sent the team home. They'd need their rest for the long slog to come, but Moss was still speaking.

"I met with Superintendent Jeffery and Dr Joy Hall earlier." His eyes kept darting to PC Finn. There was a nervy glint to them. "We know Perkins was in the area and had been lying low in Port St Giles." Once again, he glanced at PC Finn. "That is where Operation Quick Net comes in. Top secret, of course. Details are to stay within the walls of this room."

Fenella took another sharp bite from the chocolate bar. It would be a late night now. There'd be no time for a hot milk with Nan or to chat with Eduardo about his day. She pulled out her notebook and pen then sat up straight, ready to listen.

The door opened. The smell of disinfectant wafted into the room, along with the high whine of a vacuum cleaner. A man peered in, gave a quick nod, and shut the door. Croft, the caretaker, had cleaned the room for years. *He'll not be back*, Fenella told herself. *Even he knew when to go home to his family*.

Moss said, "From here on in I need one hundred percent commitment from the team. PC Beth, are you all in?"

"Yes."

"And Jones?"

"Yup."

"What about you, PC Hoon?"

He nodded.

Moss turned to Fenella.

"Aye," she said.

At last, he pointed at Dexter. "What about you?"

"I was born all in, sir."

"Good." Moss flashed a self-satisfied smirk. "We believe Hamilton Perkins will return to St Bees for a fresh kill within days."

There was a murmur of disbelief. PC Hoon

became very still. Dexter nodded slowly as he tapped a finger on his notebook, Jones crossed his arms, and PC Beth Finn stared. Fenella put down her pen and leaned forward.

Moss jabbed a finger at a large-scale map of St Bees pinned to the whiteboard. "Operation Quick Net, a night-time surveillance operation in Hemlock Woods. Locals walk their dogs on the trails. Lots of bushes, tall trees, cover for Perkins to pounce."

Fenella was on her feet; she had led surveillance operations and knew they'd need a lot of resources. "What is our head count?"

The room fell silent. A tuneful whistle sounded through the closed door. Croft always trilled out pop songs as he neared the end of his shift. The team stared at Moss and waited.

"We are it," Moss said.

That's when the thought struck Fenella. Moss wasn't the Tin Man or Cowardly Lion. He was the Scarecrow—he didn't have a brain. She said, "Six isn't enough; we need more."

"The goal is to keep it low profile." Once again, Moss jabbed at the map. "Four uniforms will join our team. We'll have Team A hiding here, Team B there, a base camp on the east side with two patrol cars. Air cover from the St Bees Royal National Lifeboat Institution helicopter. They can be on-site inside four minutes. We've funding for five nights and begin tomorrow."

Fenella was still on her feet. Quick Net was a long shot. Too much of the plan depended on luck, which could go either way. "What is the plan? Are we supposed to hang around in the bushes and hope Perkins wanders by?"

Moss pursed his lips. "We'll have a tasty bit of fish bait for our man. A nubile, young woman decoy. PC Beth Finn, are you all in?"

CHAPTER 35

It could not get any worse.

Or at least that's what Fenella thought.

Since 7:00 p.m. she had been in position, leaning against the rough bark of a gnarled oak tree, scanning the dirt trail that snaked through Hemlock Woods. The third night of Operation Quick Net. The previous two nights had been a long, drawn-out bust.

Moss had been his usual self, wolf whistling and making comments about women as they walked by. "Wouldn't mind her with a dab of mint sauce," or "Might be an old hen, but I bet she can cluck," or "The knacker's yard would be too good for her."

No sign of Hamilton Perkins either. Only a handful of people walking dogs on the trail after dark, and none between 9:00 p.m. and midnight, so Moss called off the watch at 12:15 a.m. each night, and the team drifted home.

Now it was 10:15 p.m., two hours left of the watch. A thin mist was drifting from the sea, not genuine fog yet, but clouds of ghostly swirls that hovered in the dark night seemed to twitch like spooks brought to life. The only sound out here was the low whoosh of the wind, shriek of an owl, or the moan from a tree. There was a bite to the night air which might've turned bitter if the wind picked up.

Suddenly Fenella had the feeling she was being watched. She glanced towards the distant clump of trees where Jones waited, then across to Dexter's spot. Both were well hidden, despite the bare trees, and couldn't be seen from the trail. No one had entered the area since 7:35 p.m.—a middle-aged couple with a pair of French bulldogs walked through the woods at the same time each night. Always for an hour and five minutes. Always along the same path. Anyone else in the area would have been spotted by the team, even though they were down to nine because of a uniform calling in sick. And once again, Dr Joy Hall had joined to help point out where they should stake their watch. There was no one about. No one watching. How could there be?

Again, Fenella scanned the trail, this time for PC Beth Finn. She spotted her rounding a sharp bend which disappeared behind a clump of dense trees. When she vanished out of sight, Fenella glanced at the tracker on her dimmed phone to locate PC Finn's exact spot. Jones would have sight of her now, then Dexter.

"Base to team," the voice of Moss hissed in her earpiece. "Dense fog rolling in from the sea. It has covered the cliffs and part of St Bees and is coming our way. No air cover tonight; the helicopter is grounded. PC Finn, head back to your car. Over."

Base camp was an unmarked van a stone's throw from the public toilets. The type of place where Perkins liked to clean up after the kill. A taunt to the police that he could take his time. No rush. No hurry. The dumb cops would not catch him.

A swirl of frigid night air whipped up a clump of dead leaves, scattering them in all directions. The temperature was definitely dropping now, cold enough to freeze bones. Fenella wondered if Dr Joy Hall was wrong. Maybe Perkins wouldn't strike again in St Bees. But Dr Hall had studied the man in prison. It was her job to know how his mind ticked. And Fenella had worked the case way back—knew Perkins liked to show off, outwit the police, got pleasure in that—a week ago from the night Viv Gill died.

Fenella was as convinced as Dr Joy Hall that he'd be back.

"PC Hoon to base. I've pulled onto the verge at the south end of Old Hen Lane, a flat tyre. Over."

"Bloody hell!" The earpiece crackled with Moss, this time an octave higher.

"No problem, sir. I'll get out, change it; quicker than calling for help. Over."

Moss cursed long and hard for a good thirty seconds, then the earpiece fell silent.

Again, Fenella had the unshakeable sense of being watched. With a slow 360 degree turn, she scanned the area for signs of movement. Shadows danced in the blue light of the moonless night. From some distant branch, an owl hooted. Other than that, there was nothing but the low hum of the trees and the distant rumble of sea against the shore. Still, a sense of unease sat with her like an unwelcome uncle at Christmas.

The wind yowled. Tree limbs creaked. The dimmed screen on Fenella's phone tracked PC Finn as she walked through dense overgrowth along the trail that led to her car. Jones or Dexter or a uniform would have her in their sight until she climbed in. Now, though, it was a strange quiet. The kind where Fenella sensed the wait was almost over, the action about to begin.

Mumbled voices fizzed in her earpiece. The words were not clear. One sounded like the angry bark of Moss, the other, a higher pitch. That had to be Dr Joy Hall. She was supposed to stay in the unmarked van. What the hell was she doing out on the trail with Moss?

Shreds of thick fog billowed across the woods, a dark shroud that hung in the air and made the visible invisible to sight. Suddenly Fenella had a feeling that things were going to go wrong. Very wrong.

A scream echoed through the dark. Loud.

Pitiful.

Fenella bolted from the oak tree, down the slope, and across a patch of grass. Black fog swirled and danced. There were shouts coming from the bushes. She clambered over a fence and scrambled along the dirt trail, cutting through the scrub to gain time. She could hear more excited voices and tore through a stand of silver birch trees and over a shorter fence. When she hit the car park, she stopped, doubled over with her hands on her knees, sucking in deep breaths. Jones, Dexter, and three uniforms stood in a semi-circle. Dexter half turned as if he sensed her approaching. Through the gap, she saw PC Finn, hands on her hips, in a posture that made it clear that she was baffled.

That's when the high-pitched wail of a police siren blasted through the night air, and moments later came the frantic voice of Moss through the earpiece.

"Jesus! Mr Shred has done in Dr Joy Hall. The blood. Oh Christ!"

CHAPTER 36

When her phone buzzed at 6:00 a.m., it did not dawn on Fenella that a fresh wave of crap was flying at full speed towards the fan.

She sat at the kitchen table with a mug of black coffee. Each bitter sip eased the fog that swirled around her head. Only an hour's worth of sleep filled with restless dreams of the night before. Fenella thought out of all those jumbled visions heaped upon one another without cease, that something would worm itself to the surface, crystalise into a clue. For an instant she caught a glimpse, an image that nibbled and needled at the fringe of her brain. Then it moved into the distance to taunt and goad. What happened to Dr Joy Hall?

The phone continued to dance in violent bursts, but she did not answer at once. Now her mind searched once more for clues and found none. There'd been so much blood when she got to base camp, with fog so thick and the air so cold, it felt like shards of ice. Moss knelt at Dr Joy Hall's side, pale as fresh-drawn milk. He was out of his depth and no medical skills. Fenella did what little she could. The medics and more officers appeared in minutes, but there was no sign of Hamilton Perkins despite a hunt that went on through the night.

The phone continued its frantic dance. She knew who was on the other end and took a deep breath as her hand twitched it into her grasp.

"This has turned into a hellish fiasco," Jeffery said in a waspish voice. "How did it happen with the team on the watch?"

Fenella took a quick gulp of coffee, did not know what to say, and waited.

"Did you hear me? How in the name of God did he get his hands on my friend Joy Hall?" Jeffery was shouting now.

Still, Fenella waited. She was good at the wait.

"Carlisle have called, said if we can't clean up the mess... this is the sort of screw-up that costs senior officers like me their career. I put my trust in Moss to lead the team, to find Perkins. And what does he do?"

Again, Fenella waited.

"Balls it up! He's out. You are in charge until further notice."

Fenella wasn't sure whether it was a gift from God or the curse of the devil. But nothing ventured, nothing gained. "And Dr Joy Hall?"

"She'll live, no thanks to Moss. I've ordered an armed guard on her hospital room. No visitors."

"Is she conscious?"

"I said no visitors." Jeffery barked out those four words with the venom of a black mamba snake.

There was no point arguing with Jeffery about that. Now wasn't the time for Fenella to push her luck. Moss had tried, and look where that got him.

"Okay," Fenella said, thinking. "As you wish, ma'am."

"Gather the team for a briefing at eight."

"It's Saturday, ma'am. We'll meet at noon. Give them a bit of a lie-in, eh?"

"Your call." Jeffery let out a sigh. "I've enough on my plate with all these cottage fires. Another one last night in the village of Egremont. The bloody politicians are hounding us. But it's not arson, just random blazes in old houses with lots of dry wood. Still, they've got to point the finger, haven't they? Keep me informed."

Jeffery hung up, and ten seconds later Fenella heard the grinding rattle of an engine. She went to the window. Dexter's Volvo eased into the drive. He walked with quick steps to the door.

"Bit late, aren't you," Fenella said, inviting him inside. He always got the news first, had his ear glued to the ground. But for once she'd beaten him to it. Knew about Dr Joy Hall. Knew about Moss. Knew that she was back in charge.

He said, "Have you heard?"

"About Moss being kicked off the job?" She grinned. "And that I am the senior investigating officer?"

"Old news."

"What, then?"

"They have found another body, Guv."

"Where?"

"Hemlock Woods."

CHAPTER 37

Lisa Levon, the head crime scene tech, met them in the car park at Hemlock Woods. The dark of night still clung to the dawn, and the warmth of the sun that bathed St Bees in the daytime had not yet risen to chase the chill from the air.

"No one understands how the body could have been missed," Lisa said, "but it's another one, just like Viv Gill."

"Aye," Fenella replied. When Jeffery found out about another death, there'd be more crap flung at the fan. None of it would land on the Teflon woman even if Fenella ducked. Was it a mistake to take over from Moss? "Any idea of the time of death?"

Lisa puffed up her cheeks and let the air out slow. "We'll need to run tests, get the labs to take a look. That will take time. The force's medical examiner is on the way."

"Who?"

"Dr MacKay."

"He's on vacation: Africa."

"Oh!"

Everyone knew Dr MacKay would speculate on the time of death until the cows came home. That's one of the things Fenella liked about him. He'd make a good guess and was more often right than wrong.

"Come on, Lisa," Fenella said. "I'm not asking on the record, just your best guess."

"So long as it doesn't end up in any reports."

"I'd not do that to you."

"Or get quoted back to me in a mad voice if I am wrong."

Lisa Levon was as new-school as Dr Mackay was old. She worked hard, followed the rule book, waited for lab results, and stayed well within the lines. No grey areas—everything black and white. Fenella knew all of this, knew how to sprinkle in a drop of grey, and said, "What are you doing tomorrow afternoon?"

"Eh?" Lisa looked at her in surprise.

Fenella said, "Sunday, what you got on?"

"A lie-in till noon… nowt planned, to speak of."

"My place at two p.m. Bring a bottle." Fenella turned to Dexter. "You are coming, right? No booze for you. Bring a plate of cookies. Nan is cooking black-eyed peas with rice and browned chicken."

"Wouldn't miss it for the world, Guv," Dexter

replied.

Fenella turned back to Lisa, flashed a smile, and said, "So, I'll see you at my place, then."

"I... don't know."

"You've got nowt else on, luv."

"It is just that..."

"My team will be there... and Detective Constable Jones."

"Is casual wear okay?"

"Aye, luv." Fenella's lips quirked at the corners. "Time of death?"

"About ten p.m., maybe a little later."

Fenella exchanged a look with Dexter. That's when the team were in the woods. There was no way a murder could have happened then; they would have heard the screams.

Fenella said, "It had to be earlier than that."

"An hour or two, perhaps," Lisa replied, then shook her head. "You asked for my best guess. I'm sticking with ten p.m."

"We were here till close to three a.m., and there were officers searching the woods for Perkins all night. How did we miss the body? How did we not hear the screams?"

Lisa shrugged. "I'm only a crime scene tech, you're the detective. Let's look, shall we?"

They eased around people and equipment to the edge of the roofless crime scene tent. A siren blasted from the car park, ten seconds of ear-splitting shrieks. Fenella paused at the entrance, for only a beat, then followed Lisa and Dexter inside.

The smell of death hit Fenella's nose and turned her stomach. Huge lamps shone fierce white light on the crumpled body, partly covered by white sheets. She blinked, took in the details, then looked away.

It was a woman, but they'd have to confirm the rest through medical records. Her eyes returned to the face and lingered. After what felt like hours, she tilted her head up and traced the outline of a cloud as the rising sun chased away the dark sky. *Such a sad way to go,* she thought, *butchered in the dead of night. Did the poor lass have a husband? Kids? A family?*

Lisa was talking. "We believe it's a Mrs Pearl Smith of Thirty-Eight Oak Grove Lane, St Bees. A local."

Fenella stared at Dexter. The look of shock on his face must have mirrored her own. They had visited with Mrs Pearl Smith a few days ago. Alarm bells rang. Did their visit trigger the attack, or was it another coincidence?

With slow steps, Fenella walked around the body, her head bowed in total concentration. The face was unrecognisable, but those lardy arms and legs. Yes, she was the same Pearl Smith they'd visited. And she was in a relationship with Rodney Rawlings, the newspaper reporter. That complicated matters. She circled twice, then said, "Mrs Smith's handbag?"

"What about it?" Lisa replied.

"A big, orange strappy thing, leather, and not cheap. What did you find inside of it?"

"No handbag or purse found on-site," Lisa replied, then added as if to be helpful, "But Mrs Smith wore stilettos, orange with black-lace buckles."

Fenella thought about that for a long while, pursed her lips, and said, "I want that handbag."

"Wasn't with the body," Lisa said.

"I'll arrange a search, Guv." Dexter gave a quick nod to Lisa and strode off.

As she watched him weave between the white-clad crime scene techs, Fenella considered the odds that two women in St Bees would venture out into the dark, cold night in high heels and no handbag. A sense of unease crept deep into her bones.

Crime scene techs scuttled back and forth. There was the low mumble of voices mixed with the growl of a diesel generator. They were setting up more lights even though the night had waned into day. A figure in white appeared at Lisa's side and whispered. She nodded, and the figure hurried towards the car park.

Fenella took a slow breath and said, "One more question, then I'll let you get on. Do you know who found the body?"

"A Mr Chad Tate," Lisa replied.

"Not a police officer, then?"

"Just a man out for a quiet walk in the woods. American, owns the village store."

CHAPTER 38

In the briefing room, the team waited for Fenella. She glided in as the chimes from the Port St Giles town clock rang out the noon hour, with her mind back in the crime scene tent and wondering how the whole mess began, and where it would end. They say there is nothing you can do for the dead, but there is one thing. Justice for the living.

Now she was in charge of the team once more, tired for sure. Excited? Hell yes. She could barely contain her thrill at taking the lead from Moss, and began the meeting with words that would lift the team high.

"You will be pleased to know Dr Joy Hall is on the mend."

They got to their feet and cheered. PC Beth Finn quickly raised a clenched fist, and Jones let out a wolf whistle. Dexter slapped PC Hoon on the back. The St Bees bobby's lips curved up, but the grin seemed forced.

Fenella waved the team to their seats. "I know there have been rumours about Inspector Moss. Today I can confirm that he has left Port St Giles to spend more time with his family."

More cheers. Dexter shuffled in a two-step dance.

"Save it for Sunday," Fenella said, her lips split into a wide grin. "You are all invited to my place tomorrow at two p.m. Bring a bottle of wine or case of beer, casual dress, no airs and graces. We'll kick off our shoes and relax for a while. No talk of work."

There were nods of thanks.

Fenella raised both hands, palms out. "From here on in, let's take things nice and slow. Work with care so there is no doubt that we have been thorough. We'll chase down each lead to the end of its road." She pulled a chair from the front row, turned it around, and sat so she faced the team. "Let's put our egos to one side, strip this case down to the bare bones. What is our number-one goal?"

There was a flurry of mumbles, but it was PC Beth Finn who spoke first. "To put Perkins back behind bars, ma'am."

"Aye, that'll be good for a start." Fenella half turned and pointed at the whiteboard. A picture of Viv Gill hung next to a photo of Mrs Pearl Smith. "To do right by these two ladies is what I want you to focus on. Keep your mind on that, and we'll do all right."

PC Finn nodded as if in the presence of a great sage. Fenella's heart squeezed. The job made cynics of many and rotted the souls of others, but PC Beth Finn would do all right. She cared.

Fenella said, "We know Mr Perkins spent a few nights hiding in the grounds of the Seafields Bed & Breakfast. He was spotted with a woman. Who is she? Where is he now?"

Jones said, "Since Perkins escaped, there has been a track on his financial assets—bank and investment accounts. He hasn’t touched the money."

Fenella said, "And what do you think about that?"

"He's using cash or has money stashed in a place we don't know about."

Fenella liked the way Jones thought. He might be new to the police force but learned fast and was good with computers. She'd never quite got the hang of the blasted machines, and said, "Could an admirer like Mrs Pearl Smith have funded him?"

"Possible. I'll check into that," Jones said, clearly thinking.

"And while you are at it, see if you can find out if she visited Port St Giles in the past two weeks. Was she the woman seen at Seafields Bed & Breakfast with Hamilton Perkins? Easy enough from her phone, right?" Fenella didn't wait for an answer and stood. "We have a box of letters from Perkins to Mrs Pearl Smith. PC Finn, go through them, will you? See if anything pops out."

"Will do," PC Finn replied.

Fenella said, "Okay, what do we know about Viv Gill? Pays her rent ahead of time and goes out in the dead of night to the Pow Beck bridge. There are so many things about her actions that do not compute." She paused a beat. "Like, where is her handbag?"

PC Hoon said, "It was late at night, ma'am. There'd be no shops open. That's why she didn't have a handbag with her."

PC Finn chimed in. "When a woman wears high heel shoes, she always carries a handbag."

"Aye, my thoughts exactly," Fenella said. "Track down their mobile phone numbers, credit cards, and the like. Find out when they were last used and where. And let me know if that handbag shows up in the search of her house. Maybe PC Hoon is right, and she left it at home."

PC Finn took out her notebook and wrote. Fenella could tell she enjoyed being in plain clothes and working with the detectives.

"I've not seen a statement from Chad Tate yet." Fenella pointed at PC Hoon. "Why don't you have a chat with him? Being local, he might open up and recall something that might help."

"Will do, ma'am." PC Hoon gave a slow grin. Fenella thought there was a slyness to it as if he couldn’t be trusted. "He's not a local, though. Likes to creep about St Bees in the early morning. I've even seen him hovering about the graveyard. Not illegal, just odd. He's from America, New York, but has been running the village store for years."

Fenella said, "Aye, so I've heard. Take PC Finn with you when you interview him." She paused, thinking. "Jones, what have you found out about Viv Gill's financials?"

Jones jabbed at the screen of his tablet computer. "Up until about six months ago, her income came in irregular spurts from Jabbar's nightclub in Whitehaven. Since then it's been cash deposits." He glanced at PC Beth Finn and lowered his voice. "I hear it is a place of... uncertain virtue run by a Madam—"

"DuPont, real name, Nellie Cook," interrupted Dexter. His eyes gleamed as he spoke. "Our paths crossed way back in the day. Nellie was a sex worker. Must be close to seventy by now, thought she'd retired from the game."

For a long moment Fenella struggled to speak. When she was in uniform, she'd saved Nellie Cook from a savage beating by a street pimp. They'd put the bloke away for years. What was his name? She couldn't remember, frowned, and said, "It's been a long time. Dexter, why don't you and I drive over to Whitehaven for a nice cosy chat with Nellie."

CHAPTER 39

The young girl sang in a ragged voice about undying love.

That's when the detectives inched into the dim lounge of Jabbar's. A shroud of sour booze and stale cigarette smoke clung to the black walls like a well-worn coat. They watched from the back.

It was a little before 2:00 p.m., lull time in the party district of Whitehaven. A polished bar stood at one end of the room, and a dance floor with booths along the far wall, and dim spotlights shone bleary-eyed on the stage. There was no barman about, no one visible in the room, but the girl continued to sing. She looked like a teen star, wore a gold bustier, short skirt, high heels and sang like a wind-up clock losing time—off-key and offbeat. A wannabe in search of gold. One of hundreds who had passed this way before. Girls whose dreams of fame died the day they passed through Jabbar's doors.

"Bravo." The praise came from a booth close to the bar. "You have a voice like an angel and a body like a goddess. You are in. All our girls start as waitstaff, so be here at six, and I'll walk you through the paperwork."

"Thank you," the girl replied, breathless.

"Oh, and there's one more thing. You'll need a stage name. Gretchen Stodge is nice but won't cut it in Hollywood. That's where you are going, isn't it? When you are on duty, it will be Bo Prim. I'll get a name tag worked up."

"Bo Prim?" The girl sounded uncertain.

A tall, wiry man in a black pinstripe suit, wire-rimmed eyeglasses, a button-down cream shirt and dark tie, emerged from the booth. "You want stardom? It comes at a price. Bo Prim is so much more..." He swung around and pointed at the detectives. "Who the hell are you?"

Before he finished his sentence, two men with shaved heads were at his side. Big biceps, splayed noses, men who knew their way around a fight.

"Just passing through," Fenella said. "Thought we'd take a look around."

"We are closed, don't open till eight. Come back then."

The henchmen took a step forward.

Fenella said, "I'm Detective Inspector Sallow, and this nice man by my side is Detective Sergeant Dexter."

"You got ID?"

Dexter flashed his warrant card and grinned. He still liked a good scrap, even when the odds were weighed against him. Fenella thought he was too old for that; she certainly was. She said, "Okay if we have a look around?"

The man in the pinstripe suit said, "This place is clean. We don't sell drugs, if that's what you're after. All our girls are waitstaff, nowt else. We are above board."

"So, you don't mind if we have a look around, then?"

"You got paperwork?"

"I can get it."

He stared for a moment as if weighing up his response. When he spoke there was a hint of doubt in his voice. "What is this about?"

"We'd like a word with Nellie Cook."

"Ain't no one by that name works here."

That's when Fenella remembered the last time she'd seen him. He was a snotty-nosed teen back then. Now he looked like a business executive up from London for the day.

"Troy, I'd like a quiet word with your gran, please."

He didn't need telling twice, turned, and said, "This way."

CHAPTER 40

Nellie Cook sat at a desk in a pine-walled room, her elbows leaning on a pile of papers. She wore a bright-red blouse with a string of white pearls around her neck. If she'd aged since the last time Fenella saw her, it didn't show in the well-powdered face. She could pass for a woman in her fifties, not a lass close to the big seven-O.

Nellie stared for a long beat, then got slowly to her feet. "Well, I never. Look what the cat's brought in." She moved across the room, flung her arms around Dexter. "Thought you'd forgot about your Nellie."

"Nay, lass. I've not forgot you." Dexter rubbed her back and nodded at her grandson and his henchmen. "We'd like a quiet word."

"Give us ten, luv," Nellie said. "These two are old friends from back when you were peeing your pants at the thought of the bogeyman."

Nellie watched as the men left the room. "He's got a head on him, that one. Smart, good with numbers. I've a year or two left, then it is the quiet life in a cottage in the hills. Green fields and trees, always wanted that."

Fenella said, "It's not what it is cracked up to be. Not when the snow comes, anyway."

Nellie laughed, a high-pitched snort from the throat. Not quite the howl of a hyena, but if she ever took to the stage, she'd have steady work as an extra in *The Lion King*. "Come on, let's go to my private rooms where we can talk about old times." Nellie went back to her desk and pressed a button. A loud click, and a door opened in the pine wall. "I like my little devices, James Bond fan all my life. Gin and tonic anyone?"

They followed her through the door. Rose scents puffed in great plumes from an electronic blue-and-white potpourri pot. It was a room filled with bright silks and soft lights and a mirror that ran the length of one wall: the lush style of a Paris boudoir. *A bit posh for my tastes, but each to their own*, she thought as they sat on a plush couch by a low glass-top cocktail table.

"A drink?" Nellie was at the bar and pouring.

"Aye, if the guv don't mind."

"Go on, then, for old times' sake," Fenella said. "You know how I like it, touch of lime."

Nellie floated across the room, silver tray in both hands and sat in a wing-back armchair opposite the detectives.

"To the past," Nellie said, and they clinked.

Fenella sipped, remembered she'd not eaten, and put the glass down.

Nellie downed half her glass before she placed it down with a clink.

Dexter didn’t touch his.

"Now," Nellie said, a glow coming to her cheeks, "tell me what I can do for you?"

"Do you know Viv Gill?" The question came from Fenella.

"What has she done now?"

"On your books, is she?"

Nellie smiled. "That is all in the past."

"Come on," Dexter said. "We need to know about Viv."

Nellie picked up her glass and took a long sip. "She is a good lass. Keeps her nose clean. Yes, she was on my books for a few years, then left maybe six months ago."

"Why did she go?" Fenella had her own ideas but wanted to hear it from the horse's mouth.

Nellie stared at the glass. "I asked her to leave. The world doesn’t think much of us, but we have our standards. The last I heard she had left town, set up shop in St Bees. What has she done?"

"She's dead," Fenella said.

Nellie downed the rest of her drink. "Suicide,

eh? I thought she was clean, but you can never tell these days."

"Murdered," replied Dexter.

"My God!" Nellie stood and hurried back to the bar with her glass in hand. She poured, took a long sip, then looked at the detectives. "Are you going to tell me what happened?"

Fenella ignored the question. "Tell us why you asked her to leave. It'll not go any further than these walls."

Nellie sipped her drink but stayed at the bar. It was clear she was in a state of shock. "I'm sorry she is dead. If only I could turn back the clock. I don't like to think about the past, but she... well, she got along well with men. They liked her. I told her to save cash, then get out of the game, train for a decent job, or keep an eye out for a rich bloke, the type that like to play Prince Charming. I don't know if she saved any cash, but she..."

Her voice trailed off, and she just stared as if she were deep in the past. Fenella glanced at Dexter. He raised his hand to signal they wait. Her face contracted as if reliving a dark memory. It was almost as if the detectives were not in the room.

At last, Nellie said, "Don't know if you remember Royce?" Her voice drifted through the air as soft as butterfly wings. And she suddenly looked her age. "Nasty piece of work."

Dexter said, "Aye, I remember the toerag. He used to run his business from the lounge of the Red Sheaf bar. That's where I met Priscilla. She'd sing on Friday nights. Royce had his eye on her. Wanted to get her on the game. I dealt with the toad, real good."

"Aye," Fenella said. Now, she remembered. Royce Lee was the street pimp who beat his girls to within an inch of their life just for the hell of it. She'd caught him in the act, a violent assault on Nellie. "Can't say I shed a tear the day Royce Lee went down. What happened to him?"

"Royce is still inside." Nellie walked back to the armchair, sat, and crossed her legs. "I'll not lie if I say that I'll go to my grave in peace if he dies a horrible death in his cell. That's why I had to let Viv go."

"I'm not with you," Fenella said.

"I do my best for my girls, treat them well, give them good advice because I don't want them to end up like me. We are like a family, look out for each other. No pimps; no one gets beat; leave when you want—and come back if you must. Five years on the game, and most have enough cash to make a new life, if they stay off the drugs."

"That why you let her go, use of drugs?"

Nellie shook her head. "Listen, I found out from a little bird that she wrote to men in prison."

"Let me guess," Fenella said. "Royce Lee?"

"That was bad enough! I thought that girl had

sense, might have kept her on but I couldn’t." Nellie paused a beat. "Not when I found out she also wrote love letters to Hamilton Perkins. Mr Shred."

CHAPTER 41

Fenella left Dexter to reminisce with Nellie Cook. The two had a lot of catching up to do. He'd ask about Viv Gill, get more details as they spoke. No need to hang around for that. There was something else she wanted to do, a task that would help piece the puzzle together. If she had the nerve to see it through.

The gin had whipped up her hunger, so she drove her Morris Minor across Whitehaven to Granny Wong's for a late lunch. Battered haddock, chips, curry sauce and a can of dandelion-and-burdock pop to wash it all down. A meal of stodge-filled bliss. She'd burn it off with a long jog on the beach when she got home, else it would go straight to her hips.

As she popped the last piece of crisp batter into her mouth and chewed, she wondered why women like Viv Gill and Pearl Smith wrote love letters to men behind bars who'd committed crimes that churned the gut. *Not for me to judge,* she told herself, although she was tempted to anyway. She knew the lunch and the can of pop and the thoughts were a stalling tactic, and decided the task could not wait. It was now or never.

It was a pleasant drive along the coast back to Port St Giles, but she missed the chit-chat with Dexter and wondered what he had found out from Nellie Cook. Then it occurred to her that Nellie might have been his informer back in the day. Dexter played his cards close to his chest, had a knack for what was about to go down, and an ear that separated the wheat from the chaff of gossip. He got along with all sorts, and they told him things he wanted to know. Yes, Nellie must have been on his list.

Fenella's heart picked up a beat as she pulled into the car park of Port St Giles Cottage Hospital. She turned off the engine and for a long while stared at the front doors. Maybe she'd see Eve? She knew that was just a phantom hope but watched for her sister anyway.

When she thought about Eve, she mostly thought about laughing. They laughed a lot together and sang songs that made them cry. Then they'd talk through the night, each sharing old wounds which were yet to heal. When they were done, they'd sing along to sad songs that made them cry even more. She missed her sister.

It began to rain. Hard. Each drop a frenzied slap, a slap against the car roof. If it kept up like this, there'd be no chance of a jog on the beach when she got home. *Not good for the waistline, the rain*, she thought.

A nurse in a grey overcoat hurried from the doorway and out into the car park. Eve probably left through that very door. Which way did she go? Left? Right? Did she hitch a ride? What had happened to her sister? Once more Fenella felt the empty pit of those left behind from an unsolved crime.

She slung her handbag over her shoulder, locked the car door, and strolled to the entrance. What she was about to do could land her in deep water. She would nip in and out. No harm done. No one needed to know.

There was an armed officer outside Dr Joy Hall's room. A thin-lipped man with eyes that matched his scowl. Fenella knew him. An old-timer by the name of Jake Kent, who wore the scars of the job, going by the two gashes on his left cheek.

"How do, Inspector," Jake said, folding his arms.

"Wife still on the mend, is she?" Fenella had formed a group who cooked meals for police officers whose spouse fell ill. It was her way to give back to the other half. Jake's wife had been told she'd not have long but had outlived the doctor's dire claims. They'd been cooking meals for the family, once a week, for almost a year.

"We are keeping our fingers crossed," Jake said. "More tests next week. The last lot came through all clear."

"I'll pop around next Friday to have a natter."

"Aye, she'd like that."

Fenella nodded towards the closed door. "And Dr Joy Hall, how is she getting along?"

"She'll live."

"Any visitors?"

"I've not had to turn anyone away."

Fenella lowered her voice. "Can I nip in and have a quick word?"

"The superintendent said no visitors."

"Aye, she says a lot of things, doesn't mean we always listen."

He stepped aside.

"Be quick."

CHAPTER 42

Dr Joy Hall heard the hard drum of rain in the dusk-like dim of the room. On the edge of a dream, she jerked awake. The spine-chilling memory of Uncle Fred was back. The dream had taken her to childhood but no further than a dark, traumatic stain. She had no girlhood memories of before. Only after. And those memories were hellish.

Joy breathed hard and tried to focus instead on what happened in Hemlock Woods. When they first wheeled her in, she seemed to float up and then look down at herself as a child. It was dark and their Uncle Fred was—grinning. An out-of-body experience? It had filled her with alarm and she screamed. Blind panic soon dissipated into a floaty calm. The result, she thought, of the drugs they'd pumped into her.

She let out a soft sob. Uncle Fred had attacked her. Brutally. She was only fourteen when it happened. She had wanted to keep the baby, but it died, and a nurse took it away. That's why she became a psychologist. To peer into the minds of the broken and fix them. The peering was easy. Not so, the fix. She touched her cheek. Slowly, she worked her hand over the rough ridges of the bandages. Would she recognise her face when they took the dressing off?

The click of the door changed her focus. Not another nurse! They prodded and poked and stuck her with so many needles that her limbs felt as heavy as lead and her mouth as dry as sand. She opened her eyes, but the room began to spin, so she closed them.

"Nurse, I need a sip of water, please."

She felt the glass against her lips and took a long sip.

"Feel better now, luv?"

She recognised the voice. Her eyes snapped open and focused on the grey-haired detective, then they slowly closed.

"Thought I'd see how you were getting along," Fenella said. "You're not supposed to have visitors, but I thought I'd pop in to have a natter. A quiet chat will cheer you up. No need to tell the doctors or anyone else I was here; you know how antsy they get about after-hours visits."

Joy's mind felt dead. She couldn't think what to say, so she raised her hand and gave the thumbs up.

"How you doing?"

Again, Joy gave the thumbs up.

"Aye, lass, that's what I thought. Tough as old boots, us ladies." Fenella fell silent for so long that Joy wondered whether she was still there. But she didn't open her eyes for fear the world would start to spin. Then came the detective's voice, soft and low and cautious. "Can you remember what happened, pet?"

"It is all a blur." Joy almost jumped at her own voice. She thought it would sound dry and raspy, not so strong, not so full. "I think I screamed, and everything went blank."

"Aye, lass, that was probably for the best." Another bout of silence and then, "So you didn't see anything, then?"

"No."

"Maybe you picked up a whiff of his aftershave?"

"No."

"Or saw which way he ran?"

"It was so dark."

"Did he say anything?"

"No. "

"So, you didn't recognise his voice?"

"Like I said, he didn't speak."

"Aye, that's what I thought you said." Fenella felt disappointed. There hadn't been a struggle, so there would be no fibres or DNA on Dr Joy Hall's clothes. Still, she'd suggest they be sent to the lab. No point telling Jeffery about that. "How are you feeling?"

"Groggy."

"Aye, luv. I'd not be able to think with all those tubes in me. You are doing great."

Joy moved a slow hand to touch her cheek. "My face?"

"Best focus on getting better, luv. Doctors can do magic these days."

"But—"

"It will be fine. You will be fine. Like I say, they can do magic."

Rain continued to pound against the window in the rhythmic beat of a boxer's fists working a punching bag. There'd be no let-up until after dark, and if the temperature dropped, there'd be a hard frost.

"Can you tell me anything about the attack?" Fenella asked.

Joy wanted to tell her something, anything, but she couldn't and shook her head.

"Not to worry, Dr Hall. We'll get him."

Again, Joy slowly raised her hands to give the thumbs up.

"I'll leave you to get some rest, then."

Joy was glad of the visit, felt somehow connected to the outside world. But thinking was so draining, and her thoughts were already fuzzy. "Thank you," she said.

"There is one other thing you might help with," Fenella said. "We know Viv Gill wrote letters to Hamilton Perkins in prison. Do you know if he received letters from anyone else?"

Joy eased herself up. She had to help but kept her eyes closed as she spoke. "It was not part of my job, but I used to hear things, you know. Perkins never opened up to me about that, but I know he got letters from a woman called Smith. Mrs Pearl Smith." She kept her eyes shut but could hear the raspy breathing of the detective. And she knew they'd not caught anyone and sensed things were going to get worse. "You must find Pearl Smith and warn her. She'll be next."

No answer.

Joy's eyes flicked open for a beat, and she reached out a hand to grasp the detective's arm. "Please warn her. Please warn Pearl Smith."

There was a long pause, and for a while, the only sound was that of Fenella's ragged breathing. One minute. Two. At last, she spoke. "She's dead, luv. He got her."

Sweat prickled Joy's forehead and dripped on her closed lids. She wanted to scream, over and over until her throat was hoarse. But she fought through the fear and fog of the drugs until her brain cleared. As she breathed in a slow breath, her mind focused on the questions to come. She knew what the detective would ask but wasn’t sure she could answer.

"Did"—Fenella paused for a beat—"any other women write to him?"

"I know nothing more than what I've told you. I wish I could be of more help."

"You've been a great help, luv. And you are safe now."

"But he'll be back, though, won't he? Hamilton Perkins will be back to finish the job."

CHAPTER 43

Chad Tate could feel himself coming to a slow boil as he stood by the door in his store and watched the police officers walk down the lane. Grey clouds hung low with the threat of more rain. They'd been in again, sniffing around, asking questions. PC Hoon with PC Beth Finn. And it made him anxious:

"No, I can't tell you anything about Mrs Pearl Smith."

"Everyone shops in the store; they like to support local business."

"No, I'd not seen any strange faces... well, apart from the police officers who came in to buy snacks."

"Yes, I check the storeroom every day. Only boxes and an industrial freezer. Not enough room for a small child to hide, let alone a grown man."

When PC Finn asked what he kept in the freezer, the postman walked in with a white envelope in his hand. He avoided Chad's eyes, placed it on the counter, and glanced at PC Hoon and PC Finn. Everyone knew there'd been another murder. Everyone knew Pearl Smith was dead. That meant more police poking about in village matters. If you got caught up in their net, there'd be no easy way out. Everyone knew that too. So the postman legged it with a quick goodbye shout, but PC Hoon and PC Finn followed him out.

All the questions had turned Chad's gut sour. He wanted to run. Where would he go? Not back to New York. Not away from St Bees either. He was tethered to this place. The shop was all he had. He suddenly felt like a fly caught in a web. Wriggle as he might, he couldn't get away, only watch with wide eyes as the spider got close. He went to the counter, reached a hand under, and pulled out Bert.

"What should I do?"

The one-eyed sheep with three legs stared back.

Chad turned to the window. A shaft of gold broke through the clouds. It shone on the officers as they ambled along the lane and chatted with the nervous postman. He watched until they disappeared around a sharp bend.

"Bert, they are gone," Chad said, his eyes still on the window. "I think it will be all right."

Footsteps clattered on the cobblestones. He saw Vicar Briar hurrying towards the store, black cassock hitched up an inch with both hands so his feet could move with speed.

"Was that PC Hoon I just saw?" Vicar Briar's

question came out in a breathless gasp. "And the woman is PC Beth Finn, I believe?"

"They asked nothing they haven't asked before." Chad tried to control his voice, but he couldn't hide his alarm. "The woman officer is from Port St Giles, sharp but young. She asked about the storeroom."

"What did you tell her?"

"The usual. It's a storeroom, not enough space to hide a five-year-old girl. What else could I say?"

Vicar Briar fished around in his cassock and pulled out a cigar. "I feel sorry for Pearl. She was born and bred in St Bees, wrong side of the street, though. Still, I hear she brought comfort to many in her brief life. One hopes the Lord will give her a little credit for that. God knows she'll need it."

Chad felt a pang of sadness and with it the need to talk. "We were close, once."

The vicar's puffy cheeks reddened and his deep-set, small, dark eyes stared. "You were in a relationship with Pearl Smith?"

"I get lonely. I thought it would be good to have a woman in my life again. I thought it would help."

"Did it?"

"No."

"You still have the anger?"

"I control it."

The two men fell into silence.

Vicar Briar looked tired now, almost haunted. He lit the cigar and took a long slow suck. A plume of white smoke hissed from between his lips. He stared through the window at the sharp turn in the lane where the officers went.

"That poster in the window should drum up a nice bit of business." The vicar grinned. "Everyone loves a church fête, don't they? And a Saturday at the end of the month is when folk are flush with cash—bank accounts brimming with their pay cheques."

Chad licked his dry lips. "Do you think there will be lots of little girls?"

"Hoards." Vicar Briar spread his arms wide. "Bring plenty of boxes of those lollipops. Kids can't get enough of them."

"Will do," Chad replied. "I'll have more than enough."

Once again, the vicar's eyes drifted to the sharp bend in the lane. "We can't expect much from the likes of PC Hoon. Pearl Smith and Viv Gill's deaths will end up in a file collecting dust in the cold-case archive in Carlisle."

"They asked a lot of questions," Chad said. "So many questions."

The vicar offered Chad a cigar. "It will help. Come, let us smoke awhile."

For several more minutes, the two men smoked and watched the lane. Each in their own thoughts. Each enjoying the savoury aroma and waiting for the tobacco to work its magic. The low clouds turned a shade darker.

Vicar Briar said, "So, did you… see anything?"

"No."

"What about the attack on Dr Joy Hall?"

"Nothing."

"Then it is God's will, my son."

"But the killing… it is not finished."

"No man knoweth the ways of the Lord."

Chad looked at his hands, and he looked at the fat cigar. Yes. It was God's will, and he shouldn't feel any guilt for what happened. None. Rest in peace, Pearl Smith. Rest in bloody peace.

CHAPTER 44

PC Hoon had only nipped home for a quick cuppa and forty winks, but Maude was at him like a dog on a bone.

"What you doing back here?"

"Give me a chance to take my coat off, dear."

"Don't you 'dear' me."

He shook off his coat and hung it with care on the rack. "What's that smell?"

Maude looked at him coldly and said, "Fish pie."

PC Hoon loathed fish pie. The smell turned his stomach, and then there were the small bones that Maude always missed when she dished it onto his plate. He'd have to pick through it with care, while Maude ate giant forkfuls, bone free.

Maude nodded towards the kitchen. "Sit yourself down, and I'll dish out a plate."

"Can't, luv. PC Finn is at Don's Café. I said I'd join her in an hour." He planned on a large plate of fries with beans and two fried eggs with a mug or two of Don's strong tea. Maude's fish pie would end up in newspaper and very deep down in the dustbin. "I'll have some fish pie when I get back. Right now I need a quick kip."

"Sid, we need to talk."

There was something about Maude's tone that sent a chill along his spine. He followed her to the kitchen where he sat at the table and watched in morose silence as she scooped out a generous forkful of fish pie onto a platter-sized plate.

"There you go," she said. Her mud-brown eyes stared until he picked up a fork and toyed with the glutinous stodge. "What's the matter; don't you like it?"

"Well..."

"Sid, you went through my dresser, didn't you?"

PC Hoon wasn't sure how to respond. He thought he had thrown her off the trail, covered his tracks, but here she was again asking about that bloody dresser. He couldn't tell her he knew about the life insurance policy. Not until he'd worked out all the details of how to get rid of her. His mind went over his plan. It wasn't ready yet, so he smiled and said, "What you on about?"

"Don't lie to me." Her eyes locked with his, daring him to disagree.

The cold stare sent another chill along his spine. She knew. Somehow, she knew. *This was it,* he thought, *the showdown*. It had been years in the making, and now the day had arrived. Anger began to brew. The cow had sucked him dry. Even wanted to cash in that policy over his rotted bones. No! He'd outlive the witch. He wasn't going to stand for any more of her crap. Not for a second.

"Okay," he said. "I went through your dresser and saw the bloody life insurance policy."

"How could you?" Maude stared, her eyes mud-brown pinheads.

"How could I?" PC Hoon couldn't believe his ears. "I'm the one whose been cheated here. When I croak, you'll be counting the cash over my bones. I know your game, now. I know what you are up to."

"Silly sod, did you actually read the bloody thing?" Maude stared as though he'd just dropped from the rear end of a pigeon. "The policy is for me. If I die you get the money."

She fell silent, but the air crackled with rage.

PC Hoon looked at his plate of glutenous fish pie goo, scooped up a forkful, then put the fork down and said, "Are you sick?" He regretted the words as soon as he spoke them. They sounded like he was eager to know she was ill, on her last legs and ready to croak. "I mean, is something wrong?" But once again his voice came out with too much levity. He wasn't a bloody actor. How could he hide his true feelings?

Maude was screaming now. "This is the final straw. It is over. I want a divorce."

PC Hoon had dreamt of this moment, prayed for it. Still, he couldn't believe she would agree. But she said the words, hadn't she?

He said, "Well, that's—"

"Don't bother. We both know it has not worked."

This was mad; she'd agreed to a split, and he'd soon be free. Now all he needed was to make sure the witch didn't snatch more than her fair share of his cash. He'd give her ten percent and call it quits. A wave of joy washed over him, a lightness as though heavy weights had been lifted from his shoulders. Unable to quell the excitement, he blurted, "When will you move out?"

"That's what we need to talk about." Maude waved a hand as if she were swatting a fly. "I need you to sign the cottage over to me."

"What!"

"You can't stay here tonight." She gazed towards the door. There was a suitcase packed—his.

"Hey!" PC Hoon jumped to his feet. "I'm not going anywhere."

"I don't want to fall out with you, Sid. I want our break-up to be on good terms. It is what you need. A fresh start with no strings. Me too. Come on, let's not argue." Maude reached under the table, pulled out a box, and tipped it onto the floor. Handbags. All sizes and shapes—an expensive one made of burnt-orange leather with straps, another, small and gold.

PC Hoon stared, eyes wide.

"You'll leave now and not come back, or I'll have a nice chat with your friends in the police." Maude grinned. "You get five hundred pounds. It is in the zip section of the suitcase. Now, finish your fish pie and get the hell out of my house."

CHAPTER 45

Dr Joy Hall opened her eyes, felt the pull of the IV line in her arm and realised two things. First, the room was awash with flowers, and there were cards in bright colours lined up on the windowsill. Second, she was being watched.

"Are you all right?" Jeffery walked to the flowers, sniffed, picked up a card, read silently, and put it back. "From PC Beth Finn. She'll go far."

Joy gave a weak smile.

Jeffery said, "And you, how goes it?"

"The drugs took my mind for a while, but I'm back now."

"It'd take more than drugs to kill that sharp brain of yours." Jeffery sat in the chair by the bed and touched her friend's arm. "But you do look like crap."

"Wish I could say I feel like crap, but I don't." Joy felt a pang of… she didn't know what. "In truth, I feel worse."

"I'll not stay long, then. The nurse told me they'll bring your dinner at five. I see the team sent their best wishes." Jeffery fell quiet.

"I don't blame you for what happened," Joy said. "I don't blame anyone."

"Moss made a right balls-up of it." Jeffery's words came out in a rush. "Can't understand why they sent him to lead the case. I told the top brass as much this morning. Leave it to the local team; they'll clear it up. Not my fault if you sent a dud."

Joy said, "Did any of the crap hit you?"

"Nah. But if we don't get a result, that might change."

"And Moss?"

"Carlisle have unleashed the dogs."

"It wasn't his fault. I should have—"

"He'll be nowt but a bloody pile of fat and gristle when they are through. I gave him a good kicking, damn fool. I just hope they—"

Joy raised her hand. She wasn’t in the blame game. "I'm just trying to make sense of it. Weighing up what happened. What it means. I've worked with men like Perkins all my life. I get a kick from climbing inside their heads, figuring out what makes them tick wrong, and putting it right as best I can."

Jeffery said, "You are not to blame for this in any way."

Joy didn’t reply.

"Do you hear me?"

"Hmmm, I dunno. I could have—"

"Moss is carrying the can, and that is that." Jeffery paused a beat. "You need to focus on getting well."

"There'll be others."

"We've got that covered. Hamilton Perkins will not come near St Bees again for fear of getting snared in our net. We'll get him."

"I want to help."

"Don't let yourself get obsessed, Joy. You need to heal. What you went through is not just physical."

"I want to get out of here and help."

"Joy, no!"

"I can't just lie here for days on end. They'll need the bed soon, and if the doctor says I can convalesce at home, well, why not?"

There was a very long pause.

Jeffery said, "And is that what the doctor has said?"

"It would make me feel better to be at home." Joy knew how Jeffery's mind worked. Knew if she could spin it to her friend's benefit, she'd have an in. "Look, I know Perkins, know what he'll do. He'll be back and I can help."

Jeffery went quiet for two beats, then said, "I don't like it… but if in a few days the doctor says you can go home, well, I won't stand in your way if you still want to help. But you'll not be allowed near any night-time surveillance. Understood?"

CHAPTER 46

Fenella placed a log on the fire. She was in the lounge where they'd gathered after Nan's Sunday meal. They only used it when Nan had one of her fancy do's. The room was large with wide bay windows which looked onto the lawn. It was not yet dark, although dusk was creeping across the hedged fields which sloped away to the cliffs and sea. She loved this cottage on Cleaton Bluff. It was home sweet home. Always.

She turned from the fireplace to watch the room. Dexter gnawed on a chicken bone with a plate full to the brim of rice and peas, with sides of fried okra and plantain. His third. He'd been in a jovial mood since the visit with Nellie Cook. There was a mysterious gleam in his eyes. Not that most would notice, but Fenella had worked with him for years. Once, years back, when they first worked together, she'd seen that look. It took her a week to wheedle it out of him. His great-aunt had left him land in Tobago which he'd sold for a handsome sum. This time she'd not wait a week to get at his news. What was he over the moon about?

Nan and Malc Buckham sat in wing-back

armchairs in a quiet corner by the floor lamp. Malc's mop of white hair gave him the look of a statesman, and he wore a pinstripe suit. *Old school,* Fenella thought. He grew up at a time when "Sunday best" was a thing. Nan, too, had changed into a floral dress, all floaty and frills, which matched the grin still stuck to her face after Fenella had first introduced them.

"So that's Dexter, eh?" Gail Stubbs stood at Fenella's side, holding a bowl crammed full of pie and cream. She wore a mauve blouse, stretch jeans with heeled clogs, and looked ten years younger out of her nurse uniform. She kept her voice low. "Likes his food."

"Aye." Fenella couldn't help herself; her matchmaking brain was full on. "He's a touch gnarled and grizzled, but I think he looks a lot like Leo, if you squint."

"Nothing like," Gail snorted. "Leo is water under the bridge. Like I said, if he didn't leave me, I would have left him. It was over a long time ago." She took a spoonful of pie, then nodded towards Jones, who had Lisa Levon on one side and PC Beth Finn on the other. "Your young detective is in demand. There'll be sparks with him for sure."

Fenella watched out of the corner of her eye. They were flitting around Jones like butterflies showing their colours. She'd not interfere in the private lives of her team, but she'd have a think about Jones, see if she couldn't find him a match. Neither Lisa Levon nor PC Beth Finn were a good fit. Too close to the job.

She thought about PC Hoon. He'd not shown up. Shame. She'd hoped to meet his wife, Maude. Not that she wanted to pry, but the wives always talked, didn't they? At some point she'd pop over to St Bees to say hello. You could never have too many friends, and being the spouse of a police officer wasn't easy. It wouldn't take her long to find out all about Sid Hoon. She touched Gail on the elbow. "And what do you think of Dexter?"

"How come you never introduced us before?"

"I thought you were happy with Leo."

Nan got to her feet and began to wander over.

Fenella leaned in close and whispered, "Come on, Gail, what do you think?"

"Might be sparks."

"Enjoying the pie?" Nan asked.

"The best." Gail took a large mouthful. "Might have thirds. Nice tang."

"That'd be Mr Bray's apples. He runs an organic farm not too far from here. I added them in with the blackberry for a change. Glad you like it."

Eduardo came into the room. He, too, held a bowl in his hand, glanced around, and went to sit next to Dexter.

Gail said, "Looks like Eduardo is a fan of your pie too."

"That sod will eat anything," Nan replied. "Had to keep the bugger away from the pot whilst it was still cooking. He's supposed to be on a diet."

Eduardo looked over, raised his spoon, and grinned.

"The man's got ears like radar," Nan said, then went over to sit next to him.

"And you," Gail said, "how goes the job?"

Fenella had long mastered the switch between work and home and dodged the question. She'd think about work later. This was her family time. She needed it to recharge, and said, "Work is as work does. How do you like life in the hospital?"

Gail paused for half a beat. "Nice. I've signed up for agency work a couple of evenings a week. I need the cash. The split with Leo came at a cost and I've got to rebuild." She took another spoonful of pie. "Think I'll have a natter with Nan's new fancy man."

She went to sit next to Malc. His rich, smooth voice boomed across the room as she told him something that made him laugh. Dexter, Nan, and Eduardo were all laughing too, and Jones grinned like a man in a jewellery store who'd been offered his choice of diamond rings. *A pleasant time had by all,* Fenella thought as she watched the room. *Much better than the past few days and,* she suspected, *better than the week to come.*

CHAPTER 47

PC Hoon sat on the single bed in Mrs Lenz's spare room and shivered.

It was Sunday evening and so cold that his breath curled in the air like puffs of white smoke. Not exactly the lap of luxury. The card in the village shop window mentioned mod cons. He wondered if this referred to the electric light which gloomed a dim glow from a low-wattage bulb. There was nothing else modern in the room—a giant, grey-coin gas meter, yellowed net curtains, and a faint trace of mould. And he saw the shopkeeper staring at him through the glass as he read the card. Why couldn't Chad Tate leave the past where it belonged?

He swore.

It was dark outside, and he'd no coins to feed the meter. Who the hell had coin gas meters these days?

A knock came at the door.

"Only me," Mrs Lenz said. She carried a tray with a plate covered by a silver dome. "Sunday meal included. I'm not a fancy cook, but it'll warm you up."

PC Hoon glanced about the narrow room. Mrs Lenz understood his concern. There was no desk or chair. The bed filled the space and even she had to sidle in with elbows pressed flat to her side.

"Not to worry, PC Hoon. You sit on your bed and enjoy. Sunday is the one time I let guests have food in their room." Mrs Lenz placed the tray on his lap and lifted the lid with a flourish. "Fish pie! My Alf's favourite. Leave the tray outside your door when you are done."

PC Hoon stared at the food. Bloody fish pie! He wanted to fling the plate at the wall and wrap his hands around Mrs Lenz's scrawny throat.

"Go on, then, take a bite," Mrs Lenz said. "It's my grandmother's eel recipe."

"Lovely," he said as he lifted a forkful to his mouth and sniffed. He nibbled. He would have to do without food tonight. What he really needed was warmth and that meant a few coins to drop in the meter. He'd known Mrs Lenz for years and decided to use his charm. *Piece of cake*, he thought, and gave a broad smile. "And that gas heater..."

"What about it?"

"I don't have any coins to put in it."

"I wondered why it was so cold in here. Some like it hot, others not so much. There is no accounting for taste, is there, PC Hoon?"

"It’s a strange world, Mrs Lenz. Things are

never what they seem. Take that glass jar in your front room, for example. It is filled with coins, isn't it?"

"Like to dump in my change and take it to the bank once a year. A few coins each week adds up. Hundreds of pounds in a year, PC Hoon. You ought to try it."

"I wonder if you might—"

"No! I don't extend credit. Not with rent or heat or anything else. I'm old school on that. If you can't pay for it, you can't have it. It is cash up front or nowt. Saves folks from getting into bother with bills they can't pay. I'm sure you understand that, with you being in uniform." Mrs Lenz wagged her finger. "Credit wreaks havoc in poor folks' lives. Am I right? I am."

"But it's bloody freezing in here!"

"We'll not have language like that under my roof, else you can pack your bags and go."

"Only a couple of coins until tomorrow."

"I've made my position clear. We'll hear no more of that if you please."

PC Hoon swore again under his breath, without moving his lips but with venom, nonetheless. From somewhere along the hall a dog yapped.

Mrs Lenz said, "Max is so excited at our new guest."

"He's been barking all day."

"He wants you to play with him."

PC Hoon didn't like the sound of that, but he had no choice. This was home until he sorted things out. He didn't like dogs that yapped non-stop. He didn't like the room, and he didn't like the look of the steaming hot plate of fish pie on his lap. There was nowhere to dump the pie. He'd have to eat the bloody thing or else throw it down the toilet. But he knew Mrs Lenz inspected the loo, counted the sheets on the roll and would know.

He said, "I suppose Max can eat my scraps. Make a pleasant treat for the little fellow. I'll be sure to leave him enough for seconds."

"He'll not want it after you've been at it," Mrs Lenz said. "Anyway, he's had his. You got what's left." She sniffed and marched away as Max yapped.

Once again PC Hoon swore. This time at everyone and everything and most especially at Maude. Oh, how well he knew his wife. She was a greedy cow. Once he signed over the cottage, she'd turn him in. Maude had him by the balls, and no matter what he gave her, she would squeeze. Yes! He'd do her good and proper. She wouldn't see it coming. No one would. They never did.

CHAPTER 48

If Fenella had the smallest inkling of the devastating impact her meeting would have, she might not have left home.

The next morning, she sat at a table by the window in Don's Café with a large cup of tea, two slices of buttered toast, and a pot of plum jam. The sun had yet to show any sign of life, but she could make out figures as they flitted by the window lit by the orange glow of a street lamp. She was waiting for Rodney Rawlings.

The pressman was late.

"Where are the hungry mob?" Fenella said to the café owner whose name she'd found out was Don. "Thought you'd be packed by now."

Don said, "We get a few on their way to the train station, but lunchtime is the real rush hour, with kids and staff from the school." He stopped and looked at her closely. "You're that detective I saw on Pow Beck bridge!"

"Aye, luv, that'd be me."

Don wiped his hands on the apron. "Welcome to the beating heart of St Bees. If you want to know what goes on in this village, you've come to the right place."

"Aye, is that so?"

He grinned. "Well, here, the pub, St Bees Priory, and the village store. But they all come to Don's Café for lunch." He jabbed a finger in the air as if about to make a point. "The vicar shows up Mondays and Fridays, pub landlord on Wednesday, and the owner of the village store swings by every Thursday at two p.m. like clockwork." Again, he rubbed his hands on his apron and lowered his voice. "Viv Gill was bad enough, but now Mrs Pearl Smith."

Fenella said, "When did you see her last?"

"Viv Gill?"

"Aye."

"She'd pop in once or twice a week at lunchtimes." He closed his eyes for a beat. "Last Thursday around one. "

"Notice anything different?"

"She seemed normal, ordered her usual. Crab cakes with chips and mushy peas. Even smiled at me. She had a wonderful smile, melt the heart of an iceman, it would."

"And what about Pearl Smith?"

"Yes, she came in regular as clockwork. In fact, she was here last Tuesday for breakfast. Ordered a

King Kong fry-up, but you know about that, don't you, seeing as she spoke with PC Hoon, and he paid for her meal."

"Oi, Fenella, sorry I'm late."

Rodney Rawlings scurried into the café. He wore a dirty, green duffel coat, and his eyes darted this way and that. *A trait of his job*, Fenella thought, *always in search of the big story.*

She said, "Ten minutes late, Rodney!"

"Was a rough night." His sharp eyes watched her closely. "It is not easy when one of your women friends is found dead and no one is talking."

Fenella knew it would leak out. Knew it would be all over the news this week. That's why she wanted to speak with Rodney, that and the fact he was in a relationship with Pearl Smith.

"Aye," she said in a soft voice. "I'm sorry about your loss."

"King Kong fry-up for one over here," Rodney yelled. If he was in mourning, it didn't show by his appetite. "And don't spare the grease, your man over here needs it to soak up the booze he downed last night at the nightclub."

"Righto, Rodney," Don said, looking across the café with a sad smile. He whistled a slow tune as he went to work on the fry-up.

Rodney Rawlings said, "Got to keep my strength up, been working a story about all those fires in the old cottages, trying to find a link. I hear *Look North* are working an angle for their television news show. I want to get in ahead of the buggers." He paused to look towards the kitchen, his nose twitching. "There was another blaze in the village of Egremont last Friday, doesn't look like arson, though. Just random. No one died. Shame."

Fenella said, "Right, tell me about your relationship with Pearl Smith."

Rodney popped a tab of gum into his mouth. "I hear she was murdered." There was no alarm in his voice or sense of concern that Pearl Smith was dead. His face was an unreadable mask. "Am I a suspect?"

Fenella said, "You know how it works."

"Save the taxpayers' cash, look elsewhere." He chewed the gum for a few moments, his sharp eyes never leaving Fenella's face. "Two deaths in St Bees, that's why you called me. What you got, are they related or something?"

Fenella knew it would not take much to join the dots. When he did, she'd need his help. If she gave him enough to chew on, he'd put a good spin on things. That would buy time and slow the bigwigs from sticking their oar in.

She said, "Yes, they are related."

Don whistled softly from the kitchen; it was the only sound in the café. Shadows flitted by the window, but no one came through the door. Fenella watched Rodney Rawlings and waited.

Rodney's eyes narrowed. "I didn’t know Viv Gill; you hear that?"

"Aye. But I want to know everything about you and Pearl. How long?"

"Dunno... five or six months. Nothing serious. Once a week, casual. I'd call ahead. It wasn't going anywhere fast, a bit of fun at first. Not so much over the past few visits." He spat out the gum in a napkin. "She'd turned a bit odd."

"How do you mean?"

"I don't want this bandied about."

"Do you see a notebook?"

"King Kong for one," Don said, as he placed a steaming plate of fried food on the table. He looked at Rodney for a moment who nodded in appreciation, then disappeared into the kitchen, whistling.

Rodney made a face and gave a slight eye roll. "There was nothing I could put my finger on with Pearl. I mean, she was an attractive woman, and that's what any red-blooded bloke notices first. Plump and so pale you could see her veins. Just how I like 'em." He grinned bearing two sulphurous teeth that looked like bat fangs.

"Go on," Fenella said. "I'm listening."

"After a while I got the sense that Pearl was...

off." He tapped the side of his head. "Once, she asked me what I thought about knives. Didn't know how to answer that one. Another time, during... well, she wriggled out from under and went to the window. Said she felt as if she was being watched. I should have ended it then, but... she was a looker." He glanced at the kitchen. "Pearl claimed to have powerful friends in the village. Men in high places who knew everyone's secrets. When I asked her who they were, she laughed. Gave me the creeps, but like I said, I couldn't keep my hand out of the honeypot."

"Was she seeing anyone else?"

Rodney shrugged. "I'm a free agent, so was she. Wouldn't be surprised, though." He paused for a long moment. "Look, I met up with her once a week at most. I'd stay over. In the morning, she'd make breakfast, or we'd come here. If we ate out, I'd pay. Strange thing is, when we ate at her place, she always said the sausages were a gift."

"From who?"

"No idea, but in a village this size, it wouldn't take Sherlock Holmes to figure it out."

"I'm more of a Dr Watson; can you give me a hint?"

Rodney grinned, exposing those sulphur-coloured teeth. "The bloke who runs the village store, I reckon. Goes by the name of Chad Tate. Only place round here that sells Alston pork sausages. That's what she cooked if we stayed in." Again, he exposed his yellowed teeth. "I didn’t ask because there was no commitment. We understood each other."

Fenella considered his answer for a long beat. "Do you think she was seeing Mr Tate?"

Again, he shrugged. "A bloke don't give away his sausages for nothing, and he's a businessman, ain't he? From New York City. Those folks are as sharp as a whippet. Chad Tate might look like a middle-aged man with a pot belly and receding hairline, but it's the quiet ones you got to watch."

"Aye," Fenella said, thinking.

They fell quiet for a moment. The rattle of plates drifted across the café along with the low whistle of Don. Out in the lane, shadows flitted by the window in the half light of dawn, early-morning commuters on their way to the train station.

Rodney Rawlings said, "I'm going to sit on this a while and do a bit of digging. Two related deaths in St Bees… a serial killer, eh?"

Fenella sipped her tea but did not speak.

He thought a moment, then his eyes widened. "If this is who I think it is, it will be huge. An absolute monster of a story. I mean, this will make my reputation as a journalist. I won’t have to write columns about church fêtes anymore. This story will make a shed load of money."

CHAPTER 49

Fenella paused to read the poster in the window of the St Bees Village store. A fundraising fête at St Bees Priory on the last Saturday of the month. She made a note to attend with Eduardo and Nan. They loved a church jamboree.

"Hello, pet," she said above the tinkle of the doorbell.

Chad Tate sat at the counter in his store, head drooped down. He was exactly as Rodney Rawlings described. Middle aged, pot bellied, a hairline that had seen better days. She knew he was from New York, had watched American shows with her grandkids, and thought he looked like a plump and slightly depressed version of Mister Rogers. Only there was no one in his neighbourhood, and she supposed that was because it was still early.

He did not look up but stared at a stack of white envelopes. They all looked the same, typed with black ink. She thought about what Rodney Rawlings had said about Chad gifting sausages and wondered if they were love letters from Pearl Smith. Only thing was, Mrs Smith didn't come across as overly romantic, and as Fenella stepped closer, she saw they had a bank logo in the corner.

"Not the gas bill, then?" she said.

He looked up, and Fenella thought she saw a flash of something in his eyes. Remorse? Whatever it was, it touched her heart, and for an instant she felt a deep pang of sadness.

"I'm sorry, can I help you find something?" There was a New York City accent there, but it had been softened by his years in England.

"I was just saying those envelopes don't look like they are gas bills." Fenella had tried to curb her nosiness when she was younger. But had given up years ago. "Who are they from?"

He ignored the question and said, "Our milk is in the fridge and bread on the shelves at the back, but we are out of baked beans."

Fenella said, "Do you sell Alston pork sausages?"

"You are in luck. I've a fresh batch in the storeroom, was about to put them out. They fly off the shelves as if they have wings."

"Are you Mr Chad Tate?" Fenella pulled out her warrant card.

"Ah," he said. When a detective showed up, most people looked either scared or guilt ridden. But she couldn't read his face except perhaps a brief flicker in the eyes. He looked towards the back of the store. Fenella followed his gaze to a door which she suspected led to the storeroom. He gave a weak smile. "I am Mr Tate. How can I help?"

Fenella said, "I'm making inquiries into the deaths of Viv Gill and Mrs Pearl Smith; you'll have heard?" She saw it again. A flicker in his eyes. His face might be a blank, but she knew nerves when she saw them.

"There must be some mistake," he said fast, his accent bubbling through. "I've already spoken to PC Hoon and another officer, PC Finn. They said to let them know if I thought of anything else. But nothing has come to mind. I'm so sorry to have wasted your time."

Fenella knew New Yorkers talked fast, but this bloke spoke at hyper-speed, not even taking a breath, and that made her curious.

"From New York City, eh?"

"That's right."

"Go back often?"

"I've made a life here."

"Nice, though, the Big Apple. Exciting. Not like St Bees."

"Too much changes in the city."

"That's part of the fun. Go with the flow and all that."

"It's not all it is made out to be."

"But all those tall buildings. Impressive."

"You are never more than three feet away from a roach, even in the skyscrapers."

Fenella laughed. "Tell me about Mrs Pearl Smith."

He gave a shrug. "Pearl was a regular customer. Came in once or twice a week. I believe she was born in St Bees, lived here all her life." He nodded to the window, where the first rays of sun shone down on the lane. "Went to church and paid her bills on time."

Fenella wondered about that. She'd met Mrs Pearl Smith and her fancy man, Rodney Rawlings. He'd scrambled to pull on his trousers when she and Dexter entered the bedroom. She didn't think church would have been high on the list and said, "A good looker, by all accounts."

"If you like the pale-dough look… I mean, she had a bit of meat on her."

"Not skinny like a New York fashion model, eh?"

"Pleasant enough."

"That why you gave her free sausages?"

"Pardon?"

"Alston pork sausages. Seems you gave them to Mrs Pearl Smith. A gift, eh?"

"You are mistaken."

"Or was it payment in kind… for her services?"

"I was not in a relationship with Mrs Pearl Smith."

"Know anyone who would give her free sausages?"

"No."

"Aye," Fenella said. "That's what I thought you'd say."

CHAPTER 50

When Fenella left the village store, the sun was up, a giant vexed eye in the east that spat its orange glow on the cobbled lanes of St Bees. Its glare matched her irked mood. Impatience had driven her to the shop. She had wanted to find out more about Pearl Smith before she drove back to Port St Giles to meet with her team. But her chat with Chad Tate had left frustration. Why would he deny gifting Pearl free sausages? Men give gifts to lasses all the time. No. There was something hidden beneath Chad Tate's fast New York accent and pleasant middle-aged smile. And she sensed it was deep and dark and unpleasant.

Fenella took a few steps along the pavement and turned to look back at the store. Chad Tate watched through the glass and didn't look away when she caught his gaze. *Eyes like a bloody hawk,* she thought. *Did he see something and not say?* With barely a moment to consider that, a van trundled along the lane. It belched a black plume, and her mind flitted to Viv Gill and Pearl Smith. Both women wrote to Hamilton Perkins; both died at the hand of a knife. Yet, no one had seen a thing. No one had heard a scream. In a small village, that just didn't feel right. She glanced at the red brick covered in moss and lichen of St Bees Priory. Hamilton Perkins was like a bleedin' ghost.

As she fished for the keys to the Morris Minor, she had the firm sense of being watched. Not from Chad Tate, who still stood by the window, but from elsewhere. She turned to scan the lane. Two cars and a white Ford van parked on her side, their windows dark. By the curb, a pigeon pecked at the cobblestones. A thin plume of smoke curled from the church doorway. As she peered, she made out the outline of a figure.

"Hey you!" She crossed the road and hurried towards the entrance. "Can I have a word?"

A man in a cassock emerged from the gloom. He held a cigar in his right hand. "It appears you have caught me on a smoke break. I'm Cain Briar, Vicar Briar to everyone around here."

"Nowt wrong with a puff or two," Fenella replied, taking in his thin face, purplish bulbous nose, deep-set, small eyes and black cassock, which she assumed he wore every day, for it needed a wash. He struck her as the kind of man who would not bother to wash his socks either. "I'm Detective Inspector Sallow."

"Yes, yes, I know who you are. We all do. How may I help?"

He must know what she was here about.

One of his flock had gone astray and got herself murdered, and by a man who seemed to vanish as if he were a spook.

Fenella said, "Can I have a word about one of your flock?"

"Bit nippy out here." He turned, pushed open the heavy oak doors, and led her to the vestry where a gas heater took the chill out of the cold air.

"Cup of tea?"

"I'll not say no."

Fenella watched as he walked behind a lattice screen, heard the click of the kettle, and a few minutes later the hiss of steam. Vicar Briar returned with a small tray, teapot, and a plate of custard creams. She loved the sandwich biscuit, liked to split it in half, lick out the cream filling and dunk it in her tea. *That'll do nicely*, she thought as he poured.

After the vicar had wolfed down two biscuits and gulped a mouthful of tea, he looked at Fenella and said, "Is there any news on the... deaths?"

"That's what I'm here for." She said it even though she was aware he'd known who she was before she had introduced herself. After all, he'd been watching her, hadn't he? He knew what went on in this village. "Pews full these days?"

"We give the pub and the village store a run for their money. The church is at the heart of St Bees. Most things come my way in the end." He smiled.

"How is Dr Joy Hall? Such a shame what happened, and with her being new to our village. I will pop around to say hello when she comes home from the hospital."

Fenella stared. They had tried to keep Dr Joy Hall's attack a secret. But he knew, and she could tell by the gleam in his eyes he'd not told her all his secrets.

She said, "Suppose it helps to be in tune with the big man upstairs, eh?"

"And with the mouths of those who like to talk," he replied.

Fenella thought he'd know a lot about everyone's business, whether or not they came to church. But she hadn't read a statement in the files from the vicar. PC Hoon was tasked with that job. Now she wondered whether she'd missed something, and made a mental note to go back and check. Then she had a better idea and said, "I don't want to go over old ground, but it would be helpful if I could ask a few questions. For clarification."

"Old ground?"

"You spoke with PC Hoon?"

"I thought he might stop by this week for a chat, but no. I hear he spent a lot of time in Don's Café. That's another place worth a visit if you're interested in village gossip, and the pub too."

Fenella took a sip of tea and wondered

whether PC Hoon had visited the pub to speak with the landlord. She stared at the plate of custard creams and said, "Any new faces about the village?"

"There is always an ebb and flow." Vicar Briar picked up his cup, took a sip, and held it in his hand. "We knew Dr Joy Hall had bought Mrs Rye's old place when the workmen moved in."

"From out of town, the workmen?"

"Not a one. All local. All good men. Hard workers who do more than they are paid for. No, there have been no recent new faces in the village." Suddenly his face clouded, and he put the cup down. "Only person I can think of is Hazza. He does a spot of gardening about the village, keeps the graveyard tidy. Showed up about two months ago. Does a good job."

Fenella fished in her handbag for a notebook. "Last name?"

Vicar Briar shrugged. "I pay him from the petty cash. Twenty-five pounds a time, keeps the paperwork down." He lowered his voice. "He is disabled, walks with a limp. Don't know his last name. Everyone calls him Hazza."

"Happen you've not got an address, then?"

"Maryport, I think." Vicar Briar looked at the cup as if it might confirm, then shook his head. "To tell you the truth, I'm not sure. Hazza said something about living in a hostel, or was it a bed

& breakfast in Port St Giles? No. I don't recall where. Why don't you ask him yourself? He'll be in the village tomorrow. Comes every other Tuesday."

Fenella beamed. "Aye, we'll do just that."

There was a silence. Fenella wondered whether she should grab a custard cream or two. They'd go down a real treat with her cup of tea. But before she decided, Vicar Briar said, "You want to know about Pearl Smith and Viv Gill?" He took another gulp of tea, but his eyes never left her face. "They both came to weekday service."

That surprised Fenella. She hadn't pegged Viv Gill as a church lass, not given that she worked for Nellie Cook. Still, she didn't interrupt. There would be plenty of time for questions. Best to wait. She picked up a biscuit, wanted to split it in two, eat the filling, and dunk it in her tea, but instead she bit half and chewed.

Vicar Briar was speaking. "I've known Pearl the longest, so perhaps my thoughts might add some insight into her background. She was born a stone's throw from the cliffs, on Oak Grove Lane. The house went to her when her mum passed, must be ten years back. She married, but it was troubled and ended in divorce." He spoke slow, as though he weighed each word before letting it out. "I don't want to speak ill of the dead, but she had a... challenge when it came to men. Seemed to fall in with the wrong sort. It always turned bad; that's when I'd see her at church, and I'd know another relationship had broken down."

"So she wasn't a regular?"

He picked up a custard cream, examined its ridges with one eye half closed as though a jeweller looking at a precious stone. "When her waters were troubled, she'd seek out the calm of the sanctuary."

"Been in lately, had she?"

He popped the biscuit into his mouth, munched for a long moment, then shook his head. "She'd not been in for a while. The last time... maybe five months ago. Yes, it was still warm, late summer."

Fenella wondered if that was when Chad Tate had broken up with her. He'd said he wasn't in a relationship now and that might have been true. But she knew he lied about the sausages. Still, she'd dig, find out more, so she could get a clear picture of Pearl Smith.

She said, "What can you tell me about Viv Gill?"

"New to the village. A good looker, nice sway to the hips." Vicar Briar picked up another custard cream, split it in half, licked out the soft centre, and dunked it in his tea. "Viv Gill was more regular. One of my women, liked to help out."

That baffled Fenella. Viv Gill had been a sex worker who'd moved from Whitehaven to set up shop in St Bees. What was she doing on her knees in church?

"The pews are full of the wounded," Vicar Briar said as if he'd read her mind. "You'll not find a single saint in my congregation, and that includes me."

CHAPTER 51

Chad Tate watched as the detective left St Bees Priory. She moved as quiet as a cat on the prowl and kept close to the shade of the red brick wall. He guessed she wanted to keep out of sight. He didn’t want her to see him either. Earlier, he couldn’t help but watch, but now he'd had a little think and knew it wasn't a good idea to let her see him stare. He didn’t want her to come back and fire off another round of questions.

But he struggled to control the urge to look, hesitated for a beat, then eased the shop door open a notch to peer along the lane. A sharp chill rushed in despite the glare of the risen sun. Detective Sallow crossed by her car and searched her bag for the key. Her head flicked towards the store. He darted back inside.

Whoa! Did she see him?

Chad leaned his back on the door, took thin breaths. She didn’t believe him about the sausages. The police were all about links. Once they found one, they'd haul in what they caught. He took another breath and waited for a sharp knock on the glass and the detective's soft voice, but heard the car engine splutter into life and the low growl as it drove off.

He wiped the sweat from his brow and stepped into the lane, hands shading his eyes. Two black-backed gulls hovered with slow wing beats, dark shadows against a globe-sized sun. It was peaceful and bright with a crisp bite from the Irish sea. The slap of waves drifted from the cliffs as soft as distant thunder. Idyllic. Except for the police poking their nose where it didn't belong.

"I wonder if we might have a quiet chat."

Chad spun around.

Vicar Briar said, "Best in your store, eh?"

The two men walked in silence to the store. Chad sat on the stool by the checkout and stacked the white envelopes carefully into a neat pile. They teetered but did not fall.

Vicar Briar's eyes darted between the aisles. He sucked in a breath, which rattled against the back of his throat. "No one else in the shop?"

"Just us." Chad wondered whether he should flip the sign on the door to CLOSED, but he needed the business. "It's early; we have a few minutes."

Vicar Briar said, "Detective Sallow strikes me as a woman who gets her ducks in a row, then fires." He reached into his cassock and pulled out a cigar but did not light up. "The job is an addiction for her. She enjoys lifting stones to see what is underneath."

"Like you."

"A man of the cloth is by his nature a curious fellow. We search for God and point folks to the right path. If I'd not gone into the Church, I might have made a good detective."

Chad stared at the window. "She asked about gifts I'd given Pearl Smith."

"You said it was a brief fling."

"Only a few months."

"Then what is the problem?"

"Pearl was needy, wanted things for free." Chad swallowed hard. It was almost upon him. The rage. It had taken control of him for the first time years ago. He was inside St Bees Priory when a cloak of anger gripped him hard. With his bare fists, he smashed the altar, scattered folks from a pew, shook it from its anchor, and hurled it through a window. It happened at a funeral. He'd not been inside the church since. He knew he wasn't a violent man, but once the rage came, it would not leave until satisfied. " I... only wanted to... help Pearl out. Do a good deed. You understand that, don't you?"

"I worry about you, my son," Vicar Briar said softly. He twiddled the cigar and, with a slow movement, lit it. "Getting yourself all upset and obsessed won't bring the dead back to life."

"Look, it was only a brief fling with Pearl. That's all it was. Yes... I hoped for more, fell head over heels... and that does things to a man, doesn't it?" Chad balled his fists. "You talk about obsession. Yes! I was obsessed. I admit it. It is who I am. I don't like it, but can't control what it makes me do. When it takes me, I'm like wildfire, burn everything in sight."

"Saying something like that just makes me even more concerned that you'll..." Vicar Briar sucked on the cigar and puffed out a plume of smoke. "A fool uttereth all his mind: but a wise man keepeth it in till afterwards. Please remember that, my son."

"But that detective is asking questions. She'll find out about—"

"We can't stop the police from doing their job, but we can do our good works with wisdom."

"But they'll find the link."

"What are you on about?"

Chad placed his head in his hands. "I... I... when Viv Gill came to the village... we became friends... very close friends."

Vicar Briar shook his head as if to clear it. "What are you saying?"

"I'd close the shop at lunch and go visit her at her home. We—"

Vicar Briar held up a hand. "You're a dark horse, aren't you, my son?"

"Then I found out that she was a... PC Hoon

was a regular," he said through clenched teeth.

"It is not our place to judge," Vicar Briar said in a soft hush.

Chad pounded his fists on the counter. The stack of envelopes toppled. When he lost it, he couldn't think straight, just acted on his violent impulses. Now he wanted to smash his own shop to pieces. He swallowed again and focused on flexing his hands. But anger flared, licking at his heart like wild flames.

CHAPTER 52

Dr Joy Hall yelled at the top of her voice.

It was early Monday morning, and she knew it wasn't the best way to get her point across. But if she didn't make a fuss, she'd be trapped in this loony bin for God knew how long. That it was a hospital room designed to save her life didn't matter. She was fed up with lying on her back staring at the ceiling. She felt like an Egyptian mummy, wrapped in tight rags and locked in a tomb.

"No, you stay here, get well," the doctor said in a heavy Kenyan accent. She was tall and slim with bushy black hair that seemed to have a life of its own. "We need to monitor you, check that everything good."

"I want out of here."

"You not like the food?" The doctor looked concerned. "I speak with nurse; we have good choices on staff menu."

Joy sighed. "Lying here, I'm spoilt for choice for needles in my arm. Granted, it's just pretty much the only thing I'm spoilt for choice for."

The doctor laughed. "You make good recovery

soon. I see that."

"I feel fine, really." If Joy could have got off her bed and gone down on her knees to beg, she would have done so. She couldn't stand another day in this dim room, where it was impossible to tell day from night.

The doctor peered at a clipboard, tapped it with a pen, and said, "A few more days, and we can discuss, eh?" She moved the chair and sat on the edge of the bed. "Listen, everyone knows what happened. We take good care of you."

"But you'll need the bed for someone else in more need, won't you?"

"You are in need."

This was crazy. Joy was going round in circles. It had been like this for a good ten minutes. All she wanted was to check out and go home. Then she remembered home was a cottage in St Bees, not the flat she just moved out of in Whitehaven. Back to the house with the door lock that jangled as if Uncle Fred was about to come in, and where walls creaked and groaned with the soft whisper of the ghost of Mrs Rye. Did she really want to go back to that place? Wouldn't it bring back memories of all that had happened?

Joy closed her eyes and saw the scrunched-up face of her Uncle Fred, smelled the cigarettes on his sour breath, felt his rough stubble against her breasts. He was never arrested. Never charged.

Never convicted.

Her eyes snapped open. A week after the attack, he was gone from her life. No one knew what happened to him. He vanished. Just like her dead baby when the nurse took it away. No! She would not let spooks or the creak of the old house or Uncle Fred or anything else knock her off course. She and Veronica Jeffery were Team Superwomen. They didn't back down in the face of a threat. Yes, she felt sore and still under the influence of drugs. Those things would not block her path. Nothing would get in her way.

"Then I'll discharge myself," Joy said. "I'm in my rights to do so, you know."

The doctor pulled out a notebook and a pen and furiously wrote notes as she inspected the electronics around the bed. Joy couldn’t help but wonder if she might be more ill than they'd let on. But she heard no beeps, and that meant everything was okay, didn’t it?

"You not well." The doctor shook her head and said, "And your friend will not be happy if you leave."

That's when Joy first sensed the hand of Veronica Jeffery behind all of this. She knew her friend worried about her, and there was an armed guard just outside the door. Yes, it was safer to stay in this room where the police could keep an eye on her. That gave Joy pause. She needed to think a little more about her next move.

The doctor was speaking, "And I believe you work for prison service, right?"

"Yes, but how do you—"

"Low Marsh Prison will not be happy if you leave the hospital without our consent. They not let you back at work if think you sick." The doctor held Joy's gaze. "I'll have to write a report, you know."

Oh, very nice, Joy thought. And again she sensed the hand of Jeffery. "Okay, but get me out of this room, please."

If she had any doubts that Veronica Jeffery was behind all of this, they vanished with the doctor's next words.

"This ward is busy. We need bed." She gave a sly grin and once again stared at the clipboard. "I think you well enough to be moved to the convalescence ward. You'll have private room and phone so you can help police with investigation."

CHAPTER 53

At the briefing later that morning, Fenella felt the air of excitement in the room. The team were refreshed after their weekend break and eager to get started.

No one knew what the day would bring.

If they did, their mood would have been less jovial.

But the room filled with voices as if they were part of an after-party following Nan's Sunday do. Even Dexter's grizzled face carried a broad smile, and he walked with such a skip to his step that at first Fenella thought he'd been at the booze. She gave him a quick hug and sniffed hard to take in his scent. But there was no whiff of wine or beer or rum, just the faint fragrance of aftershave. That thrilled and annoyed her at the same time. He was off the booze. Good. Why was he so… happy? He'd been that way since their visit to Nellie Cook, and she still didn't have the answer.

Then the briefing phone rang, and everyone cheered when Dr Joy Hall's voice crackled on the line.

"I'm doing well and will help where I can," Dr Joy Hall said. "They've moved me to another ward, a room with French doors that open onto the grounds, so at least I've got a delightful view."

There was another round of cheers followed by shouts of "Congratulations" and "Well done."

"I may be in hospital, but I'm still part of the team," Dr Hall said. "And I would like each person to complete a psychological assessment, only takes twenty minutes on the computer. It will help boost morale."

Fenella liked the idea and said, "Any objections?" She scanned the room. There were none. "The team have agreed. We will set it up today."

"Thank you," Dr Joy Hall replied. "The results will remain confidential. Only I and Superintendent Jeffery will see the entire teams' score. Of course, you'll get your own score for personal review. It will be a great help."

"Okay, ladies and gentlemen, now that we are all warm and fuzzy inside, let's have a chat about Hamilton Perkins." Fenella's voiced brimmed with energy despite her early start in the village of St Bees. "It's time to uncover all his secrets. Where is he now? Why did he come back when he could be away overseas?"

The room fell quiet. Everyone looked at her with bated breath, as if, she thought, they were waiting for her to answer her own questions. A heavy weight pressed down on her shoulders as she scanned the expectant faces. They had a confidence in her she didn't feel she deserved. If she had the answer, she'd not have bothered to ask the questions. In truth, she felt like a priest at the edge of a grave when a small child asks, "Why did God take my daddy?"

Dexter was on his feet. "Come on, folks, the guv has asked a question. Anyone?"

"Perkins is off the obsessive scale, same for his need to control," Dr Joy Hall said, her voice surprisingly clear. "Viv Gill and Pearl Smith wrote to him in prison, where he felt a sense of power over the relationships. He escapes and finds out they have lives which focus on more than him. A man like Perkins will see that as a threat to be eliminated. When he gets an idea in his head, it is like life or death in his mind."

"Aye, happen you're right about that." Fenella was pacing. She had been worrying about the link between Perkins and those he attacked. Pearl Smith and Viv Gill wrote to him in prison. That link was easy. But what about Dr Joy Hall? She'd been his psychologist in Low Marsh Prison. *A different link,* she thought, and that's what caused the concern. Had Hamilton Perkins decided to wreak revenge on the women who'd worked with him when he was inside?

If her gut instinct held true, there'd be more deaths to come. They'd need to build a list of women who'd come into contact with him and track down the rat to his lair before the next wave of carnage began. Fenella turned her gaze to the room and said, "If you were in a life-or-death battle, where would you run?"

"Back home," Jones said. He sat in the front row with his tablet computer on his lap. "I'd run straight back to the place I know."

"Perkins was born and bred in these parts; he can't be more than a stone's throw away," PC Beth Finn added.

"We've swept the village and have found nothing unusual." PC Hoon got to his feet. He looked as though he had slept in his police uniform. "Someone would have seen him if he was still in the village, ma'am. We've not had a single sight of the man. Anyway, he's killed two women. Why come back? Why not vanish like he did before?"

"Men like Perkins enjoy the thrill of watching," Dr Joy Hall said. "Perkins enjoyed seeing the police fumble about before he was first caught. To him, it seemed they did not have a clue. He'll exhibit the same behaviour again, haunting the crime scene and striking out at the next victim until he finishes the job he..." She gasped and did not finish the sentence.

The team stared at the phone. A soft hiss

of static crawled through the speaker. Everyone in the room knew that what Perkins started, Perkins finished. He had Dr Joy Hall in his sights. The only question was when.

Fenella changed the focus before the mood went too far downhill.

"PC Hoon, have a word with the pub landlord. Find out if there are any new workers on his books. PC Finn, make a list of women who have come into contact with Hamilton Perkins since he went into prison. I know that won't be easy, but go back as far as you can." She paused to think. "I spoke with Vicar Briar this morning; he mentioned a labourer by the name of Hazza. A last name would be useful and an address. He comes in every Tuesday, keeps the church grounds tidy. Walks with a limp. Jones, I'll leave that with you."

Jones gave the thumbs up. "Ma'am, I've got more details on Viv Gill's financials, and I've tracked down Pearl Smith's bank manager, a Mr Pete Clarke. He lives in St Bees. Single. A bit of a ladies' man. Puts it about, if you get my drift."

Fenella nodded for him to continue. As he spoke, her mind went back to Hamilton Perkins and the link between the three women. He'd been caught and convicted as a schoolgirl killer, escaped from prison, and returned home to show the world —what? That he's graduated to another league? She was thinking about how long Dr Joy Hall would be in hospital and how long after that the attack would come, when she realised Jones had finished and Dr Joy Hall was speaking.

"For the past few days, I have been trapped in this hospital with nothing else to do but think about Hamilton Perkins. I've delved deep into his mind, gone places more fearful than words, and each time I come back to one thing: he never fully opened up to me. There are so many things I just don't know."

The room became still. They did not know what she was going to say next but sensed it was important. The silence stretched out so that it felt like an hour.

"Dr Hall?" Fenella said after a few more seconds. "We can hear you, luv. We are listening."

When Dr Hall's voice came through the speaker, it was as quiet as a wisp of wind. "Do you know the Teal twins?"

Fenella's head jerked to look at Dexter. He stared back and ran a hand over his chin. The Teal twins were once notorious for a drug racket they ran out of Whitehaven. They were thugs who got rich through business and brawn. Nothing unusual in that except Tim Teal and Jim Teal claimed to be twins. That was true in part; they were distinct personalities—both evil.

But they belonged to the same man.

A man who'd been locked behind bars for

twenty years with no chance of getting out.

"Aye, I know Tim." Fenella hesitated a beat. "And Jim."

Dr Joy Hall said, "I'm certain a third woman wrote to Hamilton Perkins. The Teal twins will know her name. The three men shared a cell in Low Marsh Prison."

CHAPTER 54

The downhill slide in PC Hoon's day began at the Dog Inn in the village of Egremont.

It was noon when he parked and then crossed the street, with a large black bag, to the narrow-fronted, white-stone-and-black-timber-framed pub. Once a coach stop in the days of horse and cart, lords and ladies on their way to and from Scotland would stay for a day or two. Those times were long gone, and now it was sandwiched between a car hire business and a wine cellar on a busy road. Neither lords nor ladies had visited in years.

It had been awhile since he last drank in the pub. Two years, at least. He'd stopped on his way back to St Bees because they had free showers and great bar food of the sort truck drivers enjoyed—battered, deep fried, with a dollop of ketchup on the side. At Mrs Lenz's house, the shower required coins which he had supplied in a frantic rush, but the water dribbled out for only a short while and never got more than lukewarm. He'd not bothered to shave and nearly struck Mrs Lenz when she called him back to scrub the mess he'd left in the loo, with a bog brush.

And that was the other reason PC Hoon stopped at the pub. The Dog Inn had rooms by the week on the cheap. Not a king's palace by any means. The floorboards creaked; the air smelled of stale smoke, and tiny black bugs leaped from between the bed sheets. But it was better than Mrs Lenz's. He'd book a room for a month. *Piece of cake,* he thought as he walked through the doors. He was in uniform; the black bag contained his clothes.

It was dark inside the main entrance, and PC Hoon was surprised to find a reception area where there had once been a bar with cheap ale on tap. Above a sign which said NO FREE SHOWERS sat an elderly man, nothing more than a skeleton in a cheap polyester suit with hair the colour not found in nature.

"Can I help you, Officer?" The man smiled, his skin stretching so tight, he looked like a grinning skull.

"I see you've done a bit of renovation," PC Hoon said as his eyes darted about. The saloon where he once sat and drank cheap ale was gone. As were the booths and heavy oak benches where the truck drivers ate their fried food. There was a set of sliding doors with an electric swipe-card device where the scarred oak bar once stood. The air smelled fragrant, rose petals he thought, as his nose sniffed in vain for the scent of stale beer. He spied a name tag with the word "Bob" in large black letters pinned to the man's suit. "Bob, I've not been by in a while. I used to drink here."

"You on duty?"

"Lunch break."

"You'll not be wanting a drink, then, will you?"

"A bite to eat, for old times' sake."

Bob folded his arms. "Are you a member?"

"Eh?"

"The new owners turned it into a private club. Must have been two years back. We've got a fancy bar, gym, changing rooms, the works. Only members admitted."

"And the hotel rooms… I don't suppose—"

Bob shook his head. "Long gone. Converted into a yoga studio and salon, both booming round these parts."

"I'll not take up any more of your time, then." PC Hoon took a final look around and cursed at the speed of change. Egremont used to be a black smudge on the map; now it had turned into Greenwich Village—bohemian and hip.

He turned to leave when the front door flew open, and a woman in a tie-dye dress with floral cowgirl boots hurried in. Her brown hair was frizzed into an Afro, which dangled in two curls in front of bug-eyed sunglasses that rested on her forehead.

"Thought you were coming tomorrow," she said in a breathless gasp. "I'm running late, so can't show you around. Bob, will you give the officer a day pass and let him in. He is here for the crime safety inspection. Nowhere is off limits." She paused a moment, her sharp eyes taking in PC Hoon. "Except the women's changing rooms. Stop by my office on the top floor when you are done. I'd like to know what you find."

"Will do," PC Hoon said as Bob placed a slim plastic card with a microchip into a slot in his desktop computer. "We are here to serve."

But the woman had already disappeared through a set of sliding doors.

"Why didn't you say you were here for the inspection?" Bob said as he handed over the card. He lowered his voice. "Don't get on the wrong side of the boss. She has a temper like a bloody shark. Show the pass to the waitstaff in the restaurant, and they'll see you're all right for lunch. The quinoa feta cheese salad isn't half bad."

"I'd best begin with the men's changing room," PC Hoon said." It'll have a shower, right?"

"Along the hallway and up a flight of stairs on your left," Bob replied.

As PC Hoon walked through the sliding doors, he thought his luck had changed for the better.

It hadn't.

CHAPTER 55

PC Hoon let out a contented sigh. He felt refreshed after his shower and now sat in the Dog Inn's chic dining room out of uniform with his black bag of clothes placed under the table. He planned to change back before he left but felt he blended in much better in his regular clothes. He stared at his empty plate which moments earlier brimmed with green leaves and white feta cheese with little brown things he'd never seen before that tasted sour. *It would have been a nice enough meal,* he thought, *if it hadn't been spoiled by the lack of fried grease.*

"Another glass of sparkling water for sir?"

The male waiter with his high-pitched voice and dance-like walk reminded PC Hoon of a butterfly. And that irked him. Where were the rough-looking truck drivers with their pot bellies and lumberjack shirts, who ate cheeseburgers and chips for breakfast?

"Sir?"

The waiter was still at his side. PC Hoon didn't like water. It had no taste, but they didn't serve fizzy pop. There was wine, of course, and even craft beer, but he didn't want booze on his breath when he visited the pub in St Bees. He'd made that mistake before. Drove his car whilst drunk. Fast. Very fast. Past the priory in St Bees. But he'd got away with that. It was a while ago. Still, he wouldn't chance his luck. And there was the landlord who had whined about him drinking on the job. He had threatened to file a complaint. The mess with Maude was plenty enough on his plate. No! He'd not drink while on the job.

"Just half a glass," PC Hoon said.

"Cumbria's finest water, sir." The waiter made a delighted sound as he poured.

PC Hoon didn't like that either. He might have said a foul word or two if he'd not seen the woman in the aqua dress with the emerald-green crocodile handbag. She walked across the restaurant, sat at a table in the corner by the window, and placed the handbag by her side. Pricey. Very pricey.

It had started quite by accident last spring, in May. PC Hoon had been invited to speak on a panel about safety at the Women's Institute event held at St Bees Priory. It was an annual talk with a fresh set of speakers each year—nurses, firefighters, and this year, the local bobby. There was nothing hard to do except show up and speak for ten minutes, then answer questions for another fifteen. Arrive at one, and it would all be over by two thirty.

On that fateful day there was not much going

on in the village, so PC Hoon slept in late, missed breakfast, and ended up at Don's Café. It was a mistake, he knew, to eat a King Kong fry-up. He recalled washing down the last slice of toast with a mug of sweet, milky tea, then his world went blank.

It was the rough hand of Don that woke him.

"You'll have to pay your bill now; it's after one," he had said.

PC Hoon paid, scrambled out the café door with quick steps as he raced towards St Bees Priory. When he got to the moss-and-lichen-covered, red-brick building, the main door was locked, so he walked around the side and stared into the window of the main hall. The pews were packed. Three speakers sat behind a desk on the stage with one empty chair. His.

For a moment, he considered banging on the window but thought better of the idea. Quickly, he walked along the length of the priory until he came to a door. He turned the handle. It opened, and he stepped inside.

The room was silent and cool with dull-grey walls, no windows, and a large mahogany bench in the centre. On one wall, next to a tired-looking speaker, was a brass plaque with words:

DOMINUS DEUS TUUS IGNIS CONSUMENS EST.

The Lord your God is a consuming fire. Deuteronomy 4:24

Two rails of coat stands stood on either side, filled with an assortment of ladies' coats. A single row of handbags jostled for space on the bench; each had a small, blue ticket attached. It was some kind of temporary cloakroom.

PC Hoon placed his hands on his hips and stared at the handbags. One stood out from the rest, shiny black with a gold buckle. Expensive.

That's when things got weird.

He glanced around to see if anyone was watching. There was no one about. They were all in the hall. He picked up the shiny black bag with the gold buckle, and left. Even now he couldn't explain his actions, except that it gave him a thrill.

He took it straight home. Maude shuffled about upstairs, so he went to the basement. A shiver of electricity ran from the base of his spine and surged into his brain. He felt alive. The woman's handbag was his to do with as he wanted. *This is how drug addicts must feel,* he had thought, *when they take the first hit.*

A few days later, he sold the purse and credit card to a fence in Whitehaven. He kept the handbag for his private collection. The first of many. Somewhere in the back of his mind he thought they might make nice gifts for the wife who came after Maude. But the truth was it gave him such a charge that he could not stop. Everyone trusts a policeman, and that made it easy. PC Hoon loved easy.

Now Maude had his secret collection of handbags, and with it, she had him by his balls. The witch would squeeze until his eyes popped out if he didn't stop her. And he would. But first there was the little matter of that emerald-green crocodile handbag. If he hadn't seen the damn thing, it wouldn't matter. But he had seen the glorious piece and had to have it.

Whatever the cost.

CHAPTER 56

PC Hoon shivered with quiet excitement.

The woman in the aqua dress took out her mobile phone and turned to face the window, her back to the crocodile handbag. He watched for a long moment, then glanced about the room. There were people seated at several tables all engaged in their own conversation. The light-footed waiter with the butterfly walk had vanished through a set of swing doors into the kitchen. There was no one else around.

A chance!

PC Hoon slowly got to his feet, and the clock started ticking. It was madness to do this in broad daylight, but he couldn't stop himself. There was no reason or thought as he inched towards the handbag. If his brain cells twitched at all, it was with desire.

He got to the table where the woman in the aqua dress paced in a handful of quiet strides. The woman's voice was high pitched and irate. He was close enough that her words on the phone were crystal clear. Her lunch date was late but on the way now.

With a steady hand, he leaned forward and let his fingers grasp the straps.

"I'll order a starter, then," the woman said. "Soup or salad?"

Again, he glanced around to make sure he wasn't seen, then eased the handbag off the table and swung it under his arm. Slowly, with great care, he edged back towards his table. He kept one eye on the woman, the other on the kitchen door from where the light-footed waiter would soon appear.

He was almost at his table when his worst fear struck.

In a smooth yoga-like move, the woman in the aqua dress stood, spun around, and with the cell phone pinned to her ear, marched directly at PC Hoon.

His body became a block of stone. Even if he had wanted to run, there was no strength in his limbs. If he could feel his legs at all, they were nowt but two sticks of jelly. A sour taste of bile bubbled in his dry mouth. For a brief instant, he thought of Maude and how she would laugh at the mess. Now she'd run to the police with all she knew, just to dig in the knife and squeeze his balls to a pulp. And in that moment, he was consumed by rage. He'd buggered it up, and it was all Maude's fault.

But the woman in the aqua dress didn't give

PC Hoon a second glance as she marched past him and through a door which led to the ladies' room.

He staggered back to his table. With a hand that trembled, he grabbed the half glass of water. With a single gulp, he downed the drink and once again scanned the room. No one watched. No one saw a thing. The other diners were engaged in quiet conversation.

Piece of cake.

A boldness swept over him now. It carried his mood to a new high. In his elation he turned the bag over in his hands. So fine a piece! It felt like money to touch. The first of his new hoard. It would not be the last.

The high suddenly vanished and panic set in. He had to hide the handbag, get it out of view. He stooped down to unzip his black bag of clothes. It would fit nicely in there. The thought of carrying it past the reception desk as Bob the skeleton watched gave him another thrill.

He did not hear the soft click of the door or the hurried footsteps. A movement out of the corner of his eye got his attention, a blur of aqua flitting across the room.

She'd only been gone a handful of seconds!

But there she was, standing at her table, hands on her hips, staring at PC Hoon who held her handbag in the soft caress of a mother to a newborn child. There was a moment of stunned silence, which seemed to stretch for an hour.

Then the woman in the aqua dress screamed.

CHAPTER 57

On any other day Fenella would have enjoyed the view. Dexter drove the Morris Minor south along the A595, a two-lane road which snaked through green hills and sloped fields. They were on their way to Low Marsh Prison to speak with the Teal twins. It was close to one o'clock, and the sun in the west splashed shards of gold through a thickening swirl of dark clouds. To the east, a sheen of rain hovered as fine as a mist.

Today, though, Fenella's mind was on the questions she planned to ask the Teal twins. And her eyes were on Dexter, who hummed under his breath an old Eric Clapton tune—"Tears in Heaven." She thought he sounded good.

"La, le la, la-la-heaven, de, de, da,da-way."

After the meal at Nan's, Fenella had agreed to set up a date for her friend, the nurse Gail Stubbs. A foursome with her, Eduardo, Gail, and Dexter at a nice restaurant in Carlisle. And with Dexter so happy, she thought it would be a good time to ask if he was game, but curiosity got the better of her. She had to know why he was humming, then she'd set up the date.

"I like that song," Fenella said, hoping to strike up a conversation so she could pry into his business. "One of Eduardo's favourites. A great song for... lovers, don't you think?"

"Aye, it's a pleasant number, all right," Dexter replied and continued with his hum. "De, de, de, da-da-heaven. Le, la le, le-le, be, de, da."

Fenella knew it was best to let it drop. If Dexter was in a good mood, that was all for the best. She'd just taken a management course about flexibility in leadership. They were told not to ask personal questions. That was the new standard in the Cumbria police. If a member of your team hobbles into work on crutches, you're not supposed to ask what happened. If their arm is in a sling, don't ask. If they are lying on their back and gasping for breath, don't bleedin' ask! Fenella thought it was daft. If anyone on her team fell sick, she wanted to know what was wrong. Screw flexibility in leadership! Dexter was humming and she had to know why. But she'd take her time, tease it out of him.

Fenella said, "Dr Hall's psychological assessment, pretty cool, eh? Got my results straight away: 'Competent.'"

Dexter had his eyes on the road. "Beat me, Guv. Mine said 'Adequate.' Le, la le, le-le, be, de, da."

Fenella watched him for a moment, then said, "Jones came out 'Exemplary.'"

"How'd you know that?"

Fenella grinned. "Same for PC Beth Finn and PC Hoon."

"Guess we are letting the team down, eh, Guv? Le-le, be, de, da."

The car slowed as a large cattle truck swung out of the road and ambled along as though it were a tourist. Fenella watched Dexter, waited for him to mumble a curse, but he broke out into a melodic whistle. That did it!

"Are you going to keep me in suspense for much longer?"

"Sorry, Guv."

"What you whistling about?"

"Can't a man whistle?"

"Not if his name is bleedin' Dexter, and he's never whistled before, or hummed, for that matter."

"I can change, can't I?" He began to hum, glanced at Fenella, and thought the better of it. "Anyway, I thought you had taken that management course on flexibility. Give your team room to be themselves, to flex. That's what you said."

"Well, you can flex your lips and tell me what's up."

The cattle truck slowed to a crawl as it climbed a hill.

"Okay," Dexter said after he eased the

gearstick into second. "It's Nellie Cook. We go way back. At one time she was on my list. Gave me some great info, and I helped her out a time or two. Remember that toerag Royce Lee, used to run his business from the Red Sheaf bar?"

"Aye. He were a nasty piece of work." She was glad Royce Lee was still behind bars with no chance of getting out. "Tell me about Nellie."

Dexter seemed to hesitate a moment. "Do you think she is past it?"

Fenella puffed out her cheeks. "Seventy is her next big birthday. I know it takes all sorts, but that's a bit old for her game."

"Aye, that's what I told her. Time to retire." Dexter tapped his thumb on the steering wheel. The cattle truck had reached the brow of the hill, and the road sloped down for the next mile or two. He eased the car through third and fourth as it picked up speed. "We talked about old times and she..."

The cattle truck's brake lights flashed red; its horn blasted as it juddered to a crawl. A camper van had pulled off the verge and into the road. A woman hung out of the passenger-side window taking snapshots of the view.

Dexter cursed and jabbed the high-pitched horn of the Morris Minor. It bleated like an irritated sheep. Fenella grinned. She knew he couldn't keep up his cheerful-man face all day, knew she'd get at his secret.

"So, are you going to tell me why you are humming like we are on our way to karaoke night?"

"It's Priscilla. I met her at Jabbar's, thanks to Nellie. Can you believe she is still singing? She has moved back in with me. We are going to get wed."

CHAPTER 58

When they arrived at Low Marsh Prison, it began to rain. Big fat drops splashed against the car. Deep puddles soon formed from the run-off water. *"Tears in Heaven,"* Fenella thought as they made their way across the concrete car park to the visitor centre.

The sky darkened with blasts of thunder against streaks of white light. They picked up their pace to a trot. As they ran, Fenella wondered how PC Beth Finn was getting on with the list of women who'd come into contact with Hamilton Perkins. Maybe she'd find one who wrote to him. It was a long shot, but sometimes they came up trumps. Then her mind turned to the Teal twins. Would they speak to her? Was the visit going to be a waste of time?

Inside, there was a long line. Young mums with babes in arms, toddlers running about the place, moody-looking teens and middle-aged folk with worried faces. One man wore a three-piece, pinstripe suit with a pork-pie hat. Fenella wondered whether he'd come to see a banker who had his hand in the till and got himself locked up inside.

"Keep your kids by your side and mobile

phones in hand," boomed a warden. "One at a time, please. One at a time."

There was no fast track for police officers, so they waited their turn. It took twenty minutes to get to the front of the line. Fenella flashed her warrant card. "We are here to see the Teal twins."

"Righto, we've had word of your visit. The twins will be brought up soon. Please go through the door on the right."

Fenella and Dexter stepped through a sliding door to a room the size of a small lift. There they waited for almost a minute until an automatic door swung open. A woman in a grey uniform with her black hair tucked into a bun, greeted them. "I'm the duty chaplain. The Teal twins are in the prayer room."

Fenella glanced at Dexter. He shrugged. She thought they'd meet the twins in a sterile interview room with Perspex screens, hard plastic chairs bolted to the floor, and armed guards with shaved heads.

Fenella said, "Do the twins get many visitors?"

The chaplain shook her head. "They have been in here a long time. Friends stop coming. Even family fade away. Social contact is one of our roles. There are four chaplains, all part time. So at least the twins get to see a different face every few days. We are social creatures; it helps with their mental health to see new faces. This way, please."

They followed the chaplain through a series of sliding doors, each opened by an unseen guard, then crossed a small courtyard where they heard the rain but could not feel the drops. Fenella glanced up to stare at a vast glass roof and wondered if this was the only place where the prisoners could get a breath of fresh air. There was no time to ask as the chaplain continued through another set of automatic doors, then up a handful of stairs to an iron gate which went from the ceiling to the floor.

"This prayer chapel is for our long-term guests," the chaplain said. "They are allowed in one at a time. There is CCTV and two guards on hand at all times. I have to remain in the room with you."

The gate slowly opened, and they walked along a long hallway with wooden doors on either side. The chaplain stopped at a door with a "C" painted in black. She unlocked the door and stepped aside to let them in ahead of her.

For a moment Fenella was reminded of a doll's house, for the space was so small. Then she realised that a wall with a Perspex screen inlaid split the room in two. That's when she got her first glimpse of the Teal twins.

An elderly man with a thin neck, wearing black-framed eyeglasses, sat at a desk on the other side of the screen. He wore a dark-grey suit with a pale-blue tie that gave him the look of a Baptist preacher. Fenella recognised him at once. The years had been good to him.

Dexter stood by the door with the chaplain while Fenella took a seat at the desk by the screen and wondered which of the Teal twins she would speak with today. Tim or Jim? Tim was the smiley one, and Jim, a sourpuss.

"I will not keep you long, Detective Sallow," one of the Teal twins said, then scowled.

Fenella sighed with relief. It was Jim. He might be a sour crab apple, but you could reason with him.

"Thank you for taking the time to see me, Jim," she said. She'd butter him up, make him feel special. "This chat means the world to us."

Jim Teal tapped on the screen. "Please ask your friend to come and sit with us." His voice sounded too loud. It came from speakers hidden in the wall. "Detective Sergeant Dexter, isn't it?"

Dexter joined them at the desk. Fenella saw he had a scowl on his face. He'd not forgotten, then. With the twins, it was best to mirror back their expressions. She deepened her scowl.

"It is good to see you, my dear friends," Jim said. There was something about him that was off. Nothing Fenella could put her finger on, but his words came out in the rhythm of a snake-oil salesman whose liniment cured all ills. "Are you comfortable? Then we shall begin. Please ask your questions, my friends. Fire away."

"You shared a cell with Hamilton Perkins?" Fenella opened with a softball question. It helped to loosen the tongue.

"That's right, Detective Sallow. I can see that you've done your homework." Although his lips moved, his expression remained stone cold. "The three of us got along nicely and, if I say so myself, became great friends. I have so many friends, it is hard for me to keep up. New faces visit me each day, some from the good old days. Good mates they are, every last one of them. Not too many from the police these days, though. Not since Maximum Todd sent me to stay in this place."

Maximum Todd was Todd Grey, the judge who sent the twins down.

Jim was talking. "Not that I hold it against him. He was doing his job and providing for his family. A man can't hold that against another man. That'd be like shouting for the tide not to come in."

This was a good start. It could not have gone any better. They'd got Jim to talk, and that was half the battle. Fenella let out a quiet breath.

"And you know Mr Perkins was going to help the police, don't you?"

The question was to test the water. She wanted to know how much Jim Teal knew. Before Hamilton Perkins escaped, he had agreed to show the police where he'd buried the body of his last victim. She was a schoolgirl by the name of Colleen Rae. Superintendent Jeffery had lined it all up. If Perkins led them to the body, Jeffery would take the credit. Fenella didn't care about that. She wanted to help the parents put their child to rest. And she herself needed to gain some peace. She'd not let lost children die, in her mind. Not until they found the body.

Jim said, "That child is all he spoke about. That and God."

The chaplain coughed. She was still standing at the back of the room, arms crossed, listening.

Jim's eyes travelled to where she stood. "Mr Shred found the heavenly father right here in the chapel, and wanted to atone for his sins, didn't he, Chaplain?"

"The chapel is here to help folks take the first step towards the Lord," she replied.

Jim placed his hands on the Perspex. With a slow movement, he leaned forward so his breath fogged up the screen. "Mr Shred deserves to rot in hell for what he did!"

"Redemption is available to all," the chaplain said. "Including Mr Perkins."

"The git broke out of this place without letting on," Jim replied. "If he'd have said something, I could be on a beach in Spain sipping sangria. Not a good mate, him. Rot in hell, Perkins; rot in bloody hell."

"Now, now, that is not a very Christian attitude, is it?" the chaplain said. "I can see you have a long way to go. But we'll get there, won't we?"

Jim raised an eyebrow, and the beginning of a grin tugged at the corner of his mouth. Fenella didn't want him to break out into a smile. Then she'd have to speak with Tim. And he was a bugger to work with. She half turned to face the chaplain and placed a finger to her lips. The chaplain returned a half nod. She'd got the message.

Fenella said, "Tell me about Perkins, sir."

"I want to talk about redemption and how hot the flames of hell will be that roast Mr Shred." His lips twitched. Both sides. "Since we are in the house of God..."

"We can have a nice chat about that, later."

"No. Now!"

Fenella leaned forward so her forehead touched the screen. They held each other's gaze. Neither looked away. They stayed like that for almost a minute. Then Jim's eyes moved from side to side, and the corners of his mouth twitched.

Fenella felt a moment of hesitation. She could sense he was about to smile. If he did, she'd have to start all over with Tim. Her scowl became a ball of fury as she scrunched up her face and said, "Tell me about Perkins."

Jim blinked. His lips softened into a straight line. "Hazza spoke about God often."

Fenella's chest tightened. She sat bolt upright. "Hazza?"

"Short for Harry."

Could this be the same man Vicar Briar had mentioned? The groundsman who mysteriously appeared a few months ago to work in the graveyard? Hazza was a popular nickname, but she'd not take any chances. Now she'd order the team to find Hazza, fast. She gave a sideways glance at Dexter. He cracked his knuckles. He always did that when they were onto something.

Jim leaned back and folded his arms. "When I said Hazza found God in this room, I spoke out of turn. I suppose he really found God on the operating table when he had his hip replaced. It was always 'Mr Shred' or 'Harry' before that."

That was news to Fenella. She did a spot of mental maths. Perkins would be knocking on a bit by now. Yes, he'd be ripe for a new hip. She wondered if they made it out of the same steel he used for his blades.

Jim was speaking. "Things went wrong. I'm no medical man but he almost died. That's when he saw the light and knew he had to change. He even forgave the surgeon, wrote a letter to make his peace."

Fenella said, "Why forgive the surgeon?"

Jim pressed his hands to his ears as though trying to block a voice which whispered from within. His whole body trembled as he let out a harsh wail. When he looked up, his face had changed. His features took on an angular form, jagged like the edge of a saw. Fenella could scarcely believe her eyes and shuffled her chair back an inch. Yes, it was the same man in the dark-grey suit with a pale-blue tie who stared back through the screen, but he had a gaunt, hungry expression; his eyes were wild and he was grinning.

He wasn't Jim anymore.

He was Tim.

"Tim?" Fenella said as if to confirm. She took her time now. Slowly, she plastered a smile on her face. Not an easy thing to do when you're sitting opposite an evil bugger. But Tim would clam up if you did not smile. "How are we doing?"

"I'd like to go now, please." Tim spoke in short, sharp gasps in a joyful sing-song sort of way with a nervous energy that made his face twitch, his fingers knot, and his eyes dart about the room. "We are done here."

Again, Fenella leaned forward, so her forehead touched the Perspex. "You'll go when I say. Not before. Now, answer my question."

He stared at her through the screen, eyes wide.

His nostrils flared. He shook. All the while he grinned. It was a big, wide Santa grin. Although there was no *ho ho ho*; if he'd put on a few pounds and grew a beard, you could imagine him in red robes.

Fenella watched his hands curl tight. The Teal twins were violent buggers. Quick with a knife, trigger of a gun. Their idea of a Christmas gift was to give some poor innocent sod a good kickin'.

A fist smashed against the screen.

Fenella didn't blink. "Aye, go ahead and hit it again if it will make you feel better, pet." She wasn't done yet, thought she could squeeze him for more details. "I'll be here when the two-year-old goes away and you're ready to continue. And then you'll tell me why Perkins forgave the surgeon."

Tim grinned. "Because the bugger didn't do it right, Hazza walked with a limp after the operation." His voice went higher, his thin neck constricted. The words ended in a wheezing laugh.

Fenella laughed too. As did Dexter. They sensed they were at a critical point and mirrored Tim's actions so he would not clam up. Even the chaplain was grinning. The group snorted like a pack of hyenas. Something important was about to happen. Everyone watched Tim Teal and waited.

"Ha, ha, hee hee, ha," Tim held his gut as his body shook. "Ho, ha, funny, eh?"

"He's got more nuts in him than a squirrel's belly," Dexter whispered.

Fenella agreed. It made her sick to the pit of the stomach, but they had to get the information before Tim clammed up. It was clear he could flip at any time.

When Tim settled down, she said, "You say he wrote to the surgeon?"

"Hazza didn't want the operation." Tim chuckled. It was a spiteful sound like the hiss of a spitting fire. "But the surgeon was from his hometown, St Bees, I believe." His eyes were glassy as if he were in the operating room alongside Hamilton Perkins and enjoying the cut and slice of the knife. He broke out into a wild fit of laughter. "Hazza was in a lot of pain and thought it would be all right. He was wrong... ha ha ha."

"Go on," Fenella said between chuckles. "We are listening."

"When it was over, Hazza walked with a limp. Ha ha ha ha... can't trust women to do anything right. God knows why they let her loose on him with a knife. It's like I've always said, lasses are best kept at home to make babies, not dressed up in clinical gowns and put to work in the operating room, ha ha, hee, ha ha. Hazza wrote the letter to strike the fear of God into the woman. Called herself a surgeon. Olive Thane were nowt but a bloody butcher, hee hee, ha ha."

CHAPTER 59

PC Hoon felt sick to his stomach. He stood by his table in the restaurant of the Dog Inn while the woman in the aqua dress screamed.

"He stole my handbag!!"

PC Hoon stared at the woman and he stared around the restaurant and he stared at the handbag in his hands. He felt like he was going to throw up.

Right about now he should have been in the pub in St Bees having a chat with the landlord about any new faces seen in the village. There might have been a free bag or two of prawn cocktail crisps thrown in too, because the publican would rather give away the out-of-date packets than toss them in the bin. PC Hoon had never thought of himself as getting caught; yet, in this moment, with his fingers clasped tight around Miss Aqua Dress's handbag, he knew he was looking at time behind bars. And the men behind bars didn't like police officers. He shuddered at the thought of what they'd do to him.

He spun towards the door through which he came, with half a hope of making a dash for it. It would only take three swift strides and a yank on that bloody big door handle.

But life moved faster than his thoughts.

The handle eased down. Skeleton Bob stomped in with a woman in a tie-dye dress and floral cowgirl boots—the owner. Her bug-shaped sunglasses still rested on her forehead, but her frizzed Afro curls stuck out like devil's horns.

PC Hoon's eyes darted to the kitchen door. There was always a fire escape in the kitchen, wasn't there? If he made a dash for it now...

The kitchen door flew open, and the male waiter with the high-pitched voice marched in. There was no dance to his step or butterfly flit now, just the solid jackboot step of a soldier. Behind him was a fat man with a red face dressed in white, with a soft, checked cap on his head. The fat man carried a butcher's cleaver—the chef.

What if he jumped from table to table? PC Hoon had seen something like that in the movies. Yes, it would get him to the window. But the restaurant was on the second floor. If he jumped, he'd not bounce to his feet and sprint away as they did in the film.

There was no way to avoid it now. No way out. In that moment of fear, his mind went back to that day in the cloakroom where he first stole a handbag. The brass plaque on the wall seemed to swell in his mind.

DOMINUS DEUS TUUS IGNIS CONSUMENS EST.

The Lord your God is a consuming fire. Deuteronomy 4:24

PC Hoon felt so hot, it was as if the flames of hell were about to consume him. He closed his eyes for a beat and saw nothing but the flare and flash of fire. He opened his eyes and gaped at the staring faces.

For an instant, everyone stood still. Nothing moved in the room. The ceiling fans hummed with an ominous buzz. There was still an hour or so before the end of lunch, but the savoury aromas turned sour, and the breeze from the fans cut through the air with a chill edge.

PC Hoon's head tick-tocked between the owner, Skeleton Bob, the waiter, the chef, and the woman in the aqua dress, whose face had gone a deep shade of purple. He sucked in a breath through his teeth and cast his eyes across the tables of watching diners. There was nowt in his future now. Nowt but a yawning cavern of darkness.

He forced a smile as he placed the handbag carefully on the table and reached for his pocket. "Well done," he said in as commanding a voice as he could muster. He withdrew his hand from his pocket and flashed his warrant card at the woman in the aqua dress. "I'm from the police, here to check on the security protocol of this establishment." Next, he turned to the owner and

Skeleton Bob. "Your response to this simulated theft is outstanding. I must commend you on your security arrangements."

His hand reached out for the handbag. There was no hiding the tremble. He picked it up and turned back to the woman in the aqua dress.

"Always keep your valuables in plain sight or lock them away out of sight, ma'am."

She gave a little gasp and stared at him in horror as the penny dropped. "Oh, I am so sorry... I thought... well, you see..." Her face went from purple to cherry red. "Thank you, Officer. It was silly of me to leave it on the table. It won't happen again."

PC Hoon turned to the owner, smiled, and opened his mouth but was thrown off for a moment by her piercing stare. He ploughed on. "Like I say, this outfit has strong security in place. I'll write a report and have it in the post to you by next week." He stooped down and picked up his black bag. He'd change back into his uniform in the car. "My only suggestion would be to install CCTV cameras."

He left the room with fast steps, willing his legs not to break out into a run.

Back in his car, PC Hoon breathed like a hog and sweated twice as much. He'd got away. There were no cameras. Still, he'd not pass through this village again. Ever. There was the report for the owner, of course, but he'd not write that. And he was done with those bloody handbags too. What the hell was wrong with him? It was over now. He was through with them. Now, all he wanted was a clean slate.

He started the car and remembered Maude. They'd be no fresh start while she held on to the evidence—his entire collection of handbags. He swore long and hard. The shock of that revelation stirred his brain cells to action. The plan he had been mulling over for days suddenly fell into place. After he'd had his chat with the pub landlord in St Bees, he'd deal with Maude. He thought again of the brass plaque in the St Bees Priory cloakroom and grinned.

"Dominus Deus tuus ignis consumens est," he whispered under his breath.

And now he knew exactly what he was going to do to his wife.

CHAPTER 60

Chad Tate hid in the bushes.

He peered through binoculars with such an intense focus that he didn't hear the background splash of waves against the cliffs. Nor did he hear the rustle of wind through the trees nor the warning scream of a herring gull.

It was three in the afternoon and already getting dark. He crouched in the foliage and adjusted the focus to get a better view of the kitchen window of PC Hoon's cottage. The curtains were open as usual. A soft red plume of light shone from a floor lamp next to the door.

Chad shut the store early. CLOSED FOR LATE LUNCH, BACK IN AN HOUR read the note he'd tacked on the door. But he'd already eaten, the bread and cheese digested with a doughnut for dessert. He'd been careful to take the dirt track across the Pow Beck bridge, so he was certain no one had seen him. The growing dusk offered cover for him to settle into his post.

The first night of his watch began on Sunday when he heard a rumour that PC Hoon had moved into the spare room at Mrs Lenz's house. He'd take the card out of the window the next time she came in and hand it to her in a flourish. Tell her how well written it was. She'd love that and tell her friends. He'd soon have a store window full of cards.

Nothing beats word of mouth.

Chad brought a flask of hot tea with him, because on his first night it had been so cold, he had left early and didn't get to see her. That was a mistake, one which he'd not make twice. So tonight he had his hot flask with a stick of beef jerky in case he got hungry. He liked to watch and supposed he got a taste for it as a child in New York City where he'd sit at the window and stare into the neighbour's bedroom.

Tonight, hidden in the bushes with the creeping cold, he settled in to watch the Hoon house. He told himself he wasn't a Peeping Tom or some weird creep. He loved Maude. She knew that and came to the store for free packets of fags.

It had started with a flirt a few months ago.

They'd kissed.

Chad closed the store and shut the blinds. They'd made rough love between the loaves of fresh-baked bread and tins of Heinz baked beans.

A sound rustled in the undergrowth. Chad spun around. A rabbit scampered from a blackberry bush, watched him for a moment, nose twitching, then scurried off again just as quickly.

He turned his gaze back to the cottage. It wasn't obsessive to spy on his future wife, was it? Now that PC Sid Hoon had moved out, the road was clear. He'd propose, and they'd soon be man and wife. Only then would he tell her his secrets.

In the light of the setting sun, more herring gulls flocked. They hovered above the treetops, their beaks stretched wide as they screamed and screamed and screamed.

Chad sighed. The birds were right. Viv Gill and Pearl Smith were mere tufts of cheap tat. Third time lucky. Maude was it. She had said she wanted to marry him the second time they'd made out between the bread and beans.

"I'm tired of being the wife of a village bobby who has no ambition," Maude had said as she sucked on a cigarette. "A storekeeper's wife is a step up in status and comes with free fags. Not that it matters to me. I love you, Chad."

And he loved her too. Yes, she might be a bit long in the tooth, but she could still bear him a child. A daughter who he could... play with. He closed his eyes and imagined the future. He and Maude would snuggle up together up in his dim room above the shop and watch his grainy videos. And now it looked like PC Hoon had moved out, and she was free to move in with him. Before the wedding bells tolled, she would be with child.

Chad would have phoned, but she said never to call her mobile phone or visit the house. Maude would show up at the shop for her free fags. That's when they made love, and he, his plans. But it was Monday evening, and she didn't stop by the store. Nor did PC Hoon.

The sinking sun gave one last blast of gold as if to push back the creep of night. Yellow streaks shone through dimpled clouds. Shadows mottled the trees. A blast of chill wind whistled in from the sea. Chad shivered, zipped his coat up tight, but did not take his gaze from the kitchen window.

There she was! A dark shadow flitting about the room as a moth to a bulb. Chad refocused the lens to get a better view. She moved in a floaty sort of way as if she were... dancing. Yes, Maude was dancing. That lifted his heart.

He craned his ears to hear the faintest strains of the tune. She loved Elton John. Was it "Candle in The Wind"? He waited. Waves crashed against the cliffs. The trees creaked. Wind rustled the bushes. He was too far away to hear. So he watched her dance and imagined he was with her.

After a few minutes, he glanced at his watch. He should get back to the store to reopen. But he wanted to see his Maude now. Make love in her bed rather than on a sack between the aisles. How could he wait until the next time she came to the store?

Then it struck him.

It whispered to him like an Elton John love lyric. PC Hoon was gone. The coast was clear! He clambered from his hiding spot and hurried across the lane. A frisky dog determined to get its oats.

Chad was out of breath when he reached the front door. He pounded with an urgent fist. They'd make love tonight, then plans. A small do at the registry office in Port St Giles, and he'd repaint the flat above the shop in a colour of her choice. He could hardly wait to hear that her good-for-nothing husband had left.

He pounded the door again.

It opened wide.

Chad staggered back three paces, eyes wide.

"Yes," said a fat man with the face of a walrus. He wore a blue bathrobe which stopped above his bare knees. Pink socks encased his fat feet—Pete Clarke, the bank manager!

"Who is it, honey?" Maude's voice carried above the piano melody of "Candle in the Wind."

"It's Mr Tate, from the store. Did you order a delivery?"

There was a long silence.

Maude appeared at the door in a see-through négligée.

Chad stared at his hands, then he stared at Mr Clarke's bare knees, then he stared at Maude.

"I'm so sorry," Maude said. "I should have told you. I'm getting a divorce. When it comes through, Pete and I will get married."

"We'll have a big do in St Bees Priory," Mr Clarke added.

Maude gave a girlish giggle. "Next month, I'm putting this house on the market. Pete has put in an offer for the mansion that overlooks St Bees school. I've always wanted to be the wife of a bank manager, and I shall be very soon. Not that it matters. I love you, Pete."

Chad couldn't believe his ears. Rage boiled. He did his best to keep it under control by sucking in a breath and letting it out slow.

"But what about us?"

"There is no us, Chad. I made a mistake." Maude turned to Mr Clarke and flung her arms around him. "The naughty man made me do it for a packet of fags. You'll forgive me, won't you, Boo Bear?"

"Oh yes," he said as the door closed. "But you'll have to make it up to me tonight, Hot Lips."

CHAPTER 61

"Is this really necessary?"

Dr Olive Thane sat on a huge couch in the hardwood-floor lounge of her house. She tapped a finger on her chin. It was a nervous tick. Fenella and her team had arrived as dusk faded to night. The surgeon's house, in the most expensive part of St Bees, had five bedrooms and a three-car garage. On the deck, large clay plant pots stood in elegant rows, although it was too early for shoots to show. There were pear trees and rose bushes all tidy and neat, and the walled garden's lawn sloped to a pond that backed onto Hemlock Woods.

"I mean, it seems you've brought an entire squadron. There must be ten police officers hiding on our grounds." Dr Thane continued to tap her chin.

Fenella thought she'd do more than tap her chin if the boys in blue showed up in a big pack at her home. She'd yell bloody murder and kick the buggers out. But she'd laid the groundwork with Dr Thane in their chat on the phone, one of her tricks to oil the wheels. She did not mention Hamilton Perkins on the call. It might have put the fear of God into the woman.

"Dr Thane," Fenella said, "we believe our suspect is in the area and intends to pay you a visit. We want to be here when he arrives, so we can take him back to his home."

"Oh, come on!" Dr Thane pointed at Dexter and waved her arms about in a vague way. "You guys didn't show up for some small-time crook. I wasn't born yesterday. What's going on?"

Dr Thane was in her fifties and a senior surgeon. Life and death were part of her day. Fenella considered for a moment and said, "Here's the deal. We are trying to track down a man who escaped from Low Marsh Prison. You treated him."

Dr Thane waved a frustrated hand. "We never know the backgrounds of our patients, only their medical records. If a patient came from Low Marsh Prison, I'd be none the wiser. Our job is to treat those in need. I've taken an oath to that effect, and I have done my best throughout my career to uphold it."

Olive Thane oozed such professionalism, Fenella felt in awe. She'd never be as well dressed or smooth with her speech. And she loved Dr Thane's necklace of white pearls, her peach blouse and tweed skirt. On herself, classy clothes clung to the bulges she'd rather hide. Anyway, she'd spill coffee on fancy clothes the minute she wore them. *Nowt wrong with yoga pants and a loose-fitting blouse; they get the job done.*

Dr Thane was still speaking. "What I don't understand is why he would want to come here?"

Fenella said, "We believe you performed a hip replacement on a Mr Perkins." She had checked and doubled checked that fact. "And we know Mr Perkins is very upset because he now walks with a limp."

"Perkins... Perkins... Low Marsh Prison..." Dr Thane jerked to her feet. "Are you saying I'm the target of that maniac killer, Mr Shred?"

"Aye, luv," Fenella replied, not sugar-coating it. "That about sums it up."

Dr Thane rubbed her hands. "Thank goodness Albert is away for the week. His heart is not good, and all this excitement... well, it's for the best that he is in Zürich."

Albert Thane was her husband. He'd built an empire selling medical devices. Everyone in Cumbria had heard of the man and many a sick person had been revived through the magic of his electronic boxes. Fenella recalled watching him on a black-and-white newsreel and thought he must be in his eighties by now. That his ticker still ticked, she supposed, was due to one of his own medical devices.

"Okay," Fenella said. "So you are on your own tonight?"

Dr Thane sidestepped the question. "I hope to God you catch Mr Shred. The thought of him running lose in my garden gives me the creeps."

"We'll get him. He's not run far, and he won't run long."

"Inspector Sallow, we came here for a quiet life." Dr Thane slowly shook her head. "I lived in Carlisle for almost twenty years, thought the countryside would be peaceful. Last year my handbag was stolen from a Women's Institute event in St Bees Priory. And now this!"

She walked over to the drinks cabinet where Dexter hovered, eyeing the booze and rubbing his chin.

"Please help yourself," Dr Thane said. "I know you are on duty, but I won't tell anyone. And pour me a double of whatever you're having. This all comes as quite a shock."

"Aye, I think a tot or two will help," Dexter replied. "But I'll not drink tonight. What you having, Guv?"

Fenella felt tired. A glass of something nice might put a bit of pep back into her step. She glanced about at the expensive furnishings, and oil paintings of rolling green hills and white sandy beaches. "A small glass of sherry will do the trick." It was the right sort of place for that treat, reminded her of a lush room on a television advert. She'd sip it slow as they talked. "Just to chase away the chill."

As they settled into their seats, Dr Thane

pressed a button, and the fireplace leapt into life.

"Very nice," Fenella said and took a delicate sip.

"Could get used to this," Dexter echoed.

Raised voices came from the hallway followed by a sharp knock on the door. Before anyone got to their feet, it flew open. Vicar Briar rushed into the room followed by PC Beth Finn.

"Oh, Cain, you are here!" Dr Thane moved towards the vicar and threw her arms about him. "You'll stay the night, won't you?"

"Aye," the vicar said. "I'll do that."

His green cassock was neatly pressed. There was a shine to his shoes. If Fenella didn't know any better, she'd have thought he was dressed in the clergy's equivalent of "Sunday best."

Dr Thane said, "I called Cain and asked him to come over. He is a good friend and our family vicar." She turned to Fenella. "I hope that is okay?"

Two forces tugged. On the one hand, Fenella preferred Dr Thane to remain in the house alone. It made it easier for her team to keep a watch, and the less people who knew, the better. On the other, she understood the power of friends. It seemed clear by the lingering hug that Vicar Briar was right at home.

Fenella said, "It won't do any harm to have a drop of company."

The vicar said, "Whatever everyone is having, I'll have one too. And make it a large one."

While Dexter poured, Dr Thane brought the vicar up to speed with their earlier conversation. All the while his face remained as solid as a clay mask.

There was one other reason Fenella was pleased to see Vicar Briar. It gave her a chance to kill two birds with one stone. But she waited until the vicar was settled in front of the fire with a cigar and his drink and Dr Thane at his side before she broached the subject.

"I forgot to ask before, but are you married, Vicar Briar?"

"It does not seem to have been in God's plan to grace me with a wife."

Fenella smiled. "How long have you been married, Dr Thane?"

"Fifteen years," she replied, then took a sip from her glass. "I'm Albert's third wife."

"No children?"

"There never seemed time with my career. I don't regret it, though."

"Aye," Fenella replied. She'd had five nippers and didn't regret it either. "This is a big house, for a couple."

"We have a cleaner who comes in once a week. Mrs Broz is from Poland, drives over from Port St

Giles." Dr Thane glanced at the vicar and smiled. "And I've a nice gardener, thanks to Cain."

The vicar puffed on his cigar. A plume of smoke seeped from his mouth. Then he pursed his lips and puffed out a smoky O.

Fenella said, "They teach you that trick in the seminary?"

He winked and again puckered his lips and puffed hard. A heart drifted through the air.

Dr Thane clapped. "Oh, Cain, you are so silly!"

The vicar grinned and said, "Mr and Dr Thane have a lovely English garden. You should see it in the summer. It is so good it should be on a chocolate box. I recommended the same bloke we use at the priory, Hazza." He turned to Fenella. "You asked about him earlier."

Fenella took out her phone, fiddled for a moment, then gave it to Dr Thane. It contained a photo of Hamilton Perkins.

"Is this Hazza?"

Dr Thane put on a pair of reading glasses and stared. After a long moment she said, "No. No. I've never seen this man before. What do you think, Cain?"

Vicar Briar peered at the image and gave a little start. He turned to Fenella, his eyes narrow. "Yes... yes, that's him. That's Hazza!"

Dr Thane said, "Don't be ridiculous. Hazza has a flatter..." She grabbed the phone and studied the photo again. "It's hard to say. Yes, it could be Hazza, I suppose. Does the person I'm looking at have a criminal record?"

Everyone knew the answer. His photo was on Detective Inspector Sallow's phone. He had to have done something bad.

"Aye, he's not one of life's angels," Fenella said. "That's why we want to speak with him."

Then it sank in, and the vicar was on his feet.

"Dear God, are we saying Hazza is Hamilton Perkins?"

"We don't know anything for sure," Fenella said in a soft voice. She didn’t want to start a panic. "We want to speak to Hazza so we can eliminate him from our inquiries."

"And Viv Gill and Pearl Smith... Do you think..."

"Like I said, Vicar Briar, we know nothing for certain." Fenella let her voice drop an octave, a trick taught by the police to calm things down. It conveyed the message that everything was under control. There was no need to panic. "We will get to the bottom of those deaths. Mark my words."

It did not work on the vicar.

"And to think the man's been at work in the gardens of all the expensive houses in the village, on my personal recommendation!" He spoke in a shrill. "Gracious! Mr Shred knows where all the single women live. How many more deaths before he is caught?"

"We'll get him." This was Dexter. His voice was so low it came out as a growl. "We will not let him do any more harm."

But Vicar Briar was waving his arms about and on his feet shouting. "If that fiend sets one foot in this place and tries to harm Olive..." He flapped his cassock so it billowed, making him look like a giant green bug. "I'll not stand for it!"

It was a dramatic performance almost as if he were on the stage. But there was no redness to his face or sweat prickling his forehead, and his eyes darted to Dr Thane as he sat back down. *Aye, the man should be on the telly,* Fenella told herself.

"Oh, Cain, you do make such a fuss." Dr Thane touched his elbow. "Let's leave it to the police, eh?"

Fenella smiled at Dr Thane and said, "What time does Hazza usually show up?"

"He comes every other Tuesday," Dr Thane replied in a whisper. "Always in the morning around seven. He works on a few gardens near here."

"Which houses?"

"I don't know. Just local gardens."

Fenella thought for a moment. *If they went door to door tonight, it would cause a panic.* She said,

"Anything else?"

"In the afternoon I believe he works the grounds of the priory. But he won't be here until tomorrow morning."

"Aye, happen. Happen not," Fenella replied.

But her team would watch all night anyway, just in case Hazza paid Dr Olive Thane an early visit.

CHAPTER 62

Fenella couldn't push the grim secret from her mind. It crawled like weevils in a sack of rice. As she gazed from the deck, she felt the weight of her secret. It pressed down until she could barely breathe, then twisted and turned and pressed more.

The night was still. Faint shards of white from the moon glowed into the blue dark, and the bare limbs of the trees cast long shadows. There was still five hours until sunrise. She zipped her coat tight to ward off the deepening chill.

Her team were in place. Now all they had to do was wait. She scanned the darkness once more and checked her police radio. An icy blast loosened her hood, and with her left hand she brushed a strand of hair back behind her ear, eyes alert for the faintest movement. As long as Hamilton Perkins was on the prowl, she knew it wasn't a question of *if* there'd be another death.

It had been a long day. Had she thought it all through? The sherry had not cleared her mind; if anything, it made it foggier. What if she'd buggered it up?

On the breeze, she heard the screech of an owl, and in the distance, the almost haunting crash of waves against the cliffs. From the garden, though, there came no sound.

Fenella let out a sharp breath, then relaxed. If anyone approached, they would not get as far as the house. Her team were primed and ready to pounce. They were filled with the tense focus of a beagle on the scent of a fox. She exhaled again and turned back to look at the house.

The place was dark. A few splashes of light from the moon bounced off the window so she saw her reflection, a face with a secret etched on it: pale, tired with deep hollows for eyes.

They might never capture Hamilton Perkins.

That was her secret.

Her gut churned. She would never find peace if Mr Shred remained free. There were no pills that could ease the pain of failure. Not even in knowing she'd run the case on her own terms. Inspector Moss had tried and botched the job, and he'd flopped in the search for her sister. But would she have done any better?

Eve vanished. No one knew why. Would she show up with a smile tomorrow? Or the day after? Or never? It was hard for Eduardo, worse for Nan. Fenella was prepared for the ultimate heartache.

Again, came the screech of a bird. An owl? It

wasn't a soft hoot, more like the scream of terrified fowl. *There's a fox on the hunt*, she told herself, *just like the police*.

On the dim porch, she pulled out her mobile phone, her gaze focused on the smiling face that filled the screen. It was Eve. Taken that night in London before the start of Prince's show. They were in line, waiting, not a care in the world. Unaware of the horror to come.

Fenella shivered and dredged her mind for memories. There was seven-year-old Eve at the front of a class teaching everyone how to sing for her show-and-tell. The teacher joined in and tapped her hands on the desk, pretending to play the drums. Eve's roar of laugher still rang in Fenella's ears. And there she was again, this time at fifteen, batting her eyelashes at a lad in the dining hall. Even Fenella thought he was a bit of all right and batted her eyelashes too.

And now, as St Bees slept through this dark hour, Fenella wondered about Hamilton Perkins. He'd spent years in prison planning his escape and, just as long, his revenge. Would he walk into their trap as easily as Eve had walked out of Port St Giles Cottage Hospital?

Fenella touched the screen of her phone. Like a ghost, Eve's face was gone. Like a ghost hunter, she watched for Hamilton Perkins. Silently she stared into the dark stillness and waited for the start of the show.

CHAPTER 63

"We've got him!"

PC Beth Finn's voice boomed out of the police radio with such an elated squeal, Fenella jumped. She glanced at her watch: six thirty-five, still dark and so cold that she could see a sheen of frost in the reflected light of the moon.

"We've got him," PC Finn said again. "Detective Jones and I have got him."

A wave of relief washed over Fenella so that she made a fist and stomped her feet. This was it, a breakthrough at last. Her gamble had paid off. There were shouts of joy coming from various spots in the garden.

"Where are you?" Fenella asked.

"About fifty yards from the gate at the end of the garden on a narrow track that goes downhill to the east," PC Finn replied. "I saw him creeping through the bushes. I shouted for him to stop, but he took off like a rabbit. Detective Jones and I gave chase."

Fenella hurried from the deck and cut across the lawn. By the time she passed the first pear tree,

Dexter was at her side.

"Looks like a win," he said, his voice as gruff as Fenella felt.

"Cast the net, and haul the salmon in," Fenella replied, slightly out of breath as she kept up with his stride.

They saw the white lights of the flare before they got to the end of the garden. Dexter shoved the gate open with his shoulder, then took off with long strides. He could have run a four-minute mile; Fenella was so excited, she would have kept up.

It was much darker in the woods with overgrown foliage blocking the path, so they slowed their pace to a walk. They didn't need the flare to find PC Finn and Detective Jones; they simply followed the shouts.

Dexter shone his torch at the voices. Jones had a man face down on the ground with his arm twisted behind his back. He wore a dirty, green duffel coat with stains so grim they looked like a new form of life. PC Finn pulled handcuffs from her belt and attached them to the man's wrists.

"Hey, get off me," the man yelled. "What the hell do you think you're doing?"

The first doubts crept in. Fenella stepped closer.

"Rawlings, is that you?"

"Bloody thugs," Rodney Rawlings yelled as

Jones tugged him to his feet. His rodent face scrunched into a ball, but his black eyes were wide with rage. "Get me out of these chains, or you'll not hear the last of it."

Fenella blew out her cheeks, making a sound like a deflated balloon. She thought her net had caught salmon; instead she'd hauled in a sardine.

"Let him go," she said. "Let's not upset our friends in the press any more than we have to."

Rodney Rawlings shook himself down. "I ought to take this to the police complaints board." He rubbed his wrists. "On second thought, Councillor Ron Malton would love to hear about this. It's a fiasco!"

Fenella ignored his threats. "What happened?"

"Nothing happened to me except for Supercop here jumping out of the bushes like some bleedin' ninja warrior."

A headache which had nagged made itself at home. Fenella knew it would be with her all day. She'd not slept since yesterday and her body knew it. "Mr Rawlings, can you explain why you are creeping about Hemlock Woods at"—she glanced at her watch—"six forty in the morning?"

"Fenella, come on. It's a public space. I'm quite within my rights to take a stroll."

"You live in Port St Giles, bit of a hike for a walk in the woods, isn't it?"

"I felt like a change."

"That your best shot?"

"Really is."

"Cuff him!"

"Hey, just hang on a minute, Fenella." Rodney raised his hands, palms out. "Just... hang on." He lowered his voice as if sharing a secret. "Okay, so I'm following up on a lead about an illegal badger hunt. It led me to St Bees and the woods. Looks like a wild-goose chase, though. How'd I know this place would be crawling with cops?"

"Is that a fact?"

His black eyes watched Fenella. "I suppose that is why you are here too—the badgers?"

Fenella folded her arms and sighed. "What are you doing here, and this time I want the truth?"

"Look, we both know you will not drag me to the station in cuffs. Now, why don't I just continue on my stroll, and we can forget about this. A win-win for both sides."

Fenella said, "If you want to take that chance, be my guest. Go ahead, start walking."

His lips twisted into his version of a friendly smile. It sharpened his rodent features. "I'm concerned about you, Fenella. Have you looked in a mirror lately? You look worse than I feel Saturday morning after an all-night booze-up. My God, I know the police are all into the casual look, but did someone pull you through a haystack backwards?"

"Water off a duck's back," Fenella replied and took a step closer. "Now, how about you start talking, or would you rather save your spiel for a lawyer, because when I'm done with you, you'll need one."

Rodney Rawlings stared. His rodent nose twitched. "Okay, Fenella, you win. I got word that Mr Shred might be in the woods this morning and on his way to pay a visit to a certain surgeon's house, where he intended to exact revenge for a limp he picked up in a hospital bed."

"Aye, and who told you that?"

"Can't say."

Fenella was about to press him for the name of his source when they heard the scream.

CHAPTER 64

The day had already begun on a sour note.

It got much worse after that.

Fenella rushed towards the scream, with Dexter at her side. Not an easy feat when you've had no sleep in more than a day. And in truth, it wasn't that much of a run, or a jog for that matter. No. Not even a fast-paced stride. More of a crab-like shuffle where you drag your feet and hope your body will keep up.

They scuttled through the foliage and back to the gate, which led to Dr Thane's garden. The scream came again: a woman's high-pitched voice—cries for help from Dr Thane.

A surge of energy pushed Fenella's legs on. For once, she left Dexter two paces back. But she stopped at the first pear tree, her eyes wide at the sight before her. She had seen nothing like it.

A figure in green flayed about on the soft grass. PC Hoon had his arms clasped on the figure's waist as if a weightlifter about to heave a great load. Dr Thane stood three steps back, pointing at the scuffle.

"Don't let him get away," she screamed. "Pin him down good and proper!"

The men struggled. They twisted and turned. It was hard to see exactly what was happening until PC Hoon grunted and heaved the figure in green to his feet.

Fenella let out a gasp. The figure in green was Vicar Briar, his cassock muddied and his hands clasped around a wisp of a man, with a cloth hat pulled down over his eyes.

"That's Hazza! Arrest that man," Vicar Briar yelled. "He tried to get away but we got him. Hangin' is too good for the sod."

Dexter grabbed the man by one arm; PC Hoon held the other while the vicar backed away to Dr Thane's side. The man with the cap wriggled hard for a moment like a landed fish. Then the fight drained out of his body, but he spoke in a hiss.

"Gawd blind me, the vicar's gone mad." His upper lip lifted to reveal teeth Fenella wouldn't want in her own mouth. "Came at me like a bat out o' hell, he did."

Fenella approached, reached out a hand, and took off his cap. He had a lined face, a bulbous nose, and furtive eyes.

"Oh, for Pete's sake," she muttered.

There was no way this Hazza was Hamilton Perkins. Not unless Mr Shred had shrunk five inches and gained an Irish accent, along with emerald-green eyes during his time in Low Marsh Prison.

CHAPTER 65

When Fenella's phone rang, she was on her way home to catch an hour or two of sleep. She had spent a few hours at the station in Port St Giles with the team, and now it was past lunchtime. A fine rain beat down over tall trees and low hedges. Rivulets of water ran across the narrow lane and formed shallow pools in the dips, so she had to slow her Morris Minor to a crawl. The soft *brring-brring* came as quite a shock.

The ringtone of Dr MacKay.

It echoed in the car against the soft splash of the storm on the windscreen. Why would he call her from Kenya? For a moment, she let it ring on, knowing that voicemail would kick in. She could do with a hug from Eduardo, pancakes and eggs from Nan, and a hot shower. But she slowed the car and pulled to the verge as her groggy mind kicked into gear.

"How's the weather?" she said as the wipers worked hard.

"Raining," came Dr MacKay's reply.

"Time of year, I suppose." Fenella knew little

about the weather in Kenya. They had a rainy season, didn’t they? "Best keep away from any dry creeks, flash floods, and all that."

"And it's freezing!"

"Where are you?"

"Port St Giles. I'm back in my cave in the hospital."

His voice trilled as though he were a songbird at dawn. Give him a corpse and a knife and all was good in his world. He did what he loved and loved what he did with a passion Fenella also knew. While she solved crimes, he solved the cause of death and wasn't shy about sharing what he'd found.

"Okay," Fenella said, sensing the hug from Eduardo, and Nan's ham and eggs would have to wait. "What have you got for me?"

"That Dr Oz is a bloody buffoon. Might be as sharp as a blade when it comes to running the place, I'll give him that, but when it comes to my job, he hasn't got a clue."

Fenella waited. Dr Mackay was blowing off steam. Everyone knew Dr Oz was good. As a medical director, he'd risen through the ranks because of his political skills and quick wit. Not an easy task, climbing to the top job in a hospital. No, there was nothing buffoonish about Dr Oz. Nothing at all. But she was good at the wait.

"A damn fool, a clown who can't tell jokes,

the man is a..." His voice trailed off, his steam apparently spent. "Can you come to my studio?" By which he meant the morgue. "I've been at work on Viv Gill and Pearl Smith."

The edge in his voice set her on high alert.

"What kind of work? What have you found?"

"Not over the phone. Be here in twenty minutes and we'll talk. And keep that damn notebook in your handbag. This is off the record."

CHAPTER 66

Ten minutes later, Fenella eased the car into a space at the Port St Giles Hospital. As she stared at the entrance, rain sloshed down from the low clouds with soft thudding that would lull a small child to sleep. On another day she would have let its constant beat rock her mind to dreamland. But today she needed a coffee, strong and black, to keep her awake and to calm her stomach for what was to come.

She breathed in and out. The gruesome sights in Dr MacKay's lab were not for the squeamish. She tilted her head from side to side to ease the tension, then climbed out of the car. The rain splashed as cold shards of ice against her cheeks. Whatever the good doctor had on his slab in the lab, she was ready.

She met Dr MacKay in the hallway just outside his studio. His bronze skin gleamed, as a result, Fenella supposed, of the Kenyan sun. If his flight had caused jet lag, there were no signs of it in his glittering eyes.

"Oh, there you are, Fenella," he said. He always called her by her first name, had done so since she was a rookie who had turned green as he sliced into the gut of a corpse with a giant pair of scissors.

He wasn't in scrubs but wore a tweed jacket with patched elbows and corduroy trousers. That meant one of two things. He was about to scrub up for a demo of the corpse of Viv Gill, and Pearl Smith with her in tow. Or he'd done the job and was on his way back to his office for a cuppa.

"About time for a black coffee, care to join me?"

"That would be lovely," Fenella said as she fell into step at his side.

It was a short walk to his office. After Dr MacKay boiled the kettle and spooned instant coffee into two mugs, he turned his computer monitor so they could both see the screen.

He flushed with excitement as he tapped at the keyboard. "I want you to look at this. It is… well, just look."

A dull twinge pulled at Fenella's gut, like seaweed attached to a rock—the slow tug of anticipation intermingled with a deep pool of sadness. Always the same feelings as she prepared to uncover the secrets of the recent dead.

An image filled the screen.

It was red, raw with slim, blue veins, so it looked like a slice of beef under a microscope. Fenella leaned forward and studied it for a long while. Serrated edges ran from left to right, all equidistant apart.

"Do you see it?" Dr MacKay leaned forward on the desk, eyes gleaming.

"Aye," Fenella said. "I believe I do."

"Now look at this." He jabbed a finger at the keyboard.

A new image came on the screen. At first glance, it looked the same as the previous, a slab of raw flesh magnified so the veins snaked like the Pow Beck stream. Fenella focused; the coffee helped, so it only took two beats for her to see it this time: a series of irregular, serrated edges, which ran from right to left.

"Okay, I see the patterns; what does it mean?" Fenella said.

Once again, Dr MacKay jabbed at the keyboard. This time five images appeared on the screen. Two at the top, three below. Each framed by a white edge like an old-fashioned photograph taken with film.

Dr MacKay said, "The top two images were taken today. The left is from Viv Gill's cheek, the right Pearl Smith's." He paused a beat, then grunted with satisfaction. "See it, don't you?"

Fenella leaned forward.

"Aye, Dr MacKay, I think I'm with you."

"Oh, such a bright girl. Totally wasted on the police." He lowered his hand and pointed at each image. "See that?"

Fenella jerked upright. A headache stabbed at the back of her head, then stomped on her temples. It was absolutely clear. The Viv Gill and Pearl Smith images both had a series of irregular, serrated edges that ran from right to left. The bottom three images did not. Their serrated edges ran from left to right with a gap that looked as if it was precisely measured.

"Oh shit!" Fenella said, her mind now swamped with dreadful possibilities.

"Oh shit indeed!" Dr MacKay leaned back in his chair and folded his arms across his chest. "The bottom three images are from the file, all known victims of Hamilton Perkins. I'll bet a bottle of Glenmorangie that whoever killed Pearl Smith and Viv Gill, it wasn't Mr Shred."

CHAPTER 67

There were only three tables in the Grain Bowl Café. Fenella and Dexter sat at one. The other two were empty. She had called him when she left Dr MacKay's lair. Ten minutes later, he arrived and pulled up a chair. It was getting dark, although it was only 3:15 p.m. The threat of a storm filled the air.

"What's up, Guv?" Dexter said.

He looked as rough as Fenella felt. There was a growth of stubble on his chin, and his breath wasn't the freshest. She glanced around and in a low voice told him what Dr MacKay had said.

His eyes grew wide at the news that they were looking for another killer. "Cor blimey!" He raked a hand over his rough jowls. "Are you saying we have two serial killers on our hands?"

"I don't know."

Dexter was shaking his head. "I know Dr MacKay is good, Guv. But is he sure?"

Fenella had asked the same question and replayed Dr MacKay's response. "Things are often not what they seem, even when viewed with the naked eye."

The waitress appeared with the food. Two flat white coffees and four croissants. She smiled at Dexter as she placed the food on the table.

"Enjoy," she said, then turned and walked away.

The swing to her hips seemed a little over the top, although Dexter watched with a grin for a moment, then brought his attention back to Fenella and said, "So, Dr MacKay might be wrong?"

"He bet a bottle of Glenmorangie."

"Did you take the bet?"

"No."

Dexter tore off a chunk of croissant and chewed for a moment. "So, Guv, what do we do about it?"

"The good doctor does not want us to share until he gets confirmation from the labs."

"That's not like Dr MacKay. He always goes out on a limb."

"Things change."

Dexter considered that. "Like what?"

"He's worked in the morgue labs for years," Fenella replied. "Not sure how long, must be close to forty by now. It seems the higher-ups are putting pressure on him to retire."

Dexter let out a low whistle. "The man lives for his work. He'll not last long without access to his blades and a freezer full of corpses." He thought for a moment. "Is that why he is dotting his i's and crossing his t's?"

"Aye. We'll have to wait three days for the labs to confirm, and given the nature of our investigation, they'll want a second opinion. That could take another week."

Dexter said, "What about Jeffery?"

"Let's not bother her until we have the facts." Fenella felt tired and hung-over from lack of sleep. Although she pumped her body full of coffee, it no longer had an effect. Now she wondered whether it would keep her awake all night, and she'd be even more tired the next day. "We have to work with the cards we are dealt."

"And what should we tell the rest of the team?" He sounded cautious. They'd worked together for so long that Fenella got the message. Dexter had her back. Always.

"Best wait, eh?" she said. "We don't want rumours to get out that might lead back to Dr MacKay. There's no way I'll upset his apple cart; I want him to stay."

Dexter nodded. "Same here, Guv." He took a gulp of coffee. "Don't stop us looking for the murdering bugger, though, does it?"

"Aye, maybe we'll land two salmon with one hook." Fenella thought for a moment. "What do Pearl Smith and Viv Gill have in common if it is not Hamilton Perkins?"

"Single women," Dexter said.

"Aye, and childless," she replied, thinking. "Are we looking for a person who has a grudge against childless women?"

Dexter shrugged.

As they ate and drank, they agreed to come up with a plan in the morning when their minds were refreshed. At last, Dexter left to get home to Priscilla. In the old days, he'd hang around for a chat. He seemed happy, and that meant more to Fenella than anything else. But she'd not had a chance to let Gail Stubbs know that he was off the market. She'd do that gently on the phone tonight.

Fenella's hunger had waned, but the tiredness ebbed and flowed in great waves. She wasn't ready to set out for home just yet. There was something nagging at the back of her mind, and she wanted to work it out before she began the drive. So she ordered another coffee, decaf, and stared out the window to think. *What other link was there between Viv Gill and Pearl Smith if it wasn't Hamilton Perkins?* The question gnawed at her mind. *Were the two women friends? Did they socialise?*

Nothing in the reports she read suggested they knew each other. She'd check again with PC

Hoon. Then she thought of Vicar Briar. His image floated into her mind like a puff of smoke. Maybe they met at St Bees Priory? She'd been surprised that Pearl Smith went to church. Even more so with Viv Gill. *Yes*. That was the common link! Now her mind raced to find others. The more links found, the further down the trail they'd get, even if it led nowhere.

There was a crack of thunder. Fenella glanced through the window and wondered if she could get home before the downpour. If she made a run for it, she'd be in with half a chance. She ate what was left of the croissant and washed it down with the dregs of her coffee. As she stood up, her mobile phone rang. She didn't recognise the number but took the call.

"It's Nellie, Nellie Cook. That you, Fenella?"

"Aye, what's up?"

There was a moment of silence, then Nellie continued. "Viv Gill's murder has got right under my skin. None of my business, seeing as she was off my books, I suppose, but I can't help myself."

"Nowt wrong with a drop of curiosity," Fenella said. She was curious too, wanted to hear what Nellie Cook had to say.

"I've had a chat with some of my girls," Nellie said. "Found out a bit about Viv's business in St Bees.

Not much of a market for her... services, but she had a big-paying client, bragged to the other girls about him. A righteous bugger with a fat wallet, they said."

"Do you have a name?"

"We don't use real names in our line of work. Take me: Madam DuPont to my clients, plain Nellie Cook to my friends. He calls himself Dragon."

"What do you mean by Dragon, Nellie?"

"Fire-breathing lizard with wings, let's out one hell of a roar. According to my girls, he likes to dress up in a green suit and puff hard on a cigar."

CHAPTER 68

Fenella got home as Nan set the table for the evening meal.

"Look what the cat's brought in," Nan said. "Thought you'd run away to live on the streets of London. Want a glass of Mr Bray's organic apple wine?"

Fenella sat at the scrubbed-pine table. She would have a long shower before she ate. "Maybe a quick one."

Nan poured a half glass, then wrinkled her nose. "You stink like you've been living in a shop doorway."

"Aye, that about sums up my past few days." Fenella sipped, enjoying the tart tang. "Hey, that's not bad. How many did you buy?"

"Thought you'd like it, luv."

"How many?"

"Three cases."

"That's thirty-six bottles!" Fenella said.

"It's organic," Nan said, "And anyway, Guzzle Gut will make short work of them."

"Did you call my name?" Eduardo came into the kitchen and gave Fenella a hug. He sniffed. "My wife returns, but I'm not sure you're the real one. My princess smelled like rose petals, not the fragrance of a warmed-up bowl of sour milk."

"Cheeky sod!" Fenella said, then added. "Anyway, you are on a diet, so don't be getting the greedy eye on Mr Bray's wine."

"The doctor said I had to cut down on food," Eduardo replied. "She didn't mention anything about drink."

"He's a crafty sod," Nan said as she poured him a glass of wine. "He had to be to catch you as his wife."

Now it was Fenella's turn to sniff. "What's for dinner?"

"Smells great, unlike some," Eduardo added. "Asian scents with overtones of... oh, I don't know, something delicious."

"Crispy Asian chili beef with sticky white rice," Nan replied, then wagged a finger at Eduardo. "I've made you a bowl of salad: iceberg lettuce and cucumber. Don't add any salt; the doctor told you to cut back on that."

After her shower, Fenella joined them at the table just as Nan was dishing out.

"That don't look like salad," Fenella said to Eduardo, who was digging into a bowl of crispy beef and rice.

He sniffed. "You don't smell like my wife either."

"Couldn't keep the bugger from the pot," Nan said as she spooned food into Fenella's bowl. "I'll not let him have seconds, though."

It was delicious. They chatted and drank wine until Nan said it was time for her to turn in. Eduardo gave Fenella a long hug, then wandered back to his study. He was under deadline for a new comic strip based on the Grimm brothers' fairy tales. Fenella washed up and put the dishes away, grateful for the mindless activity. It was only eight thirty when she dried the last plate and stacked it back in the cupboard. Filled with the warm glow of a delicious meal and homemade wine, sleep called her.

There was one more thing she had to do before she headed up to bed. She searched through her handbag for her mobile phone, taking her time so she could come up with the right words. For a long moment she stared at the screen. Not too late to call Gail Stubbs. But breaking the news about Dexter would spoil the warm glow of the meal. Instead, she typed a text message:

Fancy lunch, tomorrow at one?

The answer came back within a beat:

Yes. One is good. See you at the hospital canteen.

CHAPTER 69

Fenella slept through the night and awoke after nine. Eduardo had left the curtains drawn, so it took her a moment to realise that morning was well under way. Gone was the fog that had slowed her mind, as were the tired limbs. She got up refreshed, and pulled back the curtains. There was a blue sky with a globe-sized sun like she'd seen in an African movie, although by the sheen of frost on the grass, it was nowhere near as warm.

After a breakfast of Nan's ham and pancakes, she set out for Port St Giles. The briefing was scheduled for eleven, and she arrived in good time, body relaxed, her mind as sharp as a pin.

"Afternoon, Guv," Dexter said, a cup of tea in his hand. "Nice day for it."

Fenella noted his clean-shaven chin and bright eyes and once again thought Priscilla was good for him. She poured a cup of the Cumbria police brew and walked to the front of the room. The focus would be on the information she had received from Nellie Cook.

"I've had a lead from a contact who was

close to Viv Gill," she began. "It seems Viv had a regular client." She paced in front of the whiteboard, stopped at the picture of Viv Gill, and stared for a long moment. Then she turned to the team. PC Hoon leaned forward in his seat, mouth slightly open as if he were hanging on her every word. For once, Jones looked rough around the edges, and PC Beth Finn sat at the opposite end of the row of seats. She couldn't get much farther away from Jones. "The man goes by the name of Dragon."

"The Dragon of St Bees, now that's a tag for a newspaper headline," Dr Joy Hall said. She'd dialled in by phone. "Do we know anything else about him?"

"By all accounts, he's the self-righteous type with a fat wallet," Fenella said.

"That figures," muttered PC Finn. "It's always the self-righteous types, isn't it?"

Fenella ignored her comment, sensing it was aimed at someone else. Jones folded his arms and scowled. She looked at PC Hoon and said, "Does 'Dragon' ring any bells?"

He lurched to his feet and looked at his hand and he looked at the whiteboard and he looked at Fenella. "I've not heard that name before. Dragon, no. Never!"

"Likes to dress up in green, all fancy like," Fenella added, hoping it might jog his memory. "Expensive suits, you'd have noticed. Might be a regular in the village. Maybe you met him at a fête or over drinks in the pub?"

PC Hoon slowly shook his head. "I'll ask around, ma'am."

Fenella thought a village bobby should have their ears to the ground and eyes on everything that went on in their town. If a big spender in a green suit, puffing a cigar, turned up in Port St Giles, it wouldn't be long before she found out. PC Hoon didn't seem to have his eyes or ears on anything. Doubts about the man crept in. "Oh, and he has a big wallet and smokes a cigar. Anyone seen a bloke that fits that description on your travels in St Bees?"

There was a long silence as everyone looked around. It seemed no one had heard of the Dragon or seen a rich bloke in an expensive green suit. PC Finn raised a hand.

"Might be worth a chat with Mr Chad Tate; he runs the village store. They sell cigars, don't they?"

"Aye, luv. Happen they do." Fenella smiled. "Wonder if he has a green suit?"

Dexter cracked his knuckles.

Fenella said. "Right, then. Jones, you find out what you can about Mr Tate's finances, phone records, taxes, anything. He's from New York but has lived in St Bees for donkeys' years, so there should be plenty to dig through."

"What am I looking for, ma'am?" Jones asked.

Fenella shrugged. "Is he married? Kids? What

happened to his wife? I don't know, but it will jump out at you when you find it. Dexter, why don't you have a word with our mutual friend. See what else they can tell us about our Dragon." She was careful not to mention Nellie Cook by name or even her town. Force of habit.

"Right you are, Guv." He gave a salute. "And where you off to, then?"

"Lunch with Florence Nightingale," Fenella replied. "Then I'm at the magistrates' court the rest of the day."

CHAPTER 70

The hospital cafeteria was almost full.

Fenella sat at a small table by a glass wall, which overlooked the lobby. The steel and glass reached up to a domed roof, an echo chamber for the lunchtime sounds and a cooking pot of delicious smells. She was early.

For several minutes she watched the merry throng. The marble-tile floors clacked as people shuffled in. There were one or two staff about, and they cleared the tables as quickly as new diners came. Newcomers peered at the menu board, while others carried trays in search of a table.

A hollow pang gnawed at Fenella's gut. She was starving and relished the idea of battered cod, chips, mushy peas, and a dollop of brown curry sauce. It would not take much to persuade Gail to order the same; that way she would not feel so bad when she went for seconds. She was arguing with herself over the merits of a squeeze of tartar sauce or a splash of malt vinegar when she saw her friend.

Gail made her way to the table as though she were a wilted snail. If she was pleased at her day so far, it did not show through the scowl.

Fenella said, "You've got a face on you like a crab apple gone bad. Patients giving you a tough time?" It was a light-hearted jest to lift the mood.

Gail let out a long sigh, gave a half-hearted smile, glanced at the food counter, and said, "Don't think I could eat a thing, but I'm glad you came. I need to chat."

Fenella's stomach rumbled. She cast a quick glance at the line by the food counter. It was growing by the second. There'd be no fish or chips or much of anything else if they chatted before they ate. She said, "Who needs food? I came here for a chat too. What's up?"

"It's Leo. I got a letter from him this morning."

Fenella thought Leo was a soft-hearted romantic. She could see him with a quill pen in his hand, scratching out a love note to Gail by candlelight. A young nurse with the figure of a stick insect placed her tray on the next table, then sat down. Cod and chips with mushy peas, curry sauce, and a large cup of pop, Fenella noted. She wondered how such a skinny thing would down it all.

"Don't tell me," Fenella said. "He wrote to tell you he made a mistake with that young thing he ran off with and wants you to come back home?"

Gail glanced at Fenella with glistening eyes. "It was an invitation to his wedding. He is marrying

Lyn."

Her voice was so quiet and far off, Fenella could barely hear it over the clatter of plates from the food counter. The young nurse at the next table crammed the first forkful of fish into her mouth and washed it down with a swig of pop.

Gail said, "Our marriage had run its course. Leo is not coming back, and though I'd known that for years, I feel it deep down now. In my marrow. Loneliness." She pulled an old photo from her purse: Leo with his arm around her on a beach. Their youthful faces smiled into the camera, eyes bright with love. "And for now there is nothing, nothing in the world that can end it."

Fenella said, "Not really over him, then, are you, luv?"

"I thought I was… I mean, I want to move on too." Gail's breath caught in her throat, so the next few words came out as a whisper. "It's just that it is not the same for women, is it?"

"Aye, luv. Happen you're right about that."

Gail sighed. "I feel fat and ugly and old. Everybody seems so young lately, makes me feel like I'm just about ready for my pension."

"You are in your fifties, Gail. Nowt wrong with that." Fenella felt old too, especially when she looked at the childish faces which seemed to be everywhere these days. Even the new constables looked like they'd just come out of school. It felt like it was only yesterday that she was in uniform herself. She watched the young twig of a nurse stuff the last of the fish into her mouth and mop up the dregs of curry sauce with her chips. *Can eat what you bloody well like when you are young,* she thought. "Middle age just means you are ripe. Fruit's at its sweetest when ripe. Full of sugar."

"Plumpest too," Gail said with a miserable sigh.

"Aye, that's why we jog on the beach, eh?"

Gail dabbed at her eyes. "I was born before the internet, and Lyn has no idea what a landline phone is! Watching Leo move on makes me feel old. It is totally bonkers how life goes so fast. Yes, I'm over Leo. I've moved on, but I still feel hollow inside."

"So, you going to the wedding, then?"

Gail shrugged. "Yeah, I suppose, just to stick it to him." Her voice became soft and quiet, and there was acceptance in her tone. "You'll come with me, won't you? Bring Eduardo and… Dexter."

Fenella groaned under her breath. It was time. Still, she'd not beat about the bush, best to be direct; that was kindest. "Dexter's old girlfriend has moved in with him. They are going to get married."

"Oh!"

"Let's go get a plate of cod and chips with all the trimmings," Fenella said. "Stuff our faces, eh?"

Twenty minutes later, stomachs full of battered cod, chips, curry sauce, and mushy peas, they chatted about the old times, their laughter ringing off the glass walls, like echoes from the past. It was a taste of days long gone when Fenella used to stop by the hospital in Whitehaven to chat with Gail and make plans for the weekend to come.

When they ran out of stories, Gail stood. "I'd better get back. Good thing it is admin this afternoon, else I'd be snoring on the ward." She giggled. "You'll want to know that they let Ann Lloyd go home. Nothing wrong with her but a few scrapes and bruises. You saved the child's life."

"We both did," Fenella said.

Gail went silent for a moment. "I would have followed you into the sea, but I'm afraid of water."

Fenella said, "Well we can fix that, can't we?"

"Oh no, I'm a land-loving girl. Don't get any ideas." Gail raised both hands. "I heard through the grapevine about Dr Joy Hall. Not working that one, are you?"

Fenella answered with a question. "What did you hear?"

"That she was attacked by a madman. Or at least that is what Bishara told me."

"Bishara?"

"Dr Bishara Kendi. She's from Kenya and new to Port St Giles, like me. We've become friends. She treated Dr Joy Hall. Have you caught the evil git that attacked her?"

Thunder rattled in the distance. It darkened the atrium's roof. Large raindrops splashed down but for only a few seconds, then they stopped. The sky remained dark.

Fenella said, "Dr Hall's attack is part of an ongoing investigation. But yes, Dr Hall was lucky to get away with her life. Very lucky."

"That's just the thing," Gail said. "Dr Kendi reckons her injuries are only superficial. The sort of thing she sees all the time after the pubs close on a Friday night."

CHAPTER 71

Dr Joy Hall heard the ring of the phone, sat up, and swore.

It's non-stop buzz had jerked her from a dream where she was at an event in a giant book store in New York City. Cameras jostled with a sea of microphones. Everyone wanted to know about her best-selling book on Mr Shred. She had dreamt it often over the past few months, each time the images more vivid until, when her eyes fluttered open at the buzz of the phone, she wasn't sure where she was.

It was two thirty in the afternoon.

The suite was set up like a hotel room. Medical devices blended in with the lush furnishings. A watercolour of the beach hung on the wall, all swirls of brown, blue, and white. There was a separate room with a toilet and shower. An alcove formed a small kitchen. She scanned the room for her phone. It was on a low table by a chair next to the French doors. With the soft tendrils of the dream fading, she padded across the room.

"Dr Joy Hall?" The man's voice jerked her back

to the present. "There was a problem Tuesday at Dr Thane's House. What else have you got for me?"

Joy's shoulders slumped. The last pleasant shreds of her snooze leached into the ether. This was not how it was supposed to be. In her dream, they worked for her. But every time she threw Rodney Rawlings a bone, he came back for more.

She said, "I can't tell you anything else."

"Dr Hall," he replied in that slime-filled voice. "You've got mad minds to treat, and police got crime to solve. I got news to make my deadline."

"There is nothing new."

"I say there is."

"I'm sorry, it is all confidential. I wish I could help."

"This story will be huge, and not just here. The Americans will lap it up. There'll be interest from China, India too. It'll go global."

Joy listened in silence. When his news story broke, there'd be an enormous wave of interest. A tailwind to fan the flames of her book. Dollar bills would fall like autumn leaves into her purse. Oh yes, she'd ride the wave of global hype all the way to the bank. Now she counted the days until she quit the prison service—one hundred and twenty-five.

She said, "You think so?"

"Sure."

"When will you break the news?"

"Once I've got all my ducks in a row. It's like running with a pack of dogs, in my world. I've got to stay a few paces ahead. This is my story, don't want anyone to break it ahead of me, if you get my drift." Rodney Rawlings lowered his voice. "I'm the only person from the press you've had a quiet chat with, right?"

"What do you take me for?"

"Then throw me a bone."

Joy adjusted the phone. "They picked up a man called Hazza. He broke into Dr Thane's garden, not sure why, but I'd bet a penny to the pound it was with ill intent."

Joy knew the Hazza they'd caught wasn't Hamilton Perkins, knew he didn't break into Dr Thane's place. She spun the tale to buy more time. Rodney Rawlings had lapped up the trail of crumbs she'd given him so far.

"Oh, come on," he said. "That was Tuesday, and the man is a tramp from Maryport. I've checked him out, bought him breakfast in Don's Café, where he scoffed down two King Kong fry-ups and half a gallon of tea. What new leads have our friends in the police sniffed out?"

"There is nothing new. I've told you all I know."

"What, do you think I'm an idiot?" His voice

was filled with contempt. There was a long pause. "Scratch my back, Dr Hall, and I'll scratch yours."

Joy cringed. "Did you just threaten me?"

"No. No, I would never do that. I just want to be clear about our… arrangement. You've got the cash; now I want the story."

He'd dangled the money, like bait on a hook. She'd bitten hard, got snagged by the pound signs. It was their secret. One which she prayed would never see the light of day. He wouldn't tell anyone, would he? That would be her worst nightmare, her worst fear come to life. The whole mess was her own fault, but that did not stop her rage from slowly coming to the boil.

"You don't own me!"

"He who pays the piper..."

Joy clenched her jaw. The nasty wee man was doing his best to faze her. Rat-faced by looks and a rat by nature. But he was a journalist. They always protected their sources. No! He would not rattle her; she'd not give him that satisfaction. Still, he made a veiled threat, and that made her nervous.

"Dr Hall?" His voice snapped with impatience. "Look, all I want is what I paid for, access to the police investigation as it unfolds. That's the deal, right?"

Joy squeezed her eyes shut and swallowed hard. She had to throw him a scrap. "The police are looking for a man called the Dragon."

The line went so quiet, she thought he'd hung up. Then he said, "Aw, c'mon, Joy. You think I'm nuts?"

How dare the rat refer to her by her first name! It was Dr Hall to him. He didn't seem to know his place in the order of things. Flustered, Joy said, "The Dragon was seeing Viv Gill."

"Why would the police waste their time chasing her fancy man when they've got their sights on Mr Shred? That's why they brought you in, right? To help find the evil bugger?"

A thought jabbed at the edge of Joy's mind.

It struck like a sharp blade plunged with great force. And it hurt.

It was the realisation that now she had taken his cash, Rodney Rawlings would not stop hounding her until he had his story. No matter what, he'd come back. Well, two could play at that came.

Flushed and breathless, she said, "Okay, you win. There was a sighting of Hamilton Perkins in Whitehaven. One of the nightclubs, don't know which. You might want to check it out."

"Stop blowing smoke in my face, Joy."

She said nothing because it would have been useless. The man had a nose like a bloodhound, could sniff out truth from crap. A fierce rage burned her up from the inside out. The room began to spin.

It always did when she lost it.

"You owe me, Joy, and I'm cashing in."

As fury radiated through her body, and she glanced down at her left hand. The tremble was so subtle, her eyes could barely detect motion. Then it jerked in a slashing movement, right to left. It was over in an instant, and later she would not recall it.

"Mr Rawlings, our relationship is at an end. Do not call my phone ever again, or you will deeply regret it."

She clicked the phone off, snorting with anger. Little men like him had to be put back in their box, like a child puts away their toys. That's why she enjoyed her work as a psychologist in Low Marsh Prison even though the pay stank. When she was done playing with her toys, they'd be put back in their cells.

The phone rang. Joy picked up.

Rodney Rawlings said, "Don't cross me, Joy, I don't like being crossed."

"Bugger off!" Joy slammed the phone down.

In a flash of rage, she thought of the men she worked with at Low Marsh Prison. They thought they could manipulate her too! All sour faces, roving eyes, and foul breath. All her Uncle Fred. She smiled. Now she was in charge, and in her reports, she wrote that their minds could never be fixed. Punishment for each night Uncle Fred crept into her bed. Vengeance for the death of her child. A sense of power. Justice. Her way.

Again, the phone rang—Rodney Rawlings.

Joy let it ring until it clicked to voicemail. Oh, how she'd love to get him convicted and tossed into Low Marsh Prison. She'd play with him until she broke his soul. Her lips twitched at the corners. The rat-faced man did not know who she really was. Calls himself a reporter! The fool didn't have a bead on what she knew; Hamilton Perkins was not in St Bees. He did not kill Viv Gill or Pearl Smith. But, oh what a finale to her book—the killer returns to his home town, slays two women, and puff, he's gone, while the dozy police scratch their heads.

CHAPTER 72

It was close to 3:00 p.m. and getting dark when Chad Tate closed the store and eased open the iron gates of the St Bees Priory. A soft rain blew in loose swirls over the graveyard. He liked to visit when darkness reigned. He'd play a game of "flit between the shadows," like a belfry bat. Sometimes he'd crouch behind a headstone if he heard someone on the path. But in the early evening January shadows, he usually had the cemetery to himself.

And that was the way he liked it.

He made his way along a gravel path, then cut through a lawned area to an iron bench he'd bought ten years back. The damp had rusted the ornate handles, and the slats needed a lick of paint. He'd touch it up in the spring. For now he sat on the cold iron and watched. After a while, the rain stopped, and there was just the drip and splash from the trees. Chad flicked on his torch and shone it at the first headstone.

ROSE TATE: Beloved Wife and Mother.

The simple headstone was all he could afford when she died. It broke his heart every time he came to visit his wife. Two funerals in one day cost him the earth. He shone the torch on the next headstone, much smaller.

LARK TATE: I'll take care of Bert the sheep for you. Miss you, Daddy.

It had been dark outside St Bees Priory when the car came speeding down the lane, hit the curb, and killed Rose and his five-year-old daughter, Lark. The car did not stop. The police never found the driver.

How could the killer of his wife and child still be on the loose? Chad's heart slammed hard against his chest. He'd told the police who drove the car and pointed the person out in a line-up. But they shrugged, said there was no evidence, and that was that.

He reached a damp hand into his jacket pocket and pulled out a handful of white envelopes.

"Look what I've got," he said, waving the limp envelopes in the cold air. "A stack of them from the bank manager. If Bert were here, I'd let him tell you all about these." But Bert, the one-eyed, three-legged sheep, was under the counter in the store. And anyway, Chad liked to keep the stuffed animal in the shop, so when he spoke his mind it was there to listen. "I just want you to know that whatever happens, I won't close the store. I won't leave the village. Do you hear me? Are you listening?"

In the dead space between their passionate

grunts and groans, Viv Gill and Pearl Smith had listened too. But how could a childless woman understand the depth of his loss. How could they know what death was like if they still lived and breathed?

He glanced across the dark cemetery to the spots where Viv Gill and Pearl Smith would be laid to rest. They would always be with him now. Once their graves had been filled and the earth settled, he would visit to pay his respects. He planned to buy a bench so he could sit and tell them about life in St Bees. His girls would never leave the village now. Neither would he. Yes, he'd get the small dog with the grinning mouth and bring it along too.

A low thunder rumbled in the distance. If the wind changed, it would bring rain. Chad gazed at the black sky with clouds as twisted as a hangman's noose. Even the moon seemed to be hiding; only a dirty smudge of gold streaked across the dark. He opened his lips and sucked in the frigid air. The taste of the graveyard filled his mouth. Earth and moss and grass and death.

Chad had tried to move on. Build a new life. But he couldn’t stop coming back to the grave for his night-time vigil. It was a raw compulsion. One of many which he tried to keep under control. He closed his eyes and remembered his wife and child. Rose came each Sunday to the graveyard to visit her grandmum. He'd wander off with Lark, who would giggle and laugh. They would play a game of flit between the tombstones. Rose would shout and tell them not to be so disrespectful. He'd argue that there was nothing down there but a pile of muck and dry bones.

One day, Lark asked, "What is it like to be dead, Daddy?"

"Dark," he replied. "And still."

"Is there anyone else there?"

"I don't think so."

Now he wished he'd said something else. Wished with all his heart Rose and Lark were still with him. He sighed and glanced at his phone. What about Maude? She was going to marry the bank manager. But Mr Clarke was a playboy, had a fling with Pearl Smith, and used the services of Viv Gill. His Maude deserved better than that.

Chad sighed. Bank managers get transferred, don't they? Maude would leave the village when that happened. But she loved this place, told him how much she wanted to make a life with him in the village store. And Chad had even picked out a plot in the cemetery for her with a pleasant view of the priory. He'd made the down payment with a loan from the bank.

It was to be her wedding gift.

A sign of his commitment to her and St Bees. He didn’t want to ask for a refund, still hoped she'd change her mind about Mr Clarke. He stood up. No!

Maude would not leave St Bees. He'd keep the plot. She said she loved the place, felt part of the village. Chad wanted it to stay that way. Permanently.

CHAPTER 73

All hell broke loose with the sharp chirp of a phone. The sun's first rays had yet to split the dark snarl of night when Fenella's mobile trilled like a song thrush keen for dawn: loud and screaming for light.

She sat in the kitchen sipping a cup of coffee with a plate of scrambled eggs and toast made by Nan. It was 5:00 a.m., Thursday. She let the phone chirp and wondered what Dexter wanted.

"Oi, here comes trouble," Nan said. "Give me a shout if you need me. I'll be in the study."

Calls at odd hours were part of the job. But they always startled Fenella. That was her little secret. Not that she'd tell anyone. Not even Eduardo. No. This little secret shot waves of dread up her spine. The phone continued to chirp. She'd come to accept the ring of the bell with the calm of a hospice priest awaiting their next grim call. That it was tolerable at all came from another hushed truth. She had a deep-down need to snoop. And every time the phone rang in the dead of night, the fight between dread and nosiness was fought. It was no contest. The nosy gene won out. Always.

She took a quick sip from her mug. The bitter coffee danced on her tongue. She swallowed, picked up, and said, "I take it this is not a wake-up call?"

"Guv!" Only a word but as bright and urgent as a neon sign. "I've not been home. Drove to Whitehaven yesterday afternoon and had a long chat with Nellie Cook. Well, you know how the old times roll, and the day turned into night before we got to the real business. Met a bunch of her girls. Do you recall Old Barb?"

Fenella thought a moment, then smiled. "Aye, I do. Don't tell me—"

"Yep, she's still at it." He spoke with the excitement of a man who'd just discovered the fountain of youth. "And she doesn't look a day older. Mind you, she was ancient back when we were in uniform."

Fenella's nosy gene kicked in. She forgot about the early hour, about the urgent tone in Dexter's voice. There was only one thing she had to know. How on earth was Old Barb still at it?

She said, "That's impossible. Old Barb used two walking sticks when we were in uniform and shuffled about as if she were about to fall over. It can't be the same woman!"

"Still shuffling, Guv." He let out a sharp laugh. "She used to work on the stage back in the day, so I suppose it was all an act. Still, I told her whatever she's taking, I want some."

Fenella couldn't help herself and said, "Go on, then, what's her secret?"

"Said she has nowt to thank but the fags, drink, and on-the-job activity."

"Aye," Fenella said, thinking. "Happen she is right; not that a medic would agree."

"Thing is, Guv, she still has ears like a bloody elephant. Hears everything, and was a close friend of Viv Gill."

"Oh aye? "Fenella felt her pulse quicken. Dexter had some news, and she sensed it was big. "And what did Old Barb tell you?"

"Not so much tell as show." A rumble echoed down the phone. "Still driving, but you have got to see this."

"Where are you?"

"Twelve minutes away."

He was at the door in five with a satchel slung over his shoulder.

They had to wait for Nan who fussed around Dexter like a mother hen. Not that he complained or gave the slightest hint that he had news. Once the scrambled eggs had been eaten and the second mug of coffee had been drained, Nan went back to bed.

Dexter opened the satchel and pulled out a laptop computer. He pecked at the keyboard, grunted, and pecked some more.

"From Old Barb's phone," he said. "She went to visit Viv Gill in St Bees a few months ago." With a brisk snort, he turned the screen so they could both see. "Barb got a snap of the Dragon with Viv Gill."

Fenella stared for half a minute. The grainy picture was of a couple: Viv Gill, tall, hair like Marilyn Monroe, with bright red lips and giant lashes. A low-cut blouse clung to her ample chest. She wore a tight black miniskirt and tottered on high heels. The man wore a crisp green suit with thin lapels and a dark tie with slant lines. A shadow covered the top part of his face, so his eyes were hidden. Sunken cheeks gave the impression that he was sucking hard on the thick cigar which hung from his lewd lips. It glowed bright at the tip. In the background, St Bees Priory door.

"Oh my God!" Fenella said in a breathless gasp. "Oh Christ!"

CHAPTER 74

"Is Old Barb sure this is the Dragon?"

Fenella stared at the laptop screen for the fifteenth time in the past ten minutes. She stood up, then sat down and rubbed a hand up the back of her head, wanting to tug hard to make sure she was awake and this wasn't some hideous dream. Since the death of Viv Gill, there'd been nowt but dead ends. Now they had a name and an image to go with their man, but she didn't like where it led. They would have to speak to Superintendent Jeffery, but Fenella wasn't in the mood to drive to Port St Giles. Not now.

Dexter jabbed at the screen with a thick finger. "He is with Viv Gill. He is wearing a green suit. He is smoking a thick cigar. Don't know if he has a fat wallet but if he does, it's not from his job." He leaned forward to peer at the screen as though he might be mistaken. After a moment, he shook his head. "Guv, I'll bet a bottle of Glenmorangie that he is the Dragon."

Fenella didn't take the bet. She stared once more at the image on the screen. It was impossible to see the eyes, but by the shape of the jaw, she knew it was him. They'd got their Dragon.

Dexter was speaking. "I suppose we ought to head out to Port St Giles, catch the superintendent when she arrives."

Fenella picked up the empty mugs, took them to the sink, and began to wash up. It felt as if she were only half awake in a nightmare that would not end well.

"The big boss will want to know," Dexter warned. "We'll not want to blindside her on this one, Guv. They don't call her Teflon Jeffery for nowt. Best let her know, else it will come back to bite us in the bum."

Fenella grabbed the washing-up liquid and gave it a hard squeeze. There was nothing to be washed now. It hit the sink with a hard splat. When she was a child, she had wanted to be a priest. Not a nun or even a monk but a priest. They got to peep behind the curtain of normal people's lives, to see their deep and dark secrets. It was the nosy gene, she supposed, and it came with a heavy price.

She dried her hands, then sat back down at the scrubbed-pine table. The first rays of the sun were still in hiding. It was going to be a long and difficult day.

She thought for a moment. "Let's drive to St Bees to haul him in before sunrise. I don't want to humiliate him in broad daylight."

Dexter said, "A good dose of public shame will keep the rest of the buggers in line. We ought to call a village meeting and march him down the lane with the crowds jeering like they did in the Middle Ages. "He looked away from the screen, eyes filled with rage. "Ain't nowt worse than a bent—"

Fenella raised her hand. "PC Hoon is still one of us. We'll bring him in under the cover of dark. If he is the Dragon, he'll pay the price. It is not our job to be judge and jury." Once again, she looked at the image on the laptop screen. It was PC Hoon; of that there was no doubt. He was the man in the green suit. He was the man with the fat cigar. PC Hoon was the Dragon. "We now know he knew Viv Gill, and he discovered her body, yet he didn't say a word about his relationship with her."

"It stinks, Guv." Dexter's voice dropped an octave. "I'd not want to live in his skin today or any other day from now on. His life will be a living hell. I'd not be able to take it, would rather be dead."

Fenella did not answer, but stood and approached the window. Darkness still clung on tight. Wisps of fog swirled in tight circles. When day broke, it would be grey and dull with a raw bite to the air. A day to pull up the sheets and stay in bed until it was over. It was the last day of PC Hoon's freedom—the first day of the rest of his wretched life.

"We'd best make a move," Fenella said.

"Yes, Guv." Dexter was at her side. "D'you think with a good lawyer, he might stay out of prison?"

Fenella shook her head. The story would be all over the national press. There'd be questions from their political masters. The Cumbria police had a code of ethical conduct. PC Hoon's behaviour fell well below the line.

Dexter said, "Don't like to kick a man when he is down, but I heard he and his wife are having problems."

"Oh, aye?" Fenella said. Dexter kept his ears close to the ground. "We talking about Maude?"

"She kicked him out, Guv. Not a happy split by all accounts. PC Hoon is living in a rented room. Lady by the name of Mrs Lenz takes in lodgers. Old-school and fierce. I know the address."

"Okay," Fenella said. "Let's bring him in."

They were outside in the sharp chill of the yard when Fenella's phone bleated with the ringtone of Superintendent Jeffery.

"Sallow, get yourself over to St Bees right now. There's been a fire. PC Hoon's house is ablaze."

CHAPTER 75

Fenella knew things were bad five miles from St Bees.

An orange glow lit the sky. It flared above the trees and spat streaks of hot light into the low clouds. A sign to show the way to PC Hoon's house, although the red and blue lights and wails of sirens were guide enough.

As Dexter pulled the car to the curb, they saw flames a-dance on the cottage roof. The blaze was much worse than they had imagined. Two fire trucks blocked the lane, so they got out and walked the last three hundred yards. Flames crackled and hissed with sharp popping sounds that jangled Fenella's nerves red raw. The thick stench of black smoke curled up her nostrils and hit the back of her throat. It was hard enough to breathe out in the lane. What would it be like inside the cottage?

A red-faced officer pushed the crowd back as he stretched police tape across the lane. Small groups stood and watched. Others peered from their windows. Flames raked the air and spread with such speed that even the firefighters seemed to be thrown back on their heels. On the main road a fire truck screamed.

They were at the tape. A constable Fenella did not know stood guard. She showed her warrant card and said, "There may be a woman in the house. Let the fire team know, will you?"

"Yes, ma'am." He spoke into his radio.

Fenella turned to Dexter. "Have a quiet word with the crowd; see if anyone saw anything."

He took out his notebook and strode to the nearest cluster of village folk. They crowded around him, eager to share what they knew with a man from the law.

Fenella turned back to watch the house. Smoke surged through swollen window frames; flames roared through the roof. If anyone came out of that inferno alive, it would be a miracle. *They can happen*, she told herself.

"Knew it would all end in tears," came a voice from behind.

Fenella turned to see an elderly woman in a long brown coat with a green headscarf, which covered her thin head like a shroud.

"Sorry?" Fenella said, taking in the woman's alert eyes. "Did you say something?"

"My Alf said it's the curse of Pow Beck. Those waters have been blighted ever since they washed King Arthur's bones into the Irish Sea. And with PC Hoon poking around into the death of Viv Gill and

Pearl Smith... well, it stands to reason his home would be consumed by fire and flames, doesn't it?"

Fenella smiled. She'd already taken the measure of the woman, and she liked what she saw. A gossip. "And to whom do I have the pleasure?"

"Mrs Lenz will do nicely." She smiled with false teeth too large for her small mouth. "I've known the Hoons for years."

"I'm Fenella." She held out her hand.

"I know who you are," Mrs Lenz said as she shook. "You're that top-dog detective from Port St Giles. I've heard all about you."

"Aye, happen you have, and you know I'm very interested in what goes on in this village. What can you tell me?"

Mrs Lenz tugged at her headscarf, glanced over her shoulder, and said, "It wasn't a happy marriage. Maude kicked PC Hoon out a few days ago, and he took a room in my place."

"Aye, I've heard as much."

"Well then, you'll have heard about his nasty little habits. Thought it would be nice to have the village bobby stay at my place until he got back on his feet. Boy, was I wrong."

"Go on, luv, I'm listening."

"I noticed coins going from my money jar." She lowered her voice. "I mark it with a faint pen, you see. Never happened before, only since PC Hoon moved in. Had to be him. Am I right? I am." Mrs Lenz pursed her lips. "Then there was the dark business he got up to in his room."

"How do you mean?"

"He smuggled food in, although I made it quite clear it is forbidden. And you should have seen the state he left the toilet. Smears and brown stains, and he used more than two sheets to wipe. I'll say no more!"

Fenella wondered how Mrs Lenz rented a room to anyone. She'd not want to lodge in the house. "I suppose there is a settling-in period, takes time to adjust to a new place."

"And just last night there was the foul language in his room. Swearing, he was. Words that would make a sailor blush. Terrified by my little Max, he was." She paused. "Max is my cockapoo, cute doggy."

"Oh, aye?" Fenella said.

"He'd been at the bottle too. Slurred like he'd been drinking gin and rum all day. Said he was going to get even with Maude. That he would teach her a lesson once and for all."

That got Fenella's attention. She said, "What exactly did he say?"

"I don't like to gossip."

"Aye, me neither," Fenella replied. "And?"

"PC Hoon said he would do unto Maude as he had done to the others."

"What did he mean by that?"

Mrs Lenz shrugged. "He said Maude would burn in hell when he was done with her." She gazed at the blackened house. "Drunken words come to life through the curse of Pow Beck."

Fenella said, "Is PC Hoon at your home now?"

"He went out, late. I heard him sneaking down the stairs after midnight. He has not been back to his room, and now this!"

Mrs Lenz shook her head and wandered back into the crowd.

Fenella scanned for Dexter. They had let PC Hoon slip through their fingers. He might be on the prowl anywhere, lurking in some dark corner to strike again. She felt sick to the pit of her stomach. A loud crack made her jump. She turned back to face PC Hoon's house. A plume of bright flames shot up at least twenty feet. The roof fell in with a roar. Black smoke spewed up and spread like a giant mushroom.

For an instant, there was only the sound of the wind shaking the trees and the lonely distant slap of the sea against the cliffs. Then a siren screamed and fine ash drifted down like snowflakes, coating the lane in soft grey. There'd be nowt left when the fire was done but blackened beams and twisted glass. *PC Hoon's home in ruins, like his life,* Fenella thought with a grim sigh.

She waved Dexter over and asked him to radio in a call that PC Hoon be picked up on sight. The cat would be out of the bag now. And she had not yet informed Jeffery. That would have to wait. And so would she.

Forty-five minutes dragged by before the firefighters got the blaze under control. Another hour after that, with the sun scowling through the trees, two entered the house in full gear with masks strapped tight to their heads.

Fenella stood alone at the police tape and watched. The soft scrunch of their boots gave her hope for what they might find. She thought of the child she had saved on the beach. Little Ann Lloyd was alive and well despite the odds. *Miracles do happen.* And for once she wished she had a police radio at her side so she could follow what was going on. But it was back in the Morris Minor, and she rarely used it anyway. For now, she was rooted to the spot, an oak tree of hope awaiting the worst of the storm.

Ten minutes later, the firefighters came out carrying a thin stretcher with a body bag on top. Her heart sank to a new low. Another death in St Bees. Could she have prevented it?

She sensed someone behind her and turned around.

Dexter said, "Just heard about the find on

the radio. "He glanced at the firefighters. They continued to pick their way to the ambulance, heads bowed. "It breaks my heart to say this, but it was for the best, Guv. PC Hoon can rest in peace now."

CHAPTER 76

Dr Joy Hall clutched the phone to her ear and stared with glum eyes through the hospital window. It was only 8:00 a.m. Thick, grey clouds loomed. They cast ominous shadows over the bleak grounds. Workers slouched along the path with their coats drawn tight. Visitors hunched against the cold chill. Veronica Jeffery's voice hissed in her ear.

"I don't understand. How did we get it so wrong?"

"I don't know," Joy replied. "But a copycat killing is not unheard of. There was a case in—"

"If this gets out, I'm finished."

"You are not to blame, Veronica." Joy waited a beat. "Are you sure PC Hoon is the killer?"

"We know Viv Gill met a man called the Dragon. We know that man was PC Hoon. We know he kept his relationship a secret."

"But still."

"We have a photo of PC Hoon in a suit and Viv Gill in a short skirt, low-cut top, and butterfly eyelashes. She was a sex worker, and they knew each other." Jeffery's voice squeaked as though in need of a stiff drink. "And he just split up with his wife. We are working on the assumption he went back to the home to torch the place."

"To get back at the wife?"

"And destroy the evidence." Jeffery's voice rose an octave. "They found PC Hoon's body in the basement near a box of handbags. We don't have all the details yet, but one, orange, has been identified as belonging to Mrs Pearl Smith and another, small and gold, belonged to Viv Gil. I'm thinking suicide. Keep that to yourself until we get a report back from forensics."

Joy said, "What did he have against Pearl Smith?"

"Like I said, we don't have all the details, but St Bees is a small village. I wouldn't be surprised if we found that PC Hoon held a grudge of some sort. What am I going to tell the top brass in Carlisle? How the hell am I going to tell them that PC Hoon is our man?"

Joy sucked in a breath and let it out slow. "Any chance of pinning the whole mess on Inspector Moss?"

Joy heard a sharp intake of breath, then the phone line went quiet. For a long moment, she thought she'd saved her friend's butt. Not that she gave two hoots about that. If Jeffery went down, it was her own lookout. Still, it would feel great to strike another blow against Moss. Hit him hard between the eyes and watch him spin.

"No. That dog won't bark," Jeffery said. "Moss is well clear of this mess."

"It is not your fault, Veronica. You are not to blame." But Joy knew Veronica's head was on the chopping block, and the axe was about to drop. It would be a great story to add to the last chapter of her book—"The Superintendent's Walk of Shame." That would grab the public's attention, get them flicking through the pages.

But was it worth sacrificing her friend?

Hell yes! Better her friend lose her neck than she ruin her future as a *New York Times* best-selling author. She felt her lips twitch at the corners. A moment later, they swelled into a grin.

"What am I to do, Joy?" Jeffery's thin voice screeched with wretched grief.

A wave of spite tugged at Joy's heart. A grudge which had been years in the making bubbled as sour as acid in her throat. The cow always thought she was superior: Teflon Jeffery, ha! She weren't nowt but rusted tin. Now, she'd be taken down a peg or two. And Joy would stand on the sidelines to cheer and write it all down in her secret book.

Jeffery was talking. "What do you suggest, Joy? What should I do?"

Joy put on her bosom-friend voice. "Please

don't feel bad. PC Hoon had inside information and used that to fool everyone. How could you have known what he held in his heart?"

Again, the line fell quiet. Joy knew what that meant. Jeffery was in deep thought, her mind searching for a way out. But with a police officer on her team as the killer, there was no way out. She'd have to carry the can.

"Difficult," Jeffery said at last. "Bloody difficult."

Now, Joy's mind began to whir. If the public found out she was involved in this fiasco, it would tank sales of her book. The publisher might even demand their advance back. But the money had been spent on the new house. She couldn't repay. No! As long as she kept her mouth shut, the blood splattered on the wall would be Jeffery's. She felt a deep sense of relief and something else—satisfaction.

"Time to face the music," Joy said in the sweet girly voice she used to encourage patients to talk about their darkest secrets. "It will lift a weight from your chest. You know that is for the best."

"I can't do that."

Joy let her voice drop to a conspiratorial whisper. "Go see the top brass in Carlisle, hands up, palms wide. Tell them you cocked it up." She made it all sound easy. Sweet, like eating a bowl of ice cream. No more bother than a visit to the doctor. "They'll show mercy, Veronica. They like you. We all do. You can do it, and I'll come with you for support. Let's face the music together. Team Superwomen."

That wasn't enough, though. Now, Joy needed to nail the coffin lid shut. She thought for a moment. Yes. She'd ask that her involvement in the case remain a secret. That way, no one would know. Ever. And when she went with Veronica to meet the top brass in Carlisle, she'd feign illness at the door and urge her friend on. Lamb to the slaughter. Later, when the tears fell, she'd be there to wail and cry too.

Jeffery cleared her throat and said, "The headlines won't look good, Joy. 'PC Scissorhands Takes His Own Life, While Prison Psychologist Gets It All Wrong!' You'll be ruined."

"What?"

"You told us Mr Shred was the killer. That he was stalking St Bees. You got it wrong. Not to mention your assessment of PC Hoon. 'Exemplary,' if my memory serves me well. When this leaks out, you'll be roasted alive. Dear God, Joy, I'll do my best to save you. I really will."

Joy stared at the phone for a long moment before placing it back to her ear. They called her friend Teflon Jeffery. Now, she understood why. She stared through the French doors at the hospital grounds, speechless.

"We'll have to play the sympathy card," Jeffery said. "Get you in front of the cameras."

"I want my involvement to remain off the record."

Jeffery didn't miss a beat. "Nah, can't do that. Tell you what, though. I'll spin the accident angle. The blaze was just another of those cottage fires we've seen lately. An act of God. That will buy a few days to get to the bottom of this mess."

"And what if that doesn't work?"

"We go to Plan B. That is where you come in, Joy."

"If I go public with my role here, it will ruin my boo—" Joy stopped and cursed herself for almost revealing her secret. If it came out she had a book deal, Jeffery would be all over her like a bad rash: the prison service would kick her out; she'd be finished.

Then an idea struck.

The solution to her current problem was an easy fix. Very easy.

Detective Inspector Fenella Sallow.

Sallow was in charge of the investigation. Let her carry the can of blame. Yes! All it needed was a bit of spin, and the crap would fall squarely on Sallow's head. Jeffery was good at spin, a master at it. She'd float the solution with her friend. It would be easy, and Jeffery would agree. She liked Fenella, but it was everyone for themselves now. Of course, they would need time to work out the details. The perfect set-up could not be rushed.

Joy exhaled in relief and said, "I have an idea. Let's think about this."

"I already have. There is a press conference at noon. A car will be around to pick you up. Be ready by eleven. And Joy, ask the nice nurses to wrap fresh bandages around your face. We'll need you to look like an Egyptian mummy if we go to Plan B. I'll do the talking, but if things go south, I'll have you wheeled out. If they ask you any questions, put on your little-girly voice, will you?"

CHAPTER 77

More than twenty journalists gathered in St Bees Priory. It was bright and warm inside the church hall. At the front, a giant crucifix was suspended from the ceiling, and the stained glass filtered in the near-noon light. A large crew from the BBC's *Look North* news show took up the first pew. The deaths in St Bees would be all over the airwaves soon. A shed load of crap to hit the fan.

Fenella seethed. As soon as the media circus was over, she'd gather more facts, pay her sympathies to PC Hoon's wife, and chase down loose ends about Viv Gill and Pearl Smith—all that had been put on hold for the press conference. The past few days they'd run round in circles. It felt like they had dreamt their way through the entire case and missed the most important clue. One of their own was pegged as a copycat killer. PC Hoon worked his tricks right under her nose. And that's what fired her fury.

On a raised stage at the front of the hall, Tess Allen spoke into Superintendent Jeffery's ear. Tess was the press officer who faced the media when things got tough. They sat at a long bench, which looked like a scrap dragged in from the sea. What was going to happen here? How would Jeffery spin it so the crap didn’t stick?

Nothing but the wave of a magician's wand, Fenella thought. She scanned the room. Where was Vicar Briar? She double-checked. He wasn’t in the room. She thought he'd want to be centre stage, given they were in his church. Strange.

With a frustrated sigh, she sat with her team on the back row: Dexter, Jones, and PC Beth Finn. A show of support for her troops. She glanced at Dexter. His head bobbed, and he gave a sharp snort. The team were tired. They'd given everything and got back nowt but a fistful of ash.

The superintendent peered at the press and licked her lips. She was a great grey wolf and the journalists her prey. *She better make quick work of them,* Fenella thought, *or they'll rip her limb from limb.*

It was noon. Time to begin. Reporters still streamed in. Standing room only. Fenella felt as if she were at a theatre show in Carlisle. The curtain would soon rise and the actors would take their places. Everything was set up for the perfect performance, everyone knowing their lines.

And in a side room, Dr Joy Hall waited in a wheelchair, her head wrapped into a huge globe. She'd be wheeled out if things turned sour. There was nothing wrong with Dr Hall's legs and only a few scratches on her face. *Nowt but a bleedin' show*, Fenella thought.

Tess Allen stood. An excited murmur rippled through the hall.

"Okay," Tess said. "We'll keep this brief. Let's start, shall we?"

Tess nodded at Jeffery.

"Good afternoon," Jeffery said. "Thank you for coming at such short notice. I am grateful to see so many friends from the media. Our job could not be done without your support. As you know, we are here to..."

At that moment, Fenella turned to look at the back of the hall. A hunched figure in a dirty, green duffel coat scurried through the thick oak door and weaved through the crowd with the stealth of a rat.

Rodney Rawlings.

And he looked mad.

CHAPTER 78

Dr Joy Hall felt her stomach flip, and her pulse thudded so hard she could barely think. It didn't help that the room had no window. A view might have steadied her nerves. There were four brick walls painted in dull grey and two doors. One led to the main hall of St Bees Priory; the other led outside to a path which snaked around the side of the building. A large mahogany bench sat in the centre of the room. Coat stands on wheels waited patiently on either side. It was a cloakroom of sorts. Hot. Humid. Oppressive.

She sat in a wheelchair designed for an elephant. It swallowed Joy, so she looked like a china doll in a child's pram. A superb choice for making her look sick and frail. She shifted in her seat and stared at the outline of the police officer through the glass pane of the outside door. She knew his name. Jake Kent. He carried a gun. What had she got herself into? What had she done?

Joy gazed at the old speaker that jutted from the wall next to a brass plaque:

DOMINUS DEUS TUUS IGNIS CONSUMENS EST.

The Lord your God is a consuming fire. Deuteronomy 4:24

The speaker crackled into life. Jeffery sounded calm, confident, assured. But that did not slow the thud in Joy's chest or the rush of blood through her ears. If her friend got it right, nothing would stick, and no one would know she was here. But if it all turned sour, she'd be wheeled out and would have to act out the biggest role of her life. Suddenly she couldn't breathe, only stare at the speaker and listen.

"And now I'll take a few questions," Jeffery said.

"Gay Smith, *BBC Look North*. Any victims?"

"Yes," Jeffery replied in a crisp tone. "One death. A well-loved police officer, PC Sidney Hoon. He was a family man with a wife. No children. An exemplary officer who will be missed."

Joy didn't need to see Jeffery's face. She'd seen the smug grin the first time they'd met in college. The slight tug at the corners, the wolfish glint of the eyes. Jeffery was working the crowd and winning, had the dozy journalists in the palm of her hands. Joy should have felt good about that. She didn't. It irked her when Jeffery won. She let out a breath she didn't know she was holding.

The speaker continued to crackle with Jeffery's voice. Another cottage fire. Another relic of historic Cumbria gone. A tragic accident that had left the village in shock. Hadn't there been a string of fires in old stone cottages?

It sounded good. Jeffery's plan was working. Still, Joy wished she could see the hall with her own eyes. Just to make sure.

Relax.

Yes. She would get through this without a scratch. She still had her job in the prison service, still had the big money contract for the book. And there was plenty of time to write the last chapter. She could do it. Everything was going to turn out fine. No one would know what she'd done.

She closed her eyes and was in a giant bookstore in New York City. A bright room where hordes of eager book buyers lined up to get their copy signed. The soft tinkle of a piano carried over the excited hum of the crowd. There was a red carpet too, the air filled with the sweet scent of expensive perfume, and she sat at an oak desk, like a queen on her throne. It all played out like a movie in her mind.

It was as her heart slowed that Rodney Rawlings's voice hissed through the speaker.

"Are you saying the fire was an accident?"

"We have seen house fires across the coastal towns," Jeffery replied, her voice smooth. "Old beams, dry wood, and no smoke alarm. But it is the subject of an ongoing—"

"Not arson, then?" Rodney Rawlings said, his voice filled with the sly shrill of a weasel. "Have forensics ruled it out?"

"I can't comment on that."

"I've been told PC Hoon took his own life. Can you confirm that?"

"No comment."

"Is there a link to the murders of Viv Gill and Pearl Smith?"

Jeffery hesitated. "There has been a spate of house fires, and this appears to—"

"Is this attack related to Mr Shred?"

At the mention of Mr Shred, all hell broke loose. Here was a fresh news angle. Reporters yelled with the sharp yowls of a pack of dogs.

"Gay Smith, *BBC Look North*. Are the public in danger?"

Another shouted, "What can people do to protect their families?"

And yet another. "How many more deaths before you catch the fiend?"

"One at a time, please," came the tense voice of Tess Allen. "We will answer every question, but one at a time, please."

Joy began to sweat. First on her palms, then it dripped from her brow to sting her eyes. Within moments, she sat in the cloying dampness of a fear-filled swamp. Soon she'd have to put on her girly voice. But with Jeffery on the rocks, she wasn't sure she could pull it off.

Suddenly Rodney Rawlings's voice carried above the yelps of the pack.

"Can you tell us about the team running the investigation?"

"You know I can't discuss operational matters," Jeffery replied.

"Is Dr Joy Hall on the team?"

"No comment."

"You and she go way back, have a monthly pow-wow, good friends?"

"What is your point?"

"Are you aware Dr Hall has signed a big-dollar contract for a book about the hunt for Mr Shred?" Rodney Rawlings paused but only for a beat. "Has your friend cut you in on the deal? Can you comment on that?"

Another round of yelps from the pack. Wild. Savage. Out for the kill.

"This meeting is over," Jeffery yelled.

CHAPTER 79

It was quiet in the cloakroom.

Except for the hiss of the speaker as it relayed the sounds of folks leaving St Bees Priory hall. The day had broken with a glint of hope, but now melancholia weighed on Dr Joy Hall's shoulders. What could she do? What would she say? There had to be a way out.

She stared at the door that led to the hall and waited for Veronica Jeffery to appear.

Her mind was racing. She couldn't run; there was nowhere to hide, although both childish impulses gripped her tight. No! She could do better than that. She had a brain as sharp as a blade. There had to be another way. Then, as she felt the rapid thud of her heart against her tight chest, she found it. A glint in the dark.

Yes! She'd tell Jeffery she'd made a big mistake. Throw herself on her friend's mercy. The two had been a team for years. Together, they moved through their careers to get to the top. They were superwomen. Ball breakers. But even superheroes make mistakes, right?

The door eased open.

Here we go, Joy told herself. Then her mouth dropped open.

"Been a rough few days for you, luv?" Fenella said.

"Where is Veronica?"

"Why don't the two of us talk first, eh?"

But she had to speak with Veronica. Had to get to her fast, before the detective made life difficult with her questions.

Joy said, "Listen, it's not what you think."

"Tell me what it is, then, pet?"

Joy stared at the detective. The woman had such a soft face, and those eyes were so welcoming, like a priest. She'd not be fooled, though. She used the same soft voice and sad eyes when she wanted the men in Low Marsh Prison to talk.

"I've nothing to say."

"Rodney Rawlings says you sold us out."

"He's a liar! Rodney Rawlings is a liar." Joy could not stop herself. The room spun. She fought for control. If she lost it, she was done. No! There was no way she'd admit anything. The rat-faced reporter had no evidence. Not unless he'd got a copy of her contract, and that was impossible. It was top secret. The publisher wouldn't share it with anyone. It was just a guess by the rodent. She'd ride it out.

They only had the word of Rawlings. If she played it cool, there was still a chance. No one had anything on her. How could they?

Fenella looked at Joy for a long while. Then her lips quirked at the corners. "So, you don't have a book deal?"

"The only time I put pen to paper is to write psychological reports."

"Tell me about the attack."

"It was a blur. I recall nothing."

"We all thought it was Mr Shred. You convinced us of that."

"Someone tried to kill me!"

"Dr Kendi says it's nowt but a few scratches, self-inflicted. She has seen worse on Friday night when the youngsters drink too much and let it out in a brawl. Why don't you tell me what happened? You will feel so much better."

"I'm not a child!" Joy spat the words. Her left hand jerked in a slashing movement, right to left as she tore at the bandages on her face. "I'm a psychologist and your superior! Do you have a doctorate degree? I won't be talked down to; do you hear me?"

"Yes, luv. I hear you." Fenella paused a beat. "And since you are a doctor, you know it will help you feel better to talk. Come on, get it off your chest. What happened that night?"

Joy stood. "I have to speak with Veronica."

"Sit down, Dr Hall!"

Joy slowly sat. She felt like she was in a deep pit. The detective was throwing in sand so fast, it was up to her neck, and her body couldn't move. She had to think fast, outwit the cow, and get to see her friend. Veronica would know what to do. Veronica would save her. Now she grasped at the tactic the men in Low Marsh Prison used when they didn't want to open up.

"I have nothing more to say."

Fenella's voice turned harsh. "You knew about Viv Gill's letters to Hamilton Perkins, knew about his letters from Pearl Smith, knew everything about the man. After all, you spent years crawling about in his mind. I think you knew he wasn't in St Bees and led us on a wild-goose chase. Where were you the night Viv Gill died? And Pearl Smith? We know she died before we began our watch of Hemlock Woods. Where were you?"

Joy couldn't breathe. She knew the question was asked to provoke a reaction. An ominous, low grumble of rage grew, but she had to stay calm. There was still a way out of this mess, and she would find it even if she had to crawl on her hands and knees.

Joy said, "I want to speak with Veronica."

"How much did the book folks pay you for the

story?"

"It's a bunch of lies."

"Was it worth it, luv, selling your soul for a handful of coins?"

"I can't believe you are asking me that," Joy shouted. "What do you take me for? I feel like I've suddenly been attacked by a person I trust and respect."

"Three people are dead, luv. It's my job to ask questions. Tell me about this book deal?"

"I do not have a book deal." Joy scrabbled to control herself but knew it was only a matter of time before she totally lost it. "How many more times do I have to say that? Rodney Rawlings is full of crap."

"Aye, you might be right on that." Fenella broke out into a grin. "It'll be easy enough to check, though. I've asked that nice Detective Constable Jones to have a word with your bank manager. You remember Jones, don't you? He's young and handsome, a whizz with numbers. If we don't see a big payment into your bank account from a book publisher, that would clear things up, wouldn't it?"

Joy stared but did not speak. Her throat felt as if it were filled with dry sand. Sweat prickled on her forehead. Five seconds of silence. Her mind raced. There had to be a way out. Ten. Fifteen. She slumped into the wheelchair and sobbed.

Fenella said, "Aye, lass, let it all out. When you

are done, we can talk."

Joy couldn't control the tears. It wasn't her fault. She was an undiscovered genius who the world needed to hear. Her book would light the path, and now this no-mark detective was trying to take her birthright away. Suddenly she became still.

"Listen, there is a way out of this." She dried her eyes and stared at Fenella. "A win-win for both of us."

"Go on, I'm listening."

"Let's face it, we are both public servants. And you and I both know what servants get paid—peanuts." Joy let her voice drop to a whisper. "That's what they feed to monkeys. Let's forget about this book deal nonsense... twenty percent."

"Twenty percent, luv?"

"Okay, thirty. What do you say?" Joy held her breath and watched the detective. "You'll be able to buy a new car and ditch that ancient Morris Minor."

An eerie silence followed. Ten seconds. Twenty. Half a minute.

Fenella said, "I don't suppose you have heard, but since you are on the team, I thought I should tell you about the news. We've not let on to the public or press yet, as the details came in not long ago. The firefighters found PC Hoon's body behind the bolted door of the basement. He was locked in, luv. Then the place set on fire. It wasn't suicide. It was murder.

I'd not want to be part of that for any price."

"No... I... I have to speak with Veronica. Please!"

"I'm sorry, pet. Superintendent Jeffery told me to say goodbye."

Stunned, Joy jumped to her feet and screamed, "I'm not saying anything else. I want a solicitor. I want to speak with a lawyer."

"Aye, luv. I thought you'd say that." The outside door opened. Dexter strode in with Constable Jake Kent. "How about you take a ride to Port St Giles with these young men, and we'll all have a nice chat later in the police station."

CHAPTER 80

On an impulse, Chad Tate closed the store and strolled in the crisp afternoon air across the village to Don's Café. He sat by the window and ordered a King Kong fry-up. It was a celebration of sorts. A greasy meal to mark the passing of PC Hoon. He glanced down at his bulging gut and realised he'd had too many fry-ups in the past few days. One for Viv Gill, another for Pearl Smith, and now for the village bobby.

Chad glanced at his watch, then glanced at the calendar on the café wall. It was Thursday, a little after two, his usual time to visit the café. What he thought was impulse was, in fact, the knee-jerk of his regular routine. He always came to Don's on Thursdays at two o'clock. Always ordered a King Kong fry-up. He gazed at the menu. He'd order something different next time.

A sharp tap on the window caused him to look up. A woman's face peered through the glass, slender, with long, grey hair and sharp eyes: Inspector Sallow. What did she want?

Before he collected his thoughts, she was standing at his table and talking. "I thought you might be in here. Thursday at two, as regular as clockwork, that's what I heard on my first visit at this café. Mind if I join you?" Fenella didn't wait for an answer, sat down, and glanced at the menu. "Black coffee over here, Don."

"Righto," came the reply, although Don was out of sight in the kitchen.

Fenella stared at Chad for a long while. At last, she said, "A little bird tells me you called in the fire at PC Hoon's cottage."

Chad didn't want to talk about it. Felt sick. Still, he sensed he would not get away with silence. Not with those sharp eyes watching him. He felt his pulse pound in his neck and said, "The fire caught hold so fast. Flames as tall as the trees. There was nothing I could do, except wait for the fire truck and watch."

"Odd that I did not see you in the crowd when I arrived," Fenella said. "Most folk would hang about to see what happened and give a statement to the police. Not you, though. You scampered off into the night."

It was true. He'd not hung about long after the police arrived. No way. He glanced at the kitchen as if anxious for his King Kong fry-up, but his stomach roiled like an acid-filled sea. She knew. He sensed it deep in his bones. His eyes drifted to his hands.

Don appeared and placed the mug in front of Fenella. "None of my business, but I saw Maude

Hoon heading towards the priory. A broken woman. So sad." He hurried back to the kitchen.

Fenella took a sip, then said, "I read the report about your—"

"That is all"—Chad lifted his eyes and held her gaze—"in the past."

"But not forgotten, eh?"

He glanced back down at the tablecloth. "I'm not a violent man. I regret what I did in the church, paid for the damage, apologised for my foul language. What more could I do?"

Fenella waited. She was good at the wait.

Chad said, "I think about them every day."

"Your wife and daughter?"

"We were only married seven years when they were killed. A hit-and-run outside St Bees Priory. Only four in the afternoon, but in November it was as dark as midnight." He lifted his eyes and once again held Fenella's gaze. "The police never found the driver."

"Aye, luv, I read all about it in the file. That's what the fête at the end of the month at St Bees Priory is about. I saw the poster in your shop window. Lark's Wish Fund, eh?"

"Lark was only five years old when she was taken from me," Chad said. "Raven-black hair, always tied with a pink bow. She wanted to join the St

Bees Girl's Brigade but was too young. And she knew what she wanted to do when she grew up—become an officer for the coastguard. I think 'ship' was her next word after mummy and daddy."

"I see," Fenella said and waited.

"Lark's Wish is my way to honour her memory," Chad said. "This is its first year, and I wanted to raise enough to send 10 five-year-old girls to the coastguard science retreat in Prestwick." Chad dabbed his eyes. "We've had such a large response to our appeal for funds that the bank manager has been sending me statements every day. I've a stack of white envelopes under the counter in the store. It blows my mind how generous folks are. We've enough to pay for the installation of life rings along the beach as well as send twenty kids. We are only a small village. I'm not sure there will be enough takers, so I've ordered a dozen boxes of celery soda-flavoured lollipops from New York to help sweeten the deal. Encourage a few more kids to sign up, boys too. And I've got a freezer full of New York cherry ice cream and all-beef hot dogs. I think Lark would approve of that."

Chad cried.

Fenella waited. Don poked his head from the kitchen, gave her a sad look, dabbed at his eyes, and went back to work. A whistle drifted across the café. It came from the kitchen. Don. The melancholy tune touched a nerve of sadness in Fenella's heart: the

Prince song "When Doves Cry." She thought of Eve. There was a chance her sister was alive. Rose and Lark Tate were gone forever.

Chad wiped his eyes. "I'm sorry. I've not been myself lately. Since Rose and Lark's death, I've been more watchful. Keeping an eye to see if any cars are speeding through the village. I don't want what happened to me to destroy another family. Don't want another child killed at the hands of a reckless driver. Not in St Bees. Not in my part of England." He looked out the café window. A truck rumbled along the lane, well within the speed limit. When it passed, he continued. "The mention of the police file set me off. It seems like yesterday and forever ago at the same time. I didn’t think the police did anything, let alone write a report."

"Aye, pet, we always write reports. Even if nowt comes of them today, there is always tomorrow." Fenella touched his arm. "I have to ask a difficult question. Goes with the job."

"Fire away."

"I also read about your allegations. You thought the driver was PC Hoon, didn't you?"

"It was him, but I could never prove it."

"And you show up at his burning cottage last night?"

"I was the one who phoned for help."

"Why were you outside his house?"

Chad didn’t miss a beat. "I've lived in the village a long time, cherish the memories of my wife and daughter. I'll never leave this place now and have a burial plot in the priory. But I thought it was about time that I found a new wife. A woman who wanted to spend the rest of her days in the village with me. Slim pickings, really."

"Go on, I'm listening."

"I'm an early riser. I open the store at six a.m. It is normal for me to be up and about early. I enjoy the quiet." Chad sighed. "I spend every evening watching grainy videos of my wife and daughter, obsessive, I know. But I miss my wife, Rose. Would love to marry again and have another daughter. But I'm a bit of a disaster with the opposite sex."

He fell silent. Fenella waited.

"I left the scene because I had a relationship with Maude Hoon," Chad said in a soft whisper. "I thought she wanted to be my wife, but she had her sights on bigger things."

"I see." Fenella sipped her coffee, but her eyes never left his face.

Chad wanted to explain. Speaking with the detective was like confessional with a priest. "On Monday evening, I closed the shop early and went to visit Maude because I heard PC Hoon had moved out. We had become close, and I thought it was a chance to grow our relationship, but she told me it was over."

"How long had you been seeing her?"

"Long enough for it to mean something to me." He paused for a moment, swallowed hard. "Listen, theirs wasn't a happy marriage. Maude deserved better. PC Hoon was... well, I won't speak ill of the man now he is dead."

"But Mrs Hoon broke off the relationship with you on Monday?"

"She is going to marry Mr Clarke, the bank manager." Chad sighed. "I went to speak with Maude this morning, see if I could persuade her to change her mind. Mr Clarke is a ladies' man. You know he had a fling with Pearl Smith? Doubt if there is a single woman in the village who he has not bagged."

Fenella said, "Do you know if Mr Clarke had a relationship with Viv Gill?"

"I've heard rumours," Chad said mysteriously. He shook his head. "I don't see how he and Maude will last. Yes, he drives a big car, but life above a village store has its merits."

"King Kong fry-up," Don said, placing a large platter in front of Chad. "On the house, my American friend. Enjoy." He wandered back to the kitchen, whistling.

Fenella said, "Mrs Hoon wasn't in when you arrived at the cottage?"

"I didn't have the nerve to knock. When I visited on Monday, she was with Mr Clarke. He was wearing a blue bathrobe and pink socks, nothing else. So this time I just watched the cottage for a while, not sure for how long. Then I saw the flames and panicked that Maude was inside. I would have gone into the house to save her, but the fire was too fierce by the time I got to the door. That's when I called the fire service."

"Did you know PC Hoon was in the house?"

"I was shocked to hear you found his body. I thought he had a room with Mrs Lenz."

"Aye, so did I," Fenella said. "So you didn't see PC Hoon go into the house?"

"No."

"Or anyone leave the cottage?"

He looked away. "No."

"Do you know Dr Joy Hall?"

"No."

"She works in Low Marsh Prison."

"I've never met her."

Fenella thought for a moment, then said, "And Vicar Briar?"

"What about him?"

"You didn't see him at the Hoon cottage this morning?"

"I did not."

Fenella glanced through the window into the

lane. A jay fluttered onto the pavement, walked a few paces and stretched its wings before taking to the air in a flash of black and blue. She watched it until it disappeared behind a roof. The last pieces of the puzzle had just fallen into place.

She gave a sad smile and said, "I'll send PC Finn to your store to take a formal statement later today." She stood. "Oh, and when you speak with her, I suggest you tell the truth. It's a criminal offense to give a false witness statement, not a kindness."

CHAPTER 81

Fenella would like to have stayed in Don's Café and gobble down a King Kong fry-up. It had been a long day, and she was starving. But she had to get back to Port St Giles to interview Dr Joy Hall, and there were a few more tasks left to do in St Bees.

Still, she took her time as she strolled through the village. At the Pow Beck bridge, she stopped to watch the water rush along the bed of the stream. This was where it all began. Where Viv Gill was killed. They thought it was the work of Hamilton Perkins; now they all knew better.

"Dr Joy Hall," she said to the chill air. "How could you have been so... stupid!"

She sent a text to PC Beth Finn. A moment later came the reply. Yes, she was still in St Bees. Fenella replied and then said a prayer for Viv Gill and Pearl Smith and PC Hoon. She'd not let the killer get away. Her team would tie the case up so tight, there was no chance the bugger would be able to wriggle out of the charges, no matter how fancy the lawyer.

She walked the scenic route to St Bees Priory.

A puff of grey smoke curled from the

entrance. Vicar Briar's deep-set, dark eyes watched, but he remained in the shadows.

"Can I have a word?" Fenella said.

He stepped from dark to light. His cassock wasn't the cleanest.

"Detective Sallow," he said in a cautious tone. "To what do I owe this pleasure?"

"You made yourself pretty scarce at the press conference," Fenella said. "Thought you would be centre stage, given that it took place in your church."

"A man of the cloth is always on the move." The vicar blew out a plume of smoke; it curled in tight circles upwards, then faded into the still air. "There were other pressing things to be done. A man of the cloth meets death every day. There have been many in this village. Viv Gill and Pearl Smith's deaths broke my heart. They had many years ahead. Good years, I hoped." He took another pull on the cigar and let the smoke out slow. "And there was the death of Rose and Lark Tate. Such a waste of life. And no one charged. That's why I encouraged Chad Tate to pull the positive from his bleak experience."

Fenella said, "The Lark's Wish Fund?"

"I told Chad to treat fundraising as a business. Come over as professional, radio interviews, newspapers, television and so on. If things heat up, he'll have to travel the county and beyond, speak at church halls, share his experience. He is not keen on leaving the village. But I urged him to do it for Rose and Lark. He was reluctant at first, but is coming around."

"I see," Fenella said and waited.

"I had a prearranged meeting with the bishop in Whitehaven at noon today. Lark's Wish was on the agenda. That's why I missed the press conference in my own church."

"And the bishop can confirm this?"

"Of course." He took another pull on the cigar. "There were five other vicars in the meeting. Time does not stand still. I can watch the highlights on the news."

"Aye, happen you're right," Fenella replied. "It'll be the top story for a while."

Vicar Briar's eyes turned sad. "PC Hoon wasn't a regular, but I saw Maude often enough." He glanced at the thick oak doors of the priory." We spoke a little. She is still inside."

"I'd best give my condolences," Fenella said, sorrow tugging at her heart. "It's the least I can do."

CHAPTER 82

It was dark and cold inside the church hall. The stained glass filtered in the dreary light, splattered with colours of the rainbow. There were no signs of the press conference. No microphones or cameras. Just the dust-spotted pews with the altar at the front and a giant crucifix suspended from the ceiling. Maude Hoon sat on the front row, headscarf so tight it etched the pattern of the curlers underneath. Her head was bowed in silent contemplation. She did not look up at the sound of the door or the soft slap of Fenella's footsteps on the hard stone floor.

Fenella approached the front pew so filled with doubt that she sucked in a breath and let it out slowly. What do you say to a wife who has lost their husband? Nothing. But there were other words that she had to say. Words that would shatter Maude Hoon's world. And it was best to say them now before it all came out in the news headlines. Get it over with.

"Mind if I sit with you for a bit, luv?" Fenella spoke in a hush. It felt right, given the surroundings.

Maude glanced at her for a moment. There

was no recognition in her mud-brown eyes. She nodded. Then bowed her head once more.

Fenella waited. Yes, this was the woman she'd met at the Christmas do in Whitehaven three years back. She thought Maude and PC Hoon were an odd couple back then. And with the events of last night, felt a deep sorrow.

One minute. Two. Three. Then she said, "I'm Inspector Sallow, worked with your husband."

Maude's neck jerked straight. A strange movement as if a bolt of electricity tightened her muscles.

"Oh, aye," she said. "He mentioned you."

Fenella said, "I've some bad news, pet."

"He's dead, how much worse can it get?" Maude frowned. "I'm sorry, that sounds callous. I have a heart. I do. It's just that Sid and I didn’t exactly see eye to eye."

Fenella leaned forward, her eyes fixed on Maude's face. "I know this is going to come as a shock to you, but your husband was murdered."

Again came the spasm in Maude's neck. "You're crazy! I don't believe it. Who would want to kill that lazy sod?"

"He was found in the basement of your cottage, pet. The door was bolted, so he could not get out."

"I can't tell you how many times I've been trapped in that damp basement. Sid was too tight fisted to get it fixed. Now, look what's happened!"

"You two didn't get along," Fenella said. "It's nothing personal, pet. I have to ask, you understand?"

"Oh, I understand. As a matter of fact, we split up a few days ago. I'm going to remarry."

"Really?"

"Don't look so shocked. Sid and I were finished years ago. I suppose we stuck it out for the image. Now his miserable life is over. I wonder why I waited so long."

"Why'd you come to church, luv?"

Maude shrugged. "You got me there. Yes, it is for the image. Old habits die hard and anyway I want to keep the vicar sweet. I'd like to get married in this church." She paused. "I suppose I should ask about Sid's murder. Have you caught the killer?"

"Aye, lass."

Maude's back stiffened, eyes round as bronze coins. "Name?"

Fenella said, "It will all come out with time."

"What was their motive?"

"It is greed that pulls us to dark places. Of money. Of prestige. Of another person. Always greed." Fenella felt a twitch in her neck and tilted her head from side to side. "For a while I thought I'd missed it. Then I thought, it has got to be the money."

"What money?"

"That's what I couldn't figure out until the fire." Fenella looked at Maude. "It's as old as the hills, luv. Marrying a man to move up in life. I don't know all the details of why you killed Viv Gill or Pearl Smith or your husband yet, but I'd bet a good bottle of Glenmorangie it was greed."

"What are you saying?"

"Soon forensics will come back with the details. We know the fire was started deliberately. Did you use petrol or light a match to a pile of kindling?"

Maude looked as if she were going to cry. It lasted for a second. "You can't prove anything. I know how the police work; I was married to one of the buggers. Now, if you have any evidence, we can talk, else I'd ask you show some respect for the house of God."

"Funny thing is, I heard a rumour that you were close to Chad Tate but ditched him for Mr Clarke, the bank manager. Pretty nice catch for an ambitious girl. But the crafty dog gets around a bit. I heard he was in a relationship of sorts with Viv Gill… and Pearl Smith. Don't suppose you would like that, not if you had your eyes set on marrying the man. Eliminate the competition and move up the food chain, eh?"

"Don't be daft. Those women were killed by Mr Shred."

"How would you know that?"

"Sid told me."

Suddenly everything fell into place. There was no doubt in Fenella's mind now. She broke out into a full smile.

"You wrote to Hamilton Perkins, didn't you? You were the third woman!"

Maude pursed her lips, but her eyes gave away the truth.

The church door opened. PC Beth Finn stepped through the doorway with Vicar Briar two paces behind.

Fenella said, "PC Finn, will you read Mrs Maude Hoon her rights. We're bringing her in for the murders of Viv Gill, Pearl Smith, and PC Sid Hoon."

CHAPTER 83

Late that night, Fenella sat at the desk in Superintendent Jeffery's office. The winter dark had long since crept over the town of Port St Giles, and fog hovered like a great grey sheet over the police station.

"Don't think we'll get a confession," Fenella said. "Maude Hoon hasn't said much, even in the presence of her lawyer."

"I see," said Jeffery thoughtfully. She tapped a finger on the large brown folder on her desk and slowly got to her feet and walked across the room to the window, so her back was to Fenella. For a long time she stood there against the faded glow of a street lamp which shone its weak, sulphurous rays through the small window. There was a sadness to her posture. A deep sorrow hung in the still office air. "Pity. Would have been nice to wrap it up in a bow."

Fenella said, "Aye. But we'll secure a conviction even if she seals her lips tight with superglue." She paused a moment, considering, but did not speak of the elephant in the room—Dr Joy Hall. "I set Jones to work on Maude Hoon's financials, and he has already come back with a hit."

Jeffery turned. "Go on."

"Mrs Hoon recently took out a life insurance policy in the name of her husband, and the signature does not match with the one we have on record for PC Sid Hoon."

"A good lawyer will find a reasonable explanation," Jeffery said.

"Happen. Happen not," Fenella replied. "But it will take a damn good lawyer to explain away the blades found in the basement by PC Hoon's body. We believe they were the murder weapon and were fashioned after the knives used by Hamilton Perkins. We know Maude Hoon corresponded with Perkins, and we are dealing with a copycat killer."

"Still, without a confession... it is all circumstantial."

Fenella said, "We have an eyewitness. Mr Chad Tate. He saw the flames, ran to the front door as Maude Hoon hurried from the house and climbed over a fence. She didn't see him in her haste to get away. But he saw her and tried to deny it at first. He has signed a statement. And Mr Pete Clarke, the bank manager, has confirmed Maude Hoon didn't show up at his house until the early hours of this morning. We have enough to press charges."

Jeffery turned to stare at the window, and Fenella knew it was time to address the elephant. She said, "And Dr Joy Hall?"

"What about her?"

"I hear she has hired an expensive lawyer."

"I have not spoken with that woman. But if you say so."

"Don't know how she can afford it." Fenella's lips quirked at the corners. "Not on her pay."

Jeffery's voice dropped to a whisper as though she were speaking to herself. "Can't keep a secret long in this place, can we?"

"Aye," Fenella replied. "And I hear this posh lawyer is an old friend of yours, eh?"

Jeffery's lips twisted into a wolfish scowl. "Do you think I condone what Joy did?"

Fenella waited.

Jeffery said, "Joy will never work in a prison again. Still, if an old friend of mine is a successful private criminal solicitor and wants to help Joy, who am I to object?"

Once again, Fenella didn’t speak.

"And no sign of Hamilton Perkins?"

"He has gone to ground, ma'am." Fenella knew Perkins had camped in the garden of the Seafields Bed & Breakfast, but that was weeks ago and the trail was cold. She wondered if Maude Hoon was the mysterious woman who was heard with him but knew they'd get nothing from her sealed lips.

"Shame," Jeffery said. "It would have been

a damn sight easier on everyone if..." Her voice trailed off. She looked at the large brown folder and frowned. "I've another balls-up to add to the long list."

Fenella waited.

"Child smuggling." Jeffery picked up the thick folder and read for a moment, then looked up. "The regional crime squad's operation has collapsed. It seems the kingpin and his minions got word and scattered. At least the network is broken, but it would have been better to haul them in. They've asked us to be on the lookout. She slid the folder across the desk. A little light reading for you."

Fenella took the folder and stood. As night continued to creep over the town, she knew evil still lurked in the shadows. In the form of Hamilton Perkins, in the form of the child smuggling ring, in a hundred and one other forms. But she reminded herself that there were beautiful things in the world, and they far outweighed the bad. For now, she'd done her part. The memory of Viv Gill, Pearl Smith, and PC Sid Hoon would sit a little easier in her grey matter. Now it was up to the courts to hand out justice.

CHAPTER 84

It was the last Saturday of the month. Chad Tate sat on the first pew in the hallowed hall of St Bees Priory. It was his first visit since the funeral of his wife, Rose, and daughter, Lark. He fidgeted with his hands as he tried to blot out the memory of what had happened the last time. He breathed in and out slowly to calm his nerves. Would anyone show up?

The vicar had told him not to worry, that despite the empty pews, the villagers would come out in large numbers to support Lark's Wish. But only Mrs Lenz and a few of her friends had turned up. They were helping run the stalls that sold baked goods, mountains of cucumber sandwiches, and huge urns of tea and lemonade. A stern woman with tree-trunk arms monitored the cloakroom and two wisp-like figures hovered as greeters by the front door.

Chad had closed his store early and now wondered if it was all a mistake. He wanted to speak with Vicar Briar, but the man had vanished. So he sat and watched the empty hall and waited.

"How about a cucumber sandwich to cheer you up," said Mrs Lenz. "You've got to have cucumber sandwiches at a church fête. Am I right? I am."

Her voice echoed off the stone walls. Chad thought there might be another event on at the same time and cursed for not checking that out. Now he was certain no one would show up. He braced himself for the tea and sympathy of Mrs Lenz's ladies. Cucumber sandwiches for the rest of the week. They'd have to throw away the tea.

He heard the drums first. Then a bugle and the syncopated shuffling of feet. The heavy front doors of the chapel opened, with Vicar Briar in the lead ahead of the flags and pennants of the Girls' Brigade. Two girls at the front carried an enormous banner with an image of a smiling little girl with raven-black hair tied with a pink bow. Chad's mouth dropped open. Lark!

And then he saw it.

All the girls wore pink ribbons. They marched to the front of the church and lined up in front of the altar. Behind them came the villagers. They shuffled into the priory chatting and laughing and shaking Chad's hand.

Vicar Briar made a brief speech and called Chad to the front to open the fête. Although Chad sat on the front row, it seemed to take him an age to walk the short distance. He watched all the faces, then glanced at his hands and realised he was shaking. He might never find a wife he loved as much as Rose, or a daughter to dote on like Lark, but he'd live out his days here so he could always be at their side. Yes, he was a native New Yorker, but St Bees was his little piece of England.

CHAPTER 85

Fenella stepped outside. They had driven to the Lark's Wish fête in St Bees Priory. Nan loved to rummage the knick-knacks on the jumble sale stalls, and Eduardo was content to hover between the food tables, eating baked goods, washed down with hot, sweet, milky tea.

The sun shone bright in a cloudless sky, although it was cold enough to see her breath swirl in white plumes. For a long while she stood in the shadows cast by the red-clay brick walls of the priory, covered in moss and lichen, gazing out at the quiet lane. This was family time, so she didn't let her mind wander to all that had happened in the previous weeks.

Fenella had mastered the switch between work and home life.

Instead, she thought about her cottage on Cleaton Bluff and made plans for a lunch date with her nurse friend, Gail Stubbs. Her matchmaking mind sifted through suitable names now that Dexter was getting wed to his long-time on-and-off girlfriend, Priscilla. With a deep focus, she stared at her phone, scrolling through contacts in search of a good match.

She did not hear the low splutter of the engine. It was the feeling of being watched that caused her to look up. A figure in black leather and knee-length boots stood on the opposite side of the lane. They had a helmet on their head, stood by a motorcycle, and clutched a large envelope in their right hand.

Fenella became instantly alert. In a heartbeat, she took in the details. The build was so slight and the height around five feet, so she assumed it was a woman. The light-footed steps as the figure hurried towards her did nothing to change her opinion.

The figure stopped several paces in front of Fenella and raised the visor. A thin-faced man, in his late forties, with deep-brown eyes and a wispy devil's beard, the colour of faded carrots, said, "Are you Detective Sallow?"

"And you are?"

"Whitehaven Couriers, ma'am. Package for Detective Sallow."

"Oh, aye, that would be me," Fenella replied, taking the envelope and flipping it over to read the sender's address.

The neat print was too small to read with her naked eye, so she reached into her handbag and put on a pair of reading glasses. On the back, where the sender's address was supposed to be, there was nowt but a series of blue question marks.

Fenella looked up. The figure in black was across the lane and on the motorcycle.

"Hey, come back, I want a word with you," Fenella shouted as she hurried after the man.

The motorcycle spluttered to life and raced away. Fenella watched until the high-pitched whine of the engine faded into the constant rumble of waves against the cliffs. Then her eyes fell to the envelope.

Inside, on a single sheet of cream paper, there were three words:

I'm sorry.

Eve.

The Detective Inspector Fenella Sallow series continues with Twisted Bones.

AFTERWORD

If you have enjoyed this story, please consider leaving a short review. Reviews help readers like you discover books they will enjoy, and help indie authors like me improve our stories.

Details of my other novels can be found in the store where you obtained this book.

Until next time,

N.C. Lewis

PS. Be the first to hear about new releases by joining my **Readers Newsletter or visit** https://bit.ly/NCLewis.

Manufactured by Amazon.ca
Acheson, AB